# BREWED
## WITH
# LOVE

# BREWED WITH LOVE

## Shelly Page

joy revolution

Text copyright © 2025 by Michelle Page
Jacket art copyright © 2025 by Betsy Cola
Moon phases ornament by dariachekman/stock.adobe.com

All rights reserved. Published in the United States by Joy Revolution,
an imprint of Random House Children's Books, a division of
Penguin Random House LLC, New York.

Joy Revolution is a registered trademark and the colophon
is a trademark of Penguin Random House LLC.

GetUnderlined.com

Educators and librarians, for a variety of teaching tools, visit us at
RHTeachersLibrarians.com

Library of Congress Cataloging-in-Publication Data is available upon request.
ISBN 978-0-593-89762-1 (trade pbk.) — ISBN 978-0-593-89763-8 (ebook)

The text of this book is set in 11.5-point Sabon LT Pro.
Interior design by Michelle Canoni

Printed in the United States of America
1st Printing
First Edition

# For Mom

# The Coven

### Sage Bishop
A novice witch with the ability to make
magical healing mixtures known as brews
or tonics; future owner of her family's
apothecary, Bishop Brews; prone to
accidentally misbrew tonics.

### Hazel Bishop
Matriarch of the coven and the current owner
of Bishop Brews; an expert tonic brewer;
affectionately known as Nana; not one
of your little friends.

### Tiva Locklear
Nana's long-term partner and owner
of Tea for Thought, a magic tea shop;
can control all water-based liquids in
Blackclaw; a second grandma to Sage.

### The Carvers
Have treelike growth cells that give them the ability to regenerate. **Poppy**, ambitious former friend of Sage, and **Raven**, Poppy's mom and owner of a sleek interior design business, Spellbinding Spaces.

### The Kims
Have the ability to read the history of any object through touch. **Mercer**, Sage's best friend, who has an unhinged crush on Poppy; **Julie** and **Seo-Yun**, busy accountants.

### Shaye Thorn
Can clone themself; manager of the Marigold Inn, the cutest B&B in Blackclaw Valley.

# 1

**M**y tonic is out for blood. Raucous green bubbles burst from the mixing pot, spilling over the sides and rushing at my feet like starving mice. Unruly fizz chomps at the toe of my high-top Converse, instantly melting the rubber with its searing heat.

In hindsight, adding the carnations to the pot *after* my magic was a bad idea. Magic brews are fickle, and this one doesn't have neatly printed instructions in my family grimoire for me to follow. I'm creating it from scratch, a feat only a witch as skilled as Nana manages to make look easy.

A smoky haze clouds the kitchen, and the scent of charred rubber fills the air as I lurch away from a particularly large bubble.

"Sage! What's that smell?" Nana yells from her study.

"Um . . ." My gaze whips around for a way to stop the foamy mess before it escapes into the rest of the house. I'm not supposed to brew at home. Most of my supplies are at our apothecary, but after spending all night tinkering with this blend, I thought I'd finally cracked it. Joke's on me.

Nana's heavy footsteps and her signature scent—rose oil and lemongrass—meet me before she does. A second later, she's standing in the doorway, wiry bifocals sagging halfway down her broad nose. Her large gold earrings match her gold bangles. The green monstera hair clip I gave her last Mother's Day holds her tiny gray afro in place. It complements her olive linen shift perfectly. If Nana was a succulent, she'd be aloe vera—nourishing and sweet, with a hardened exterior.

"I know you are not brewing in my— Oh! Not my rug!"

The poor rug she's had for the last three decades is fighting for its life against the remnants of my failed tonic. Scorch marks decorate the patterned fabric. Nana's stricken, and my most apologetic smile doesn't help the situation.

"Which rug, Hazel?" Tiva hollers from the other room, though her footsteps are light and swift as she heads our way.

"The purple runner from Rugs R Us, but that's hardly the point," Nana replies sullenly.

Tiva pokes her head into the kitchen with our oldest pothos tucked under her arm like a baby. Her thick, waist-length hair frames cheekbones as sharp as blades.

Sizzling bubbles charge toward her on a mission to

destroy anything in their path, but Tiva's fast. She flicks her wrist, gathering magic in her palm, and extends her hand. Instantly, the angry bubbles turn into harmless puddles.

Misbrewed tonics can do anything from itch to burn if touched. They leave behind nasty stains that are nearly impossible to get out (RIP my rainbow cacti shirt), and if ingested, they can cause dizziness, fever, pain, or even memory loss.

The key to brewing the perfect tonic is not only the ingredients—all grown in the Hemwood, a redwood forest soaked with more magic than a fairy tale—but how and when you put them in the pot. If the grimoire says "toss in" an herb, you better toss it. If it says to add a burst of individual magic *after* the mixture, don't add it before. The order of operations, the attention to detail, and the witch's intentions are what make a brew glow. Brewing isn't a problem when I have guidance, but inventing something new is advanced magic requiring a deep understanding of herbal properties and the problem in need of remedying. I'm still trying to wrap my head around that.

"Explain yourself," Nana demands, her round face pinched with annoyance.

I turn to Tiva for a show of support, but she shakes her head and covers a smirk with her free hand. Her and Nana have been together longer than the rug has haunted our kitchen, long enough to be like a second grandparent to me—one who is all too amused by my predicament.

Nana levels her gaze. "Well?"

"I swear I thought I finally cracked this tonic. It's going to put Bishop Brews back on top."

"Ah yes. Your breakup cure."

"It's not a *breakup* cure. It's an emotional recovery tonic, not just for heartbreak but for anything emotionally difficult someone might experience. It's genius." All the tonics we sell are healing, and this one would mend the mind and the heart.

Nana hums noncommittally. "And this has nothing to do with Ximena Reyes starting at the shop today?"

*Ugh.* As if I needed reminding. I've been dreading today since Nana told me Ximena applied for the open cashier position two weeks ago. Back then I could pretend it wasn't happening. It was easy to imagine Ximena's full day of training with Nana last weekend as a fluke. Now I have no choice but to face the music, which is easier said than done, because I'd rather pull out my teeth than spend fifteen long hours a week alone with Ximena.

I skirt around the counter, stepping over the now harmless mess on the floor, and throw the residue floating at the bottom of the pot into the trash. "Of course not. I'm doing this for Bishop Brews."

It's not a total lie. I *am* creating the tonic for our family apothecary, but I'm also doing it for me. I just don't mention that part because it's embarrassing enough to admit to myself that I'm still not totally over Ximena, even though it's been four years since she ghosted me.

I dust my hands off on my jeans, blow a frizzy curl out

of my face, and add for good measure, "Something needs to be done about Bottled Wonders."

Bottled Wonders is an apothecary in the neighboring town of Crimson Grove, the only other town in Northern California with a reputation for magic. The store is a force to be reckoned with. Customers say their prices are lower than ours, and their tonics work faster. Nana's too tired from running Bishop Brews for the last thirty years to try to compete with them, but at the rate Bottled Wonders is growing, our business won't survive much longer. I can't let everything she's worked so hard for crumble.

Nana grabs the mop from the hall closet and starts sopping up the remainder of the fizz. "Don't you worry about the apothecary. Tiva and I will figure something out. You should be focusing on—"

"School. I know, Nana, but Bishop Brews is important too."

Nana shakes her head, probably because she knows I'm not giving up. "Actually, I take that back." She points at the charred remains of her precious runner. "If you want to worry about something, worry about getting me a new rug."

A car horn blares from outside. Perfect timing. "You needed to upgrade anyway. This thing is nearly as old as you," I tease.

Tiva covers a laugh. Nana scowls half-heartedly and pushes the mop in my direction. "I'll pretend you didn't just say that. Go on, or you'll be late. It looks unprofessional if Ximena gets there before you."

"Can't we switch shifts? You work Sunday mornings, and I'll work evenings." I don't even try to keep the desperation out of my voice. I wouldn't have stayed up half the night if I wasn't desperate for a fix to this Ximena-size predicament.

"Sage, we've been over this. You have to be eighteen to work the farmers market on Sundays. Tiva has her own stall to run. She can't manage Bishop Brews as well. It has to be me." Nana peers at me over the rim of her glasses. "Unless your birthday changed overnight?"

I'll be eighteen in four months, which is exactly how long Ximena and I will be stuck working at the store together until we go to college in August. The universe hates me.

The car horn shrieks again and my phone buzzes in my pocket, begging me to get a move on.

"I really don't want to do this," I announce, slinging my bag over my shoulder.

"Luckily, I'm the nana here."

I grunt and shuffle toward the door. The parlor palm and the hanging verbena in the hallway wilt from my mood.

Tiva follows me. "Keep your chin up, love. This helps your gran. And believe it or not, a little change can be good."

Change can also be bad, especially when it means spending time with the girl who broke your heart.

"Not," I mumble. "I wish there was another option."

"You love Bishop Brews, right? Since Tracy retired,

the store could use the extra hand, at least for the spring and summer while your gran and I work the farmers market. Ximena may not be your friend anymore, but she's a good kid and a qualified applicant. Hazel isn't doing this to hurt you. She just wants to see the two of you find common ground again."

Nana has always seen the best in people and couldn't hold a grudge against a murderer. When she overheard Ximena asking about job applications at the Forage Collective last week, she readily offered her a position at Bishop Brews despite knowing our history. She said it was "time we get over our differences," as if what happened was just a simple misunderstanding. Nothing short of a miracle would get me to forgive Ximena.

"That's not going to happen. I don't get why Ximena would accept this job in the first place. She wants nothing to do with me."

"Maybe she needed the money, or she wants to make things right. Or both. You could ask her."

"Pass. We're only talking when strictly necessary."

Tiva shakes her head amusedly. "Have it your way. I'll see you tonight."

She nudges me outside, where my best friend, Mercer Kim, is waiting for me in her mom's Prius. On Sundays, we carpool into town because we both have morning shifts: me at Bishop Brews and her at the Enchanted Emporium. As far as succulents go, she's a lipstick echeveria— bright around the edges and blooming in warm seasons. A total socialite.

Mercer brushes her silky brown hair out of her face, revealing the stripe of cherry-red dye she added last month. She flaunts a bright smile. "Morning, sunshine!"

I climb into the car and strap on my seat belt. "Hey."

Mercer reverses out of our driveway and swings around the one-lane dirt road that winds through the arboretum I live in. It's impossible to describe to someone who doesn't have magic in their blood, connecting them to every plant in Blackclaw, but living in an arboretum is magnificent, like always being surrounded by your closest friends.

"Mrs. Dunn called earlier asking me to help her find her reading glasses again. I swear that woman loses something every day, and it's getting harder and harder to find stuff," Mercer complains as we drive past the fully bloomed desert garden and the collection of lively palms. The sun hovers above us, its warm rays lancing through the trees like golden swords.

"Founders love asking us for favors. Mayor Brown comes in every week for his custom hair-growth serum—on the house on account of him being the mayor, of course. When do witches get favors?"

"Would love to see the day," Mercer replies. "I'm positive we'll talk about it at the meeting tonight. What kind of donuts are you bringing?"

"What?" I ask.

Mercer glances my way. Her perfectly shaped eyebrows stretch dramatically toward her hairline. "Don't tell me you forgot you're on donut duty for the coven meeting. I've been looking forward to them all week."

I roll my eyes. "Are you sure you haven't just been looking forward to seeing Poppy? You know your crush on her is unhinged, right?"

"It is not!"

"She thinks she's superior to everyone because she can heal herself. Ever since she started going out with Morris Brown, Poppy mainly hangs around him and the other popular kids and acts like she's too cool for her coven." Dating the mayor's son shouldn't be grounds for ditching your crew, but here we are. Poppy is the second person who seems to have outgrown me, Ximena being the first and the worst.

"She's misunderstood. And hot." Mercer glances at me out of the corner of her eye. "You and Poppy used to be friends."

"Ancient history."

Mercer drums her purple nails against the steering wheel as a SZA song drifts through the speakers. We pass towering cacti and succulents in hues of pink, purple, and blue before turning onto Dogwood Drive, which takes us into the town center. There's a cute flower shop on the corner called Bewitched Blossoms. The owner, Mrs. Hart, is a redheaded woman with a growing belly. She puts a fresh bouquet of carnations outside and waves when we drive past.

Mercer honks in return. "Seriously. What's up? You've been super off lately. Last week you forgot about our Shakespeare presentation in AP Lit, and you *love* that stuff. Seeing you finesse the plot of *Much Ado About*

*Nothing* after watching half the movie that morning was cringe."

"Nothing's up. I've just been trying to figure out this tonic for the store. Figuring out the right recipe is surprisingly harder than I thought it'd be."

I don't tell her, because it's embarrassing, that everything is harder since all the old hurt I felt right after Ximena left came racing back when she returned to Blackclaw this year. I wanted to believe I was immune to her. Turns out I'm not. Seeing her again makes my entire body tense, my thoughts turn to goo, and my heart shrivel to the size of a pea.

"Hmm . . . Are you sure it doesn't have something to do with Ximena? I can't imagine working with an ex," Mercer says.

I bristle, and a lump forms in the base of my throat. "That's not— 'Ex' is a strong word. She's my former best friend."

"An ex-friend you've kissed. Middle school dating still counts. Ever since she moved back for senior year, I've seen you two aggressively avoiding each other at school and sharing heated stares when no one's watching. You may have history, but you also have *chemistry*." Mercer wiggles her eyebrows suggestively.

I fake gagging and seriously debate hiding inside my hoodie. "We have *beef*."

"Sure," Mercer replies, the word riddled with disbelief. "What happened between you two anyway?"

"Exactly what I told you."

"Tell me again."

I slouch further in my seat as we near our destination. Victorian-style buildings painted warm yellows and browns make up downtown Blackclaw Valley. On the ground floors are both regular and magical shops, like the local barber and the magical landscaping business, the Garden Genie, owned by my great-aunt, Nana's only sister, Genie. She's a witch but rarely participates in coven business. Nana says it's because she's an introvert and a workaholic, which is probably true, but I don't mind. I love the quiet boss energy she exudes.

"Ximena left the summer before high school," I reply to Mercer, watching the flower arrangements in the Garden Genie window wiggle their petals at me in greeting. "When she came back this fall, it was like I no longer existed. End of story."

I say this as casually as I can muster and leave out all the details. Details like how Ximena and I used to be inseparable—the last two rocks on a cliff. And we liked each other, at least I thought so, because when I told her how I felt, she said she felt the same way. Two weeks later, though, she left Blackclaw and ghosted me. Our relationship went from something to nothing in the blink of an eye.

When she returned this fall, everything was different. She pretended not to know me anymore, and I hardly recognized her. She came to school rocking a sleek new haircut, stylish clothes, and a moon tattoo behind her right ear that quickly caught the eye of the popular kids. She had remade herself. Fashioned herself into someone new. But New Ximena's skin doesn't quite fit.

Even from a distance, I can see that it pinches at the seams, and sometimes I notice the old her peeking through the gaps. Her airy laugh hasn't changed, nor has her love for painting her nails different colors: purple, orange, pink, and white. She still has a sweet tooth if the packet of M&M's she eats with her lunch every day is anything to go by. The fact that the girl I used to like, and kind of, sort of *date,* is still there bothers me. That I even think about these quirks annoys me the most.

Mercer inhales, undoubtedly about to ask a pesky follow-up question. I shake my head, and she snaps her mouth shut. She jabs her finger into my ribs, right where she knows I'm ticklish. When I squeal, she snorts with laughter. It's her way to break the tension and, like always, it works.

"Today is our first shift alone together, and I'd rather eat dirt than work with her. That's why I've been distracted."

"Well, the coven meeting will cheer you up," Mercer says brightly. "There's always some drama to cling to."

"I was hoping to get everyone's opinion on that heartache tonic I've been working on." Among friends, I do call my new tonic a cure for heartbreak. But I'm too self-conscious to have that be its official name. I don't want my business on blast like that.

"I mean, curing heartsickness does seem a little impossible," Mercer says.

"Nana doesn't want me wasting my time on it. There's nothing in the grimoire about it either."

"If I could brew like you, I'd help," Mercer replies.

I smile. "If you could brew, you'd have cracked my heartache tonic days ago."

All witches in Blackclaw have magic derived from the properties of redwoods, but each family has its own unique subset of magic. Just like tree rings are snapshots of the past, Mercer can see the history of any object she touches and know exactly where it's been since it was first made. But when it comes to tonics, her gifts could only give me suggestions for herbs. Thanks to her, I know that fleawort would be more potent than myrrh. The only skill my coven shares is plant manipulation.

Mercer slows to a stop in front of the blue-and-white storefront where I spend most of my free time. "Hurry, or I'll be late too. Henry has a new batch of donated artwork he needs me to help sort. He's still waiting for the day I uncover a priceless artifact hidden among the family junk we usually get, as if I'm going to read the history of a dusty sketchbook only to discover it actually belonged to a queen."

"It could happen."

"If it does, he better split the profits with me. It's past time for a new phone." She gestures to the door.

"Can't I just stay here forever?" I ask as I drag myself from the passenger seat.

"Always so dramatic," Mercer scolds lightly. "Don't do anything I wouldn't do. See you tonight."

As I stare up at Bishop Brews, I wish more than anything I'd been able to crack my tonic this morning. It was supposed to eliminate all feelings I have toward Ximena. Nana thinks if we work with each other we'll reconcile. But that is not, under any circumstances, going to happen. If Ximena wanted to be friends, she wouldn't have ended our friendship.

Taking a deep breath, I decide not to give her the satisfaction of seeing me perturbed. I'll play it cool and aloof. Minimal conversation and a modicum of effort, same as I've been doing whenever I see her at school.

Here goes nothing.

# 2

Opening the bright-blue door of Bishop Brews for my Sunday morning shift is like stepping into paradise. Dried herb bundles filled with lavender, sagebrush, rosemary, and thyme carefully bound with woven string hang on hooks behind the counter. Bags of charms dangle above the door, warding off any kind of negative energy. The oak shelves are stocked with colorful crystals in glass dishes and jars of spices, ground herbs, and homemade tonics. Devil's ivy drapes from corner to corner like giant green spiderwebs.

The space is small, barely large enough to hold a dozen people at once, but it's familiar. Cozy. A smile tugs at my lips. This is my second-favorite place, aside from the Hemwood. Bishop Brews has been in our family for generations. I feel my parents here the most. Their memory has a home in these walls. I'd do anything to make sure this store not only survives but thrives.

I check my phone: 9:15 a.m. Our shift started fifteen minutes ago, and there's no sign of Ximena the Heartbreaker. Yes, I'm late too, but I can still give her a strike.

I drop my messenger bag on the counter. The few pins I decorated it with—a Pride flag, the phrase "More Plants Please," and a pink cactus—clang against the wood. The lights are already on, which means Nana probably forgot to turn them off yesterday. There's a laundry list of chores to do before the store opens at ten, like sweep, restock, boot up the old-as-dirt register, and enter our daily cash flow. Without Ximena, it's going to take me twice as long.

I open the blinds and start my walk through the store to see what needs to be restocked.

Singing rings out from the back room. The vocals are smooth, high notes cresting before plunging into deep lows. I don't recognize the song, but something about the voice makes my muscles tense.

I round the corner and there she is. Ximena's poking and prodding at the jars of dried herbs laid out on the kitchen's laminate countertop. Her short black hair sways as she gracefully moves about. While she drags her hand over little glass vials of essential oils, antioxidants, and vitamins, she sings about Washington Heights, coffee, and bodegas.

The air in the shop is suddenly thin and hot. I've tried my hardest not to notice Ximena since she waltzed back into my life eight months ago. It's easy to do in class with our teachers vying for our attention and easier still during lunch while listening to Mercer's dramatic renditions of whatever reality TV show she's binge-watching.

Now it's just me and Ximena with no distractions in sight. I can't seem to look away.

As soon as she heads toward our family grimoire, I remember myself. With a flick of my wrist, I command the peacock fern hanging from the ceiling to snatch the book out of her reach.

Ximena flinches. When she turns around, I catch a phantom glimpse of the old her—a spark of mischief in her walnut-colored eyes—and then it's gone, and she's hiding behind a locked jaw, a narrowed gaze, and stiff shoulders.

My palms are sweating like they did when we were thirteen and swapping secrets on my bedroom floor. I push away the memory and lean into the irritation stirring in the pit of my stomach. "What are you doing?"

"Um . . . perusing." She quirks her full eyebrow and takes the upper hand. "Were you spying on me?"

"No. I came to see what the noise was. You sing?" Why didn't I know she has the voice of a Disney princess? Maybe it's a skill she learned during her time away. It's weird to think she has hobbies and interests I don't know anything about. Then again, I've been really into documentaries and crafting and have gotten good at brewing common tonics since we were friends last.

Ximena rolls her eyes. "Since forever. Just because

we were friends once doesn't mean you know everything about me."

Scratch that. Disney villain. As far as succulents go, she's a euphorbia. She comes in different shapes and sizes, some of them eerily beautiful, but don't be fooled. She will poison you.

"You should've waited for me in the front," I say sharply. We make tonics in this room, and since Ximena doesn't have brewing magic—or any magic at all—she's supposed to be stuck on the register, helping me label, or restocking.

Ximena sighs like the conversation is taxing. "I was trying to find you, and when I realized you were late, I figured I'd familiarize myself with the merchandise."

"You won't have to do anything back here. Come on." I spin on my heel and definitely don't stomp back into the front of the shop. Before I'm out of earshot, I yell, "And that's not our uniform!"

The fact that she looks good in her purple crop top and vintage jeans is irrelevant.

)·)·)·)●(·(·(·(

Working with Ximena proves to be a test of my patience. School allows me to pretend she doesn't exist, but I can't do that with her standing two feet away. We're the only ones in the store, and there is nowhere to hide. I feel her eyes prodding my face like pinpricks as I explain the different crystals, herbs, and creams we sell and what each one does. I show her how to label the essential oils, inform her that all tonics should be glowing, and if they aren't, they're expired or misbrewed. I tell her what to do if a shopper comes in asking for a custom mixture.

All the while, Ximena stays quiet. She doesn't even ask questions. It's like I'm having this training session with myself, which is funny considering four years ago, no one could get us to stop talking. We literally had to be separated during class.

Maybe it's the rigid silence bordering on disinterest that causes me to blurt out, "Why are you working here? There are a dozen stores on this block."

Ximena folds her arms across the Bishop Brews T-shirt she's now wearing. I hate that it suits her. Mine bunches weirdly under my arms and is way too baggy in the stomach because my torso is short.

Ximena pushes aside the collection of herbs I just finished going over with her. "I need a job. The hours are flexible, the pay is good, and believe it or not, I actually like Bishop Brews. It's homey and healing."

I swallow down the retort I had planned. Tourists love Bishop Brews because even though the magic fades after they leave town, their vacation ailments—allergy flare-ups, food poisoning, hangovers—are typically cured with a single dose. For Blackclaw residents, the effects last longer. Magic works only near the Hemwood. The farther away from the forest you go, the less magic witches have and the less our creations work, until eventually both fizzle out completely.

"You need to take this seriously," I tell Ximena. "The store is really important to me—"

"I *am* taking it seriously." She moves toward the rows and rows of homegrown herbs hanging from the trellis leaning against the far wall. "I memorized most of this stuff from visiting you here daily when we were kids." She spins to face me. "Plus, your grandma explained this when she trained me last week. I even took notes."

"Why let me ramble, then?"

Ximena shrugs her narrow shoulders. "You were in the zone. I figured I probably shouldn't interrupt. You always geeked out about this stuff."

I switch the subject before she can tell me what else she remembers about our old selves. "Are you only working here for the money?"

Ximena grunts. "Well, I do need money. My UCLA scholarship isn't covering everything. I have to come up with the rest myself."

She smooths down her undercut. If I didn't know her at all, I'd say she was worried about frizz. But I do know her. Before the undercut, she rubbed the skin between her thumb and forefinger. She's nervous.

"I've been thinking," she starts. "If we're going to work together, we should clear the air."

My hands grip the edge of the table a little too hard. "Nope. We are not having a heart-to-heart about past wrongs before a six-hour shift."

Ximena and I never actually talked about how things

ended. We let it fester like an untreated wound. She never apologized. There was a single moment, earlier this year, when she did a lot of lip biting and shaking out her arms before stomping toward me. I spun on my heel and fled. No way I can hear her out without losing it. That's why I've been working so hard on my heartache tonic. Being with her brings up all the same horrible feelings she caused when she disappeared. I wish they'd fade entirely on their own, but clearly my body needs an extra push.

"Sage, if you'd just listen—"

The old-fashioned bell above the door dings in greeting as a group of tourists wearing leggings and popular waterproof hiking shoes enter the store. Perfect timing. They're our typical customers, likely passing through town to see the redwoods and to buy magic charms. Tourism is a huge part of Blackclaw's economy. People flock here and to Crimson Grove to get a rare taste of magic.

The group gasps as they take in the tonic-stuffed shelves and the herb bundles dangling from the ceiling.

If Ximena wants to work here so badly, fine. Let's see how much she really knows. "I'm going to label new merch. You take our first customers."

"Gladly," she mumbles to me. She turns toward the customers and says, "Welcome to Bishop Brews, where everything is brewed with love. How can I help you?"

Ximena doesn't stumble over the greeting like I thought she would. Then again, she must've heard it a million times by now. We spent years playing tag, darting between shelves and customers, while Nana tried to maintain her professionalism. As hard as it is to admit, Ximena still knows this store.

The tallest of the four customers speaks first. "This is probably a silly question, but do you have anything to ward off giant wolves?"

Ximena gawks.

The customer clears her throat nervously. "Blackclaw has been lovely so far, but a few hikers staying at our B&B mentioned seeing a giant wolf with strange markings on its claws lurking near the trail we planned to hike today. We just want to be extra cautious and heard this might be the place to find charms or trinkets for that kind of threat."

Typically, we don't get many customers asking for silver charms. This year has been unusual in that there seem to be a lot more sightings of abnormally large wolves. The encounters used to be more common. Blackclaw was even named after the massive claw marks found littering the forest floor. When I was growing up, Nana told me stories of people entering the woods never to return, of residents sprouting thick gray fur along their arms and their nails lengthening into claws. Until recently, we even had a curfew on full moons.

Giant, shape-shifting wolves were run out of town long ago, just legend at this point, but we keep a few charms made of silver and laced with wolfsbane, an all-natural werewolf repellent, for easily spooked tourists.

"We have silver charms in here," I say, pointing to the base of the bookcase across from me. I'm surprised to find only a handful left when I open the drawer.

Ximena regains her composure. She lets the customers rifle through the charms. Although she should have taken the trinkets out for them, the hikers seem satisfied.

The shop bell chimes as another customer enters. I hope it's a sign that today will be busy. The man has a thick handlebar mustache and hair so slicked-down not even a storm could tousle it. He's dressed in a brand-new fleece, rather than a windbreaker, and crisp hiking shoes that look more fashionable than functional. Most of our experienced hiking customers prefer thicker rubber soles and water-resistant leather.

"Welcome to Bishop Brews, where everything is brewed with love!" I call out.

He chuckles at my greeting. "Can you point me to your bestselling products?"

"Sure," I reply. "Our bestsellers are our crystal pouches, chakra-balancing bracelets, and home-brewed tonics. If it's a tonic you want, we have premade ones for just about anything: rashes, arthritis pain, confidence boosters, you name it." His interest dims slightly. He's only our second customer of the day and I'm desperate to make more sales, so I add, "I'm working on something new, though. It's going to be groundbreaking." I may be overselling it. "A tonic to cure heartbreak."

The customer stands straighter and hikes a thin blond

eyebrow. "Really? That's . . . exactly the kind of thing I'm looking for. When will that be ready?" he asks.

"Soon. Maybe even today." It's wishful thinking, but he doesn't need to know that. I can see how eager he is for this. Maybe he knows how stubborn heartbreak can be or has experienced firsthand like me how easy it is for the pain of losing someone to rear its ugly head at the most inopportune time, even after years.

The man nods gratefully. "Then I'll be back."

He leaves, and Ximena rings up the group of hikers without a word to me and doesn't ask when or why I've experienced heartbreak. It's torture to smell the faint coconut scent of her shampoo and to sense her gaze on my back. I wish we had more customers to take my mind off her. This time last year, we'd have a line at the register with more customers filing in every few minutes. Now the store is empty, customers choosing our rival, Bottled Wonders, over us.

The faster I get my heartache cure finished, the sooner we can attract more customers. I plop onto the chair behind the counter and pull a few wildflowers from the bottom of my messenger bag. I tap the cottony petals of the meadowsweet, and they respond immediately, nudging happily against my hand like a cat asking for pets. With a wave of my hand, I coax out the passionflower. It slithers across the table to join the meadowsweet. Then I grab my notebook. It's overflowing with recipes and different blends for my tonic. I cross off the one I tried this morning. Hopefully attempt number twenty-two is the winner.

I make a break for the kitchen to get some breathing room from Ximena and to take another stab at my stubborn tonic. The entire shop smells like a wildflower field, but it truly looks like one where I've been working. Freshly crushed herbs sit in glass jars along the windowsill and hanging flowers crowd the corners, stretching toward the sun. Copper pots dangle from racks on the back wall. Our family grimoire sits on the counter next to the giant black brewing pot.

The grimoire has hundreds of recipes for tonics with lists of ingredients, tips on how to grow them, and the best time for harvesting. There's a tonic or a cream or a charm for just about anything. Bugbites, the common cold, eczema. At the end are pages and pages of miscellaneous notes scribbled in various handwritings. A collection of advice, warnings, and musings from Bishops over the years, like how turmeric is better than dandelions at managing inflammation, or that lavender tea should always be sipped before bed to prevent nightmares. By far, my favorite part is the meticulous ink drawings of plants, flowers, and herbs embellishing the margins of each page.

I mentally check off a list of ingredients I'll need for my heartbreak cure. We keep water from Willow Creek, a stream running through the Hemwood, in a jar in a mini fridge. I pour it into the pot and turn on the stove. This time, I save my magic for last.

Soon enough, the mixture begins to shimmer like summer heat on asphalt. Small bubbles balloon as the tonic boils. Steam wafts off the surface and dances along the rim of the pot like dry ice. I close my eyes and focus my intentions, concentrating on my goal. I tie the properties of the herbs together with my magic like twine around a bag of goods, letting it seep into the mixture just like any other ingredient. I stir carefully. The liquid quickly turns dark and bitter. I hold my breath, waiting for that steady glow to let me know this brew is a success.

It never comes.

My hand slams against the counter. Another misbrewed tonic. Where did I go wrong this time? If it's not my measurements or my ingredients or the order in which I added them to the pot, then it's my intentions, which doesn't make sense because my intent is clear: joy.

I slink toward the front of the shop. Ximena's putting the freshly labeled merch on a top shelf. Her Bishop Brews shirt rides up ever so slightly, revealing a patch of smooth, tan skin that absolutely doesn't short-circuit my brain.

She turns her head, as if sensing me looking. Her eyebrows rise.

"I—I'm going on break early," I stammer.

Her smile morphs into a pleased smirk.

Before she can say anything or I can embarrass myself further, I dash toward the door and into a smear of afternoon sun. I move out of Ximena's sight and try to compose myself.

A sunburned couple approaching the apothecary hardly

notice me. The teen is animatedly telling her boyfriend how the store has a cream that can cure her sunburn with one use, and she needs it before tonight. Ximena did well with the last customers. She can handle them.

Once I'm no longer thinking about Ximena or the patch of skin I saw, I head down Main Street and toward Tea for Thought, the best café in town. Aside from having the strongest drip coffee I've ever tasted, they also have a signature lavender-and-chamomile latte, magically enhanced to boost its calming properties. When you're a witch with anxiety, finding ways to cope with life is key. Right now, the latte is about the only thing that's going to get me through the rest of the day with Ximena.

Standing between Tea for Thought and Mystic Muffins are my covenmate Poppy Carver and her boyfriend, Morris Brown. Poppy's voice is loud and growing louder, her heated words breaking the relative silence of the tranquil street. "What's going on?" she asks.

Morris tightens the straps of his backpack, crinkling his basketball jersey. "Nothing."

"Really? Because you've been acting sus, hiding your phone and canceling plans. You were even weird at the kickback yesterday with *your* friends. *I* had to cover for you," Poppy replies. "Then today, you said you had family stuff, but I run into you here. What's that about?"

I duck out of the way, partially concealing myself so I can listen to the drama unfolding.

Morris shrugs. "You know that I've been having some family issues. No big mystery."

Poppy shakes her head, her box braids swaying. She's wearing her cheerleading warm-up clothes. "I don't buy it," she says.

"Yeah, well, you seem suspicious too. You have your Scheme Face on. Why aren't you with the rest of the squad?"

A cramp in my leg forces me to move from my hiding spot behind a truck. Morris spots me. "Let's talk about this later. I don't want to argue in public," he says stiffly.

Poppy replies, but her voice is too low for me to hear. They part, heading in opposite directions down the street. It's odd to overhear one of our school's power couples bickering in broad daylight. I suppose no relationship is perfect.

I shake off the interaction and head inside Tea for Thought, where a line is waiting for me. Nana decorated the café for Tiva and her sister. She filled the nets looping across the ceiling with polka-dot plants and devil's ivy, with long vines ribboning above each table. Along the back cream-colored wall is a giant abstract painting of the Hemwood, vibrant reds, greens, and yellows adding the perfect splash of color. It's a big hit with tourists who come for the aesthetic and social media–worthy photos but stay for the ever-cold bubble tea and the tarot readings.

At the register, a woman in front of me has an elderly bichon, his eyes cloudy with cataracts. She orders him a Pooch Potion. As soon as she gives it to the dog, his slow-wagging tail triples its speed, his eyes clear, and he happily jumps on his owner. Along with the tea being transformative, so are their doggy drinks.

More than ready for that kind of boost, I order my tea and find a little table in the rear of the shop. I listen to the rumble of chatter, clinking cutlery, and the soft piano and violin sounds seeping through the speakers above me. The creamy taste of warm oat milk and the sharpness of the lavender make it easier to breathe, and a warm, heavy feeling settles in my chest, not too far from contentment. It offers a feeling of relaxation I'm hoping to achieve with my own tonic—only instead of lasting a few minutes, it'll last for months without needing another dose.

I don't take more than a few sips before my phone starts vibrating. The number that pops up is one I know by heart, though I've long since deleted the contact.

I've only been gone for fifteen minutes. If Ximena was listening as she claims, then she can handle a few customers, but a spark of unease prods me to answer.

"What?"

"You need to come back to the apothecary," Ximena says, slightly out of breath. "There's been a break-in."

# Sage's Heartbreak Tonic

## Attempt Number 22

## INGREDIENTS

½ cup Hemwood spring water
1 tsp. ground cinnamon
3 purple carnations
2 oz. crushed cedar

1 drop lemon balm
1 generous scoop of honey
1 ginger root

## DIRECTIONS

1. In a brewing pot, pour in the spring water, sprinkle in the cinnamon, and toss in the carnations and the crushed cedar. Add one drop of lemon balm. Let simmer on medium heat for 5 minutes.

2. Add a generous scoop of honey. Don't play yourself. When it comes to honey, we measure with our hearts. Add the whole ginger root. Stir.

3. Let the mixture steep for 3 minutes. To pass the time, listen to "On My Mama" by Victoria Monét. The bubbles should turn dark, and steam should waft off the surface.

4. Close your eyes and focus your intentions on making a tonic to forget your heartache, because that shit is for the birds.

5. When ready, tie the ingredients together with magic.

6. If successful, the mixture will glow. If unsuccessful, it's trash. Immediately dump it.

Warning: *If not properly disposed of, misbrewed tonics will stain and burn! (Nana does not play about her granite or fancy rugs.)*

# 3

*A* fresh burst of adrenaline kicks against my ribs as I race back to Bishop Brews. I fling open the front door and nearly knock into Ximena, who's standing by the register chewing on an orange lacquered fingernail. My head provides a slew of useless thoughts as I approach, like how she'll chip her polish and how worried—no, nervous—she looks.

"What happened?" I demand, my words as choppy as my breathing.

"I was helping this couple who had a million questions and bought a bunch of stuff. After I rang them up, I went to grab more intention candles from the supply closet. That's when I saw the back door open and the kitchen in disarray." Ximena says all of this in a single exhale.

I run to the kitchen. My steps stagger when I'm hit by a warm, syrupy breeze. The door's ajar. The vase of fresh wildflowers we keep by the window is overturned. The counter is covered in crushed herbs, a dusting of cinnamon, and a sticky residue, likely from the honey. The mixing pot along with the rest of my tonic is empty, plum-colored dregs staining the counter and floor like smeared ink. My family grimoire is blessedly untouched.

I gesture wildly at the mess. "You didn't hear them do this?"

"I was preoccupied with the customers, and whoever came in was stealthy!" Ximena replies from the doorway. She wrings her hands together. "I think a few tonics might have been taken."

Sure enough, several jars of our popular premade tonics, like ones for the common cold, clear communication, and attracting abundance, are missing. "They took my heartache tonic," I hear myself say as I stare at the empty bottom of the brewing pot.

"The one you mentioned to the guy with the mustache?"

"Yeah, it's— Never mind." A cobwebby sensation clings to my skin, one I can't shake.

Ximena looks as if she wants to say more but decides against it. Instead, she asks, "Why would someone do this?"

"How am I supposed to know?" The words come out harsher than I mean them to. This is so bad.

Ximena holds up her hands. "Just thinking out loud. I'm trying to help."

"If you wanted to help, you would've been paying

attention. How is it that on your first day, the store gets robbed? That's either the worst luck ever or highly suspicious."

Ximena stands taller. "I didn't do this. I wouldn't jeopardize this job. I need the money."

"So you said. Maybe you want to sell our products to the competition. I honestly can't believe you didn't hear anyone come in."

The muscles in her neck strain. "I was helping customers! You left me alone. I was trying to juggle working the register and accurately relaying all the stuff I learned."

I pinch the bridge of my nose and exhale, letting my anger seep away.

Could it have been a customer? There were the tourists asking about silver charms, the man with the mustache and thin eyebrows, and the sunburned teens that came in after him. I think the latter are freshmen at our high school, but I could be wrong. Ugh. I was so focused on my frustration with Ximena that I didn't notice their faces.

I rub the tension from my eyes. "I need to call my grandmother."

"Great idea." Ximena drags a hand across her undercut again, the new nervous tell I catalog next to her other quirks I wish I didn't remember.

Nana answers on the second ring. "What's happened?" she asks.

Nana's parental alarm bells are probably blaring. I only ever call mid-shift if there's an emergency.

"Someone broke in while I was on break. They took some premade tonics and the new one I was working on," I tell her shakily.

Nana's quiet for a beat, the only noise a muffled shuffling sound, and then she says, "Are you okay?"

"I'm fine." I glance toward the front of the shop, where Ximena's checking the register. "Ximena too."

"That's good. Did they take anything else? Cash?" Nana asks.

I start walking around the store, checking everything, but nothing is out of place, and the money in the register is accounted for. "Cash is all here."

"Did Ximena see anything?" Nana asks.

"She says she didn't," I mumble, not sure whether to believe her or not.

"I don't like it, Sage. I'm heading there now. Wait for me somewhere safe, okay? I'll call Tom."

Blackclaw Valley is a tiny town, so when anything goes awry, you call Tom Dunn. He's been the sheriff for the last fifteen years. Under normal circumstances, I'd be thrilled to leave early and not have to spend another two hours with Ximena, but these are not normal circumstances.

"Are you sure? I can call him and stay here," I reply.

"No. Your safety is my first priority. Tell Ximena we're closing for the day, but she'll get her full day's pay for the trouble. We'll report the break-in and tell the coven tonight."

"Got it. See you soon." As soon as I hang up, my

adrenaline rushes out. I slump against the shelf stocked with hand-poured candles and scan the front of the store, trying to catalog any additional damage. Nothing seems out of the ordinary, though there are a few dirt splatters on the floor, likely from today's customers, and a sprinkling of something crushed on the shelf beside me.

I swipe at it, picking up the debris with my thumb and index finger. I smush the substance around, fairly certain I know what it is. A quick sniff confirms my guess. Elderberry. It has numerous health benefits, including reducing inflammation, easing headaches, and improving digestion. Apothecaries use elderberry in a variety of tinctures, teas, and balms, which wouldn't matter, except Bishop Brews is completely out and has been for the last three weeks.

Ximena chooses the exact moment I'm sniffing random herbs to find me. "If you don't believe I'm innocent, our last customers provided their contact information. You can call and ask if they saw anything and verify that I was with them the entire time. You came in a second after they left, I swear." She holds out the form we use for our rewards program.

"We didn't get a shipment of elderberry today that I might've missed, did we?" I ask, ignoring her but seizing the form.

"No."

"Weird."

She crosses her arms. "What did your grandmother say?"

I consider telling her the truth, that Nana's sending her

home for the day with pay and we'll revisit opening the store after the sheriff has been called. But the more I think about it, the more I see an opportunity. I don't want her here all spring and summer, not when I've got enough to worry about with school and Bottled Wonders.

"She said she's calling the sheriff so we can report the break-in. He'll probably want to take your statement, and after that, you can go home. Consider it your last day."

Ximena tenses. "*What?* You're *firing* me?"

I don't tell her that, technically, *I* can't fire her. I plan to convince Nana she's a liability later. "The store was robbed on your watch."

"And I feel awful about that, but I didn't do this. Let me prove it."

I hold up my hand. "No need. The sheriff will sort this out."

"Sage—"

"No, Ximena."

As soon as her face drops, so does my stomach. It feels like jumping off a swing at the highest point, but instead of excitement I only feel shame. I tell myself it's for the best, and yet, a horrible knot in my belly remains the entire time we stand by for Nana and the sheriff.

)·)·)·)●(·(·(·(

Outside, Ximena rides circles around me on the same purple bike she's had since middle school. Across the street, Henry, the owner of the Enchanted Emporium, waves as he puts out a fresh batch of lilies that have been charmed to dance. I wave back.

Outside the town hall in the distance, I can just make out the bronze statue depicting the partnership between wolves and witches. A witch in flowing robes rests her hand on the back of a massive wolf with rippling fur and huge claws. It makes me think of the customers asking for silver charms and how before the wolves were feared, they were revered.

Ximena screeches to a halt in front of me, effectively blocking my view of the statue. "Hello? Are you listening? Your grandma said I could work from April until August. I was counting on that income."

"I'm listening. Geez. I'm sure you can find another job. They always need new servers at the Magic Cauldron."

The charming ivy sprouting along the side of Bishop Brews is a little dull. I wave my hand over the vines until they deepen in color and shine. I ignore the little voice in my head reminding me that most college deposits, including mine for Blackclaw College, are due soon. Ximena probably needs the money now. I ignore my guilt. This is Ximena the Heartbreaker we're talking about.

"Finding a new gig now is going to be hard if the other business owners in town realize your store was broken into on my watch. By the time I find someone to hire me, the summer could be over. I'm already behind on my savings." She inhales and squares her shoulders. "Besides, I don't want a new one. I want *this* one."

The desperation lacing her words gives me pause. But

I don't have long to dwell on it as Nana and the sheriff approach us.

After we give our statements, Ximena and I are sent home. To my utter disdain, she picks up the conversation right where she left off by texting me. I guess my messages the summer before freshman year got lost in the ether. Our text thread is empty, leaving a blank slate. It's the fresh start everyone seems to want us to have but will never happen. Not with all these memories in the way. I wish moving on was as easy as deleting a phone number.

**Unknown:**

> can you pls convince your grandma to keep me on?

> it's Ximena, btw

I don't respond, but while I'm here, I add her contact back into my phone and save her name as "Ximena (Don't Fall For It) Reyes" to remind myself that she is my adversary.

I have to admit she seemed sincere when I asked what happened today, but it's best not to let her off the hook yet. The store being robbed the same day she starts is too coincidental.

I plop onto my bed, the old springs hissing in annoyance, and prop my feet against the headboard. I'm careful not to disturb the morning glory, its dark purple flowers kissing the wood. The plant was a gift from my parents before they died. It doesn't keep away bad dreams of their car accident like a dream catcher or light up in the dark like the fairy lights Mercer has on her bed frame, but it does bring me comfort. And it reminds me of my parents. All of Blackclaw does, especially my magic since they were both witches.

Instead of doing boring homework, I crack open the notebook I've been using to keep track of my heartache cure and start to rework the ingredients. I should switch the cedar for licorice root. Both are good for confidence boosting, and that's part of what I need to get over Ximena. I don't know how to act around her, and second-guessing myself doesn't help. Luckily, I'll have plenty of time to master the tonic and help the apothecary now that Ximena's out of the picture.

For a while, working on my recipe takes my mind off things, but soon enough, those pesky little thoughts creep back in. Who would rob Bishop Brews? And of all people, why did Ximena have to be there when it happened?

I decide to call the customers who left their information on our sign-up sheet. Turns out they are freshmen at Blackclaw Valley High. They confirm that Ximena was graciously assisting them the entire time, and even asked if there was a customer service survey they could fill out because she was *that* good. Please.

Could they be colluding with Ximena, providing her a fake alibi during the break-in? But no, none of them could have known I would leave the store when I did. I could just as easily have helped these clients as Ximena.

I find myself still thinking about Ximena—as a possible

culprit, obviously—later that night. A line of cars snakes up our driveway. Inside, conversation rages as the witch families of Blackclaw converge in one place. The Carvers, the Kims, and Mx. Thorn mingle over hot cups of Tiva's famous oolong tea and the last-minute mint chocolate chip cookies Nana baked. I forgot the donuts, but to be fair, it's been a *day*.

The meetings are more of a social gathering than what you'd picture a bunch of witches doing together. It's mostly gossip and desserts.

Mercer hangs on my arm with flaming heart-eyes while she watches Poppy take the world's smallest bite out of her cookie. I haven't told Mercer about the break-in. I haven't told anyone other than Nana, Tiva, and the sheriff because I'm still trying to wrap my head around what happened. For the most part, the residents love the coven, the magic, and the charm we add to Blackclaw. It's hard to imagine a neighbor or teacher or friend doing this.

Nana rings the brass cowbell she keeps on the end table to start the meeting, and my heart skips.

"Witches! We thank you for coming. It has been a long, productive month," Nana begins. She's wearing a vintage green dress and wide brown belt. Her eyes crinkle at the corners, and her lips pinch when she forces a smile.

As she goes through her usual spiel about community and commitment to the craft, I bounce my leg, wobbling the plastic folding chair Nana pulled out for the meeting. Mercer gives me a questioning look, but I shake my head.

I asked Nana to let me tell the coven about the break-in since it happened during my shift.

Nana digresses, her tone taking on a more somber note. "Today's agenda is getting a change from what was proposed last meeting because Sage has a very important update that concerns us all."

*Way to set the mood, Nana.* Murmurs ping-pong around me. Mrs. Carver watches me with narrowed eyes. She's an uptight woman with a short auburn Afro, a splash of freckles across her face and arms, and a permanent scowl. Poppy takes after her.

I take Nana's place at our makeshift dais—the stone lip of our fireplace—and press my fingertips against my legs to steady myself. "So, um, this afternoon, someone—"

A loud knock on the front door cuts off the rest of my sentence. Every head in the room whips in the direction of the sound. At first, I think it's a fluke. Our meetings, while not secret, are private.

The sound comes again. "Hazel? Tiva? It's Tom," says a deep, cigarette-burned voice. "We need to talk."

Nana's and Tiva's eyes meet as the rest of my coven visibly tenses up. Tiva sweeps her shoulders back and strides toward the door. She flings it open with a flourish.

A second later, Sheriff Tom Dunn steps inside wearing his signature brown uniform. He brings with him a whiff of stale coffee and ash that overpowers our freshly steeped tea and mint chocolate treats. He's from a wealthy founding family and is a member of the town council. His hard exterior and no-nonsense attitude always put me a little on edge.

He doesn't even take his shoes off, tracking dirt on our clean floor. "Evening, ma'am," he says to Tiva. "Sorry to interrupt, but this couldn't wait."

He steps aside, revealing Mr. and Mrs. Lawson, also descendants of our town's founders, who own more than half of the businesses in Blackclaw, and their daughter, Leigh. As always, she's Instagram-perfect, wearing a yellow-and-blue dress. Her blond hair is pulled into a high bun. Her usual sharp blue eyes and resting bored face are gone, replaced by a weird doe-eyed expression, and there's a plum-colored tint to her lips that's not her normal shade. When she glances my way, there's not a drop of recognition.

The hair on the back of my neck prickles. Her parents hold her hands and lead her to a corner of the foyer. The door closes behind them with a deafening click.

Nana keeps her voice low when she asks, "Is this about the break-in? I thought you had what you needed from us."

"Not quite," the sheriff replies slowly. He raises his voice to be heard by the entire coven. "This afternoon, Leigh Lawson was drugged. Her memories have been completely erased. The poor girl doesn't even remember her name. As you can imagine, this doesn't look good for Bishop Brews or the coven."

# 4

My heartbeat skips like a scratched vinyl, and I gasp with the rest of my coven at the sheriff's declaration.

Sheriff Dunn locks eyes with my grandmother. "Shortly after your call, the Lawsons phoned about Leigh. Her memory loss, coupled with the fact that Bishop Brews was broken into earlier today with several tonics being stolen, leads me to believe the incidents are linked."

Memory loss is a common side effect of drinking misbrewed tonics. Since badly crafted magic is so rare and never sold, not many people know about its consequences. The people who do are witches, Bishop Brews employees, and the founding family members in charge of vetting all the businesses in town. Sheriff Tom Dunn is among them.

He waits for the coven to quiet before continuing. "Hazel, a *kid* was poisoned by one of your products."

"Not intentionally, I assure you," Nana replies swiftly. "My products are sound. Always."

"Evidently not. Someone dosed Leigh Lawson, which on its own is worrisome, but what's worse is that the tonic was defective. I hope you haven't lost your touch."

He says it casually, as if we're talking about the weather. Meanwhile, my hands clench at my sides. Is he insinuating that Nana's gotten careless or that the shop has gotten to be too much for her? She may be getting older and getting tired of the store's upkeep, especially in the wake of Bottled Wonders' opening, but she's never been negligent.

Nana's voice is strained when she replies, "I haven't. I don't know why any of the apothecary's tonics would be misbrewed. I've been making the same ones for decades."

Not every witch can make tonics. Although we can all move and mold plants to varying degrees, our gifts aren't interchangeable. Witches without brew magic or non-witches can certainly try to make one, but the tonic won't have any magic in it and therefore wouldn't have any magical side effects. That means whoever made the tonic Leigh drank is a witch with brew magic like me or Nana.

"Someone could be framing us," I say, because there must be at least one witch in Crimson Grove with brew magic making tonics for Bottled Wonders.

Tiva rests a hand on my shoulder. "Or couldn't Leigh have lost her memory another way? We don't know it was one of Hazel's tonics."

"Not definitively, but a healthy seventeen-year-old girl

doesn't go to a fundraising rally and come home without her memories."

The normally perky leaves of our parlor palm droop mournfully across the hardwood floor at his words.

Mr. Lawson steps forward. He's a lean man with a thin brown mustache and rectangular wire-frame glasses. His shirt is stretched and tucked into a pair of perfectly creased dress pants, and his Rolex gleams when it catches the light. "If I can provide a little more insight into the situation—"

"Please do," Mrs. Carver, Poppy's mom, demands. Her tightly clasped hands twitch in her lap. Our families may have their differences, but in the presence of anyone outside the coven, we're united.

Mr. Lawson clears his throat. "As the sheriff said, Leigh was found wandering the streets after the fundraiser and brought home by a deputy. She had no idea who we were. It took us two hours to explain everything before she calmed down."

"Her friends didn't see anything?" Mrs. Carver asks.

"They seem to have been separated at some point. They don't know where Leigh went, and she certainly doesn't remember now."

"I'll be looking into that," the sheriff says with a nod to Mr. Lawson. "As for the business with the stolen goods, this could be the tip of the iceberg. I'd hate if more defective products are making their way around town. More people could get hurt. This isn't the first time something like this has happened, but it *is* the first time a minor has been involved, and that cannot stand."

Witches and the founding families have always been partners in Blackclaw's society. Both groups sit on the town council and vote on local provisions. While the founders' descendants have wealth and power as elected officials and business owners, witches have magic and a strong influence on the town's economy. There was one occasion, years ago, when a bridal party used the mud bath at a spa owned by a witch family in our coven and ended up covered in painful sores the night before the wedding, including the bride. Something went wrong with the rejuvenating magic the witches usually infused in the mud mixture. Tensions were so high in the town, the family ended up moving away. Since then, the relationship between witches and founders has been precarious.

Worry creases Nana's normally bright face. "What are you implying, exactly?" she asks of the sheriff.

He hooks his fingers through his belt loops. "I'm just making observations. I sincerely hope, for the coven's sake, that the investigation doesn't trace that tonic back to your store, or we'll have to shut it down."

I'm on my feet in a second. "You can't close Bishop Brews! The apothecary is our livelihood."

Sheriff Dunn rests a hand across his chest. "*I* don't want to see it closed." He doesn't seem remotely sincere. "But with a council vote, it could happen."

Nana takes a moment to regain her composure, throwing back her shoulders and smoothing her expression.

"I think you're forgetting something." The sheriff sighs. "This is a magic-related mishap. Per our town bylaws, any magical misfortunes must be jointly handled by the police *and* the coven."

"Ah. Yes. You and Mrs. Carver lobbied hard for that." The hint of bitterness I detect in his voice doesn't suit him. Nana and Mrs. Carver are the only witches on the town council. The rest of the members are Sheriff Dunn, Mr. Lawson, the mayor, and two other elected officials.

"So, we will look into this too," Nana says. "Quietly, of course."

This response seems to placate Sheriff Dunn, whose stance loosens. "Good. You have my full support. Magic is such an important pillar of our community. It does wonders for the town's residents and its economy. I'd hate for that to change."

"If that were true, you wouldn't threaten to close our family business," I grumble.

"Sage," Nana warns.

"It's all right, Hazel," the sheriff says lightly. "As I said, I don't want to see Bishop Brews go anywhere, but if it comes down to it, I'm sure we'd be able to find a use for some of your products elsewhere. If the store is becoming too much, I hear there are also bigger apothecaries out there that might be looking to buy."

Anger bubbles low in my gut. He's referring to Bottled Wonders. Like hell Nana would sell to them.

"I appreciate the concern, but you have my word, Sheriff. This will resolve itself swiftly," Nana replies coolly.

The sheriff runs a bony hand along his close-cropped hair. "Good."

Mrs. Lawson, who's been quietly rubbing her daughter's head—much to Leigh's chagrin—gives the group a grimace. "How long before the side effects wear off?"

"They won't without a counter brew," Nana says gently. "It will take me at least a few days to make. It's hard to guess where the initial brew went wrong to reverse the mistake. Since we don't know which stolen tonic your daughter drank, it will be even harder to find the right cure."

"But she has school and cheerleading," Mrs. Lawson whines.

Nana ignores her. She rubs her hands together while she gathers her thoughts. "There's something else. I'd be remiss if I didn't mention that without a counter brew, the effects could become permanent."

Even though everyone knows Nana is the most skilled witch in Blackclaw, that doesn't stop the admission from sucking the air out of the room.

"How long before *that* happens?" Mr. Lawson demands.

"One week, give or take a day," Nana replies.

The Lawsons inhale sharply. That only gives Nana seven days to make a counter brew and for the coven to find the thief and save Bishop Brews. Talk about a tight deadline.

While the Lawsons press Nana further about the counter brew, I distract myself by walking over to Leigh. She's standing off to the side, looking both worried and bored. It's kinda creepy.

"Do you want some water or something?" I ask, and then freeze.

This close, I can better see her plum-stained lips and chin, the same color of the tonic residue currently splattered inside the mixing pot and all over the floor of Bishop Brews. The color of today's failed tonic. Attempt number twenty-two.

The floor sways under my feet. Or maybe it's the other way around. I knew it was a long shot that any of Nana's tonics would be misbrewed, and that's because they weren't. *Mine* was. The residue on Leigh's lips isn't harmful or permanent, but my god, is it damning. It's partly my fault she can't remember anything.

"No, I'm good. You'll find who did this, right? I'd really like to remember my life," Leigh replies.

She's not faking. There's no way Leigh would be thinking anything I did was nice if she remembered me. Leigh has hated me since I ruined her tenth birthday party by getting so excited to ride a pony for the first time that all the trees in her backyard flowered, causing her to have a horrible asthma attack. She had to be taken to the local hospital. As a baby witch, I didn't have my magic under control. She knows it was an accident, but I don't think Leigh ever forgave me. From then on, she's been trying to get back at me by turning everything into a competition. Naturally, I rise to the challenge. Best yearbook photo, loudest applause during the talent show, first picked during gym class. You name it. I rarely win (except freshman year talent show because my dancing carnations were top tier) but still. Now she can't remember any of it.

"I'll do my best," I reply, meaning it. I've got to make things right.

"Bill, Cheryl, I think you've hounded them enough about this counter brew," the sheriff tells the Lawsons, gesturing toward the door. "Let's let them get back to their meeting. They have much to do."

Leigh gives me a small nod before following her parents and the sheriff out of the house. As soon as they're gone, the living room erupts.

"How dare they storm in here!"

"Total power play."

"Why didn't you tell us there was a break-in?"

"This was *not* on my bingo card of gossip for today's meeting."

That last one comes from Mercer. She's vibrating with pent-up energy. Meanwhile, Nana has a pallor to her skin that makes me itch with guilt. I can't let her think she messed up. She didn't do anything wrong. I did.

I tug her aside while the coven discusses the sheriff's visit. "This is my fault," I tell her. "The misbrewed tonic was mine. I—I don't know who stole it or how it got to Leigh, but Nana, your tonics weren't the issue. I'm so sorry."

Nana's features soften. She pats my cheek. "It's okay, Sage," she says.

"It's not! I put the apothecary at risk by leaving the tonic out and leaving Ximena alone and in charge of the store on her first day." Just saying it aloud makes me wince. "This is my mess to clean up, not yours. Should we tell the sheriff?"

"Absolutely not. I'm the owner of the store, and you're a child, mine specifically, and an employee. Let me worry about this, okay? The sheriff tasked the coven to look into this, and that's exactly what we're going to do," Nana tells me before rejoining the rest of the room's conversation.

"For the most part, our relationship with the founding families has been amicable," Mrs. Carver is saying. "This *mishap* has put the coven in a very tough position."

Next to her, Poppy nods. There's a tightness around her eyes and mouth. She's worried. Everyone's worried.

I can't help but wonder whether things would've turned out differently if I'd just gotten the tonic right.

"I'll start working on a counter brew tonight," Nana says. "In the meantime, I think it would be best if everyone remains vigilant. The break-in might not have been an isolated incident."

"You're right. The more cautious we are, the better," replies Shaye Thorn, a witch in our coven with cloning abilities, another form of magic based on the properties of the coastal redwoods in fairy rings.

"I want to help," I tell the group. "Let me take the lead."

"We're all going to help, but the coven elders will run

point," Nana replies. She doesn't want me involved, but I already am.

"Sage can at least answer a few questions," Mrs. Carver says. "Did you see anything suspicious around the time of the break-in?"

"I—uh—I wasn't actually there. I was taking my break. Ximena Reyes was working, but she says she didn't see anything. She was helping customers at the time."

"We need to confirm that," Mrs. Carver replies.

"Agreed. We should speak with her tonight, if possible," Shaye adds.

"I already did. I doubt she'll have much more to say," I tell them quickly. I didn't exactly get the chance to convince Nana we should fire her, and Ximena doesn't know she's really still employed. Plus, today's been bad enough without having to see her again. *Can I catch a break?*

"Sage, see if Ximena is willing to come over and talk with us briefly. It won't take long," Nana says.

"Um . . ." Coven business is tight-lipped. Only witches and the town government are supposed to know of our inner workings, though occasionally that rule is broken. The fact that my coven is willing to invite a non-witch to the meeting means they're more worried than I thought. I want to push back against bringing Ximena into my space, but arguing will only make me look like a child with a grudge, which isn't exactly *wrong*, but the whole coven doesn't need to know that. "I guess I can text her."

While the adults discuss logistics and next steps, I pull out my phone and pretend it doesn't cause me actual pain to reply to her messages. I type, delete, and retype over and over again. *You can do this, Sage. Cool and aloof, remember? Cool. And. Aloof.* I'm sweating by the time I come up with the right combination of words.

> If you want to keep your job, meet me at the arboretum.

The reply comes a moment later like she's been waiting by her phone. Where was this text etiquette four years ago?

**Ximena (Don't Fall For It) Reyes:**
FINALLY! WHEN??

> Now?

**Ximena (Don't Fall For It) Reyes:**
be there in 10!

# 5

The room is abuzz. Poppy's furiously texting on her phone, likely breaking the unspoken rule of not sharing coven drama with non-coven people to update her boyfriend about said drama. To be fair, I used to do the same thing with Ximena. I feel a pang beneath my ribs at the memory.

Nana solicits suggestions from the elder witches on how to handle the investigation while Tiva shoves a plate full of cookies at me, Mercer, and Poppy. She then hands us chamomile tea. Not gonna lie, it helps my nerves since Tiva's magic allows the properties in the tea leaves to be extra potent. It makes chamomile super calming, jasmine extra clarifying, and peppermint truly pain relieving. Amplifying is a skill I wish I had. My gift allows me to mix multiple herbal properties together, not enhance individual ones. We only inherit one kind of magic, whether our parents have different types of magic or not.

The doorbell rings. I swear this house has never seen so much action. A quick time check confirms it's been exactly ten minutes since I texted Ximena. She came right away. She's taking this seriously, and subsequently her job at Bishop Brews.

I answer the door and find Ximena staring at my house, a moss-ridden cottage laden with age but quaint and cute as hell. Her hands flex and her jaw grinds back and forth. She's traded her Bishop Brews shirt for a *Wicked* hoodie and jeans. I don't see her truck parked in the driveway, so she must've gotten a ride.

The faint scent of earth and bark rushes between us, good tidings from the Hemwood in the distance, where the redwoods stand like sentries watching over the arboretum and guarding the magic that fortifies my bones.

We stare at each other for an eternity before she says, "Thanks for hearing me out."

"I didn't have much of a choice."

I step aside to let her in. I don't have to prompt her to take her shoes off. She does so on her own and leaves her Dr. Martens by the door. Orange-painted toenails poke through her purple-and-white polka-dot socks. I bite back a smile.

If it felt bizarre to have her roaming around Bishop Brews today, it's so much stranger to see her in my house. She knows her way to the living room, having been here a thousand times before. Nothing's really changed. Same cream-colored paint on the walls. Same loose floorboard in the entryway. Same ficus tree next to the coatrack, and thrifted red couch and mahogany table in the living room. Ximena used to be one of the constants in this house too. It's hard to see her here, different and yet the same. I plop back into my chair before anyone can see how unsteady I am. How unsteady she's made me.

Nana wastes no time updating Ximena on the sheriff's visit, carefully explaining in more eloquent terms that the situation has gone from bad to worse with Leigh losing her memories.

Ximena freezes in shock. When she unsticks herself, she rubs the back of her neck and mumbles, "Now that missed call from her mom makes sense. Leigh and I are friends. Is she okay?"

"She's not in any pain, but we're working with the police to discern how this occurred, so we need to hear all the facts," Nana tells her. "Do you mind relaying to the coven what you told Sage this afternoon?"

"Yeah, of course." Ximena tucks her shaking hands into the pockets of her jeans and shuffles from foot to foot. She's being put on the spot, and it *almost* makes me feel sympathetic. "So, someone broke in while I was helping two customers. I was preoccupied and didn't hear them in the back of the store. I only noticed the back door was ajar when I went to get more intention candles."

"That sounds scary, especially on your first day. I'm so glad you're okay," Tiva says kindly.

I'm not sure "scary" is the right word here. More like a giant, steaming pile of coincidence.

"Thanks," Ximena mutters.

The members of the coven take turns asking her questions. *What time did this happen? Did she move anything?* Ximena carefully chooses her words, telling them how within fifteen minutes someone carefully picked the lock on the back door, and how she didn't touch a thing.

Ximena inches forward, her back straightening as she gains her footing. "And I was thinking, since whoever did this was in and out while Sage was gone and I was busy, they must've been watching us." Ximena pauses before adding, "It was clearly planned, at least minimally."

The silence during her responses is followed by a swell of murmurs and a litany of hums. The coven is impressed. But for me, she's not in the clear yet. She still could've done this, hoping to sell the tonics for a little extra cash.

"I don't want to lose my job," Ximena says. Her nervous twitching has stopped. No doubt because she believes she's escaped suspicion. "The customers there at the time can vouch for me."

"Sage already called them, honey," Nana replies.

Ximena looks at me quizzically, like she can't believe I didn't just take her word for it. After thinking about the logistics all afternoon, here's what I've landed on: Ximena had to know I'd leave the store, and then, within the fifteen minutes I was gone, she would've had to ditch the enthusiastic customers, break the back door lock to divert suspicion, stash the charms and tonics without getting any on her hands or clothes, and then call me. It doesn't seem plausible. Unless . . . she had help.

"I'm so sorry this happened," Ximena replies. "Let me know if there's anything else you need from me."

"Of course," Nana replies.

Everyone thanks her for coming, and Tiva shoves two cookies into her hands. Ximena has barely turned around to leave when she spins on her heel, chin raised high. "I want to help look into the break-in," she declares. "I know Leigh and her friends. I can talk to who she was with today."

"That's kind of you," Nana says. "But we've got it covered. We'll work with the Lawsons to question her friends."

Ximena grinds her teeth as she processes this and tries again. "Can I at least prove I'm innocent? I need this job, Ms. Bishop."

I cringe. The faithless houseplants give me away as their leaves twitch from my discomfort.

"Your job's safe, honey," Nana replies gently, though her stare is weighty when it falls on me. I shove a cookie into my mouth to keep from giving myself away.

"Sage said . . ." Ximena pauses, her expression unreadable. She could tell my grandmother in front of everyone that I fired her without permission, or she can play along, but why would she do that? There's nothing in it for her. I hold my breath and wait for her to decide my fate. "Sage said the store could be in jeopardy."

Air rushes out of my lungs. What alternate universe did I slip into where she's covering for me?

"That's nothing for you to worry about right now,"

Nana says. "Sage will let you know if things change. God willing, they won't."

Nana thanks Ximena for coming and asks me to walk her out, which I do without complaint because I'm super mature. Right now, anyway.

We pause in the foyer. Ximena and I stand on opposite sides of the room with a distance between us that is more than just space.

"Why didn't you rat me out when you realized you weren't actually fired?" I ask.

"What good would that have done besides get you in trouble?" she counters with a slant of her head.

We watch each other in silence. She seems uncertain, like she did when she first walked in. Her teeth gnaw on her bottom lip while she picks at a hangnail. Meanwhile, my overactive brain is *whirling*. I'm not a skilled enough brewer to make a counter tonic to reverse Leigh's memory loss, but I can still save Bishop Brews. It's at risk because of me. I won't let the sheriff shut us down.

"What is it?" she asks after a beat.

I cross my arms defensively. "Nothing."

"You're planning something. I know that face."

"I'm not making a face. I'm definitely not planning anything."

"Sage—"

"Why did you volunteer to assist us in the investigation?" I don't even try to keep the disbelief out of my voice.

Ximena's eyebrows rise. "I wasn't lying when I said I

care about the store." She drums her fingers against her leg. "And I want us to be good again," she adds, a hopeful lift to one side of her infuriatingly perfect mouth.

I balk at that. "Good again," I repeat numbly. How can we ever be good again? Why would she even want that?

"Yeah. We could have a fresh start between us before college. If helping you is how I do that, then I'm in."

Well, maybe if we— Nope. Not even considering it, especially if she doesn't have the estrogen to apologize. "I'll text you, okay? I need time to think."

Ximena has the audacity to smirk. "Okay."

As I watch her leave, my brain is a shaken snow globe of thoughts, most of them about Ximena and the far-fetched idea that's forming.

While my coven tries to find out who drugged Leigh, and the sheriff works on finding out who broke into the store, I need to figure out how it's all connected, and to do that, I need Ximena. She has connections to Leigh's inner circle, and if she was involved in the break-in, keeping her close is safer than giving her free rein to strike again. Even though I want to spend as little time with her as possible, I'm the only person who can suss out her real motive for wanting to contribute to the investigation. And that's exactly what I'm going to do.

# 6

The meeting winds down soon after Ximena leaves. The adults wrap up conversations about their next steps, while Mercer, Poppy, and I hang out on the front porch.

Mercer, who could not be more obvious in her crush, tucks her hair behind her ear and scoots over to give Poppy room to sit.

"Actually, I need your help with something," I tell Poppy. Mercer shoots me a death glare. "I found a wasp nest above the herb garden. Nana's already been stung once," I add delicately.

Poppy sucks her teeth but follows me. Because she can regenerate, she's become the designated person for anything dangerous. Her family also tests all our new tonics to make sure they're ready for public consumption—not the misbrews, though, the ones that don't glow from the start. That's asking for trouble.

I grab the stool Nana keeps near her garden to relieve her back pain when she's working and plant it under the live oak tree next to us. With a gentle wave of my hand, I part the branches concealing the wasp nest.

"You're examining the break-in yourself, right?" Poppy asks as she steps on the stool and gets to work.

"I . . . What?"

Poppy grunts. "Come on, Sage. I know you want to investigate. Everyone knows Blackclaw police are slow. And your grandma will be tied up with the counter brew. I doubt either will find anything quickly. What happened doesn't affect just you but our entire coven."

I scoff, hating that she still knows me even though we aren't as close anymore. "You'd be the first person I'd question. I saw you and Morris fighting outside Tea for Thought yesterday. He accused you of scheming. That was only minutes before the break-in."

Poppy squints. "You were spying on me?"

"You weren't exactly quiet."

She grabs the nest, immediately angering a few wasps who dart around her hands. "Don't listen to Morris. I wasn't *scheming*. I was waiting for my squad. Instead of focusing on me, focus on fixing the situation. Someone got hurt because of Hemwood magic. That makes all witches look bad. And what's worse, a founder's kid was hurt. I don't want them jeopardizing my family's interior design business like they're threatening yours based on a hunch."

Poppy yelps as a wasp digs its stinger into the back of

her hand. I step forward, but she waves me off. She's managed to keep the nest completely intact.

"I'll figure this out," I tell her as we head toward a tree farther away from the garden and the house.

"Good." She averts her gaze before adding, "You should know that I might've told some of the girls on the cheerleading team about that heartbreak tonic you've been working on."

And now I'm annoyed again. "Poppy, it's not even done!"

"It's a big deal! Half of my squad has been through a breakup this year or are anticipating one because they're going to different colleges than their partners. I thought you'd be happy," Poppy says. "Can you make something for me to anchor this to?"

The wasps have started to notice the move and are restlessly weaving between us. Already, the angry red mark on Poppy's hand has started to disappear. I won't be so lucky if I'm stung. Quickly, I find a set of new branches, still thin enough to manipulate with relative ease. With my help, they bend and weave together, forming a bowl shape. The effort leaves me a little lightheaded, but that'll dissipate in a few minutes. Poppy stands on her tippy-toes and slots the nest into the hollow.

Mercer's practically drooling over Poppy when we rejoin her on the porch. "Sage is planning to do a little sleuthing, isn't she?"

"Yep," Poppy says.

My covenmates aren't the only people I need in my corner, I realize. There's also Ximena. She has skills I lack, like being able to think on her feet and charm. So much charm. She also knows everyone, including Leigh's friends, which will be useful in establishing exactly what went down at the fundraising rally. My coven may have magic, but interviewing Leigh's friends will require a unique approach, one Ximena knows more than me because part of remaking herself this year involved joining the popular crew. I don't *want* to involve her, but if I'm going to solve this mystery, I have to exhaust all my options.

Poppy's mom finds us a few minutes later and offers to drive Mercer home, but Mercer seems to notice I've got more on my mind and says she'd rather walk. It's honestly scary how well she knows me.

"Come with me?" she asks once the Carvers leave.

I hurry inside and slip on my satin-lined beanie. I also wrap an oversize cardigan around my shoulders. The days are warm, but that nighttime wind is nothing to play with.

"Walking Mercer home?" Nana says when she sees me. "Can you drop something off for me on your way?" She scurries to the kitchen and returns carrying a brown paper bag. "Mrs. Hart wanted a tonic for her morning sickness, but I did her one better."

"A custom brew? Let me guess: peppermint, calendula petals, and . . . fennel?"

"Plain old ginger ale and saltines. Why fix what isn't broke?" Nana pats my head. "Be careful."

Outside, the sound of chirping crickets mixes with the

shushing sway of the trees around us. Nature is chattiest at night, when it's not competing with the boisterous noise residents and tourists make during the day.

Mercer and I don't get more than a foot past the end of my driveway before she says, "You're not telling me something. Spill."

I take a deep breath and then rip the Band-Aid off. "Leigh didn't drink one of the premade tonics. She drank my heartache brew." Mercer's eyes double in size. "Obviously, I'm supposed to immediately dispose of misbrews, but I must've been so distracted by Ximena that I forgot! I didn't tell the coven because the fewer people who know, the better."

"Holy crap. Who else knows?"

"Nana. She wants me to stay out of it. She's trying to protect me, but I can't just sit around. Whoever broke in could've wanted to steal a few basic tonics . . . or one in particular."

It takes a moment for what I'm suggesting to sink in but, when it does, Mercer's mouth drops open. "You think someone watched you misbrew, then stole the tonic on purpose? Who? And why? To sabotage Bishop Brews or to hurt Leigh?"

"I don't know." I push a few flyaway curls out of my face. "It could be anyone. A witch. Ximena. A spy for Bottled Wonders. Even an unsatisfied customer!"

"For starters, I don't think Ximena would jeopardize her new job. And before you spiral, the community loves Bishop Brews, especially kids. Remember that sixth-grade class that took a tour and made mock tonics? The thank-you cards they made were so cute. As for Bottled Wonders, business is booming there. Why risk that by stealing from an apothecary in another town? And a tourist wouldn't have given the tonic to Leigh Lawson, of all people. More likely, they'd try to sell it to Goop."

"You know our brews only work within the town borders, and last I checked, giant wellness brands haven't planted roots here. That said, you make good points."

"Of course I do."

We've reached Bewitched Blossoms, where, out front, Mrs. Hart hangs pink-and-yellow garlands in the window, likely decorating early for the Spring Harvest Festival next Sunday. The entire town and just as many tourists attend the celebration. A live band plays music throughout the day, carnival games promising sugar and stuffed animals line the streets, and all the small businesses in town set up stalls where we showcase our goods. This year I'm hoping to debut the heartbreak tonic. Once everyone sees how amazing it is, Bishop Brews will be back on top. That is, if Nana can save Leigh before the memory loss becomes permanent.

Mrs. Hart laughs when she sees the ginger ale can and repays me with a jar of her homemade peach jam. It's better than anything you can buy in a store, somehow both sweet and mellow. Our families regularly trade favors, whether it be in tonics, help around the arboretum during busy season, or plant food for Mrs. Hart's gorgeous flowers. She's not a witch, but her natural skills with growing flowers rival Nana's.

"Do you really think the council would close the apothecary?" Mercer asks once we start heading to her place.

"The sheriff could convince the council that Bishop Brews or my grandmother is a liability."

I've never given much thought to our town politics until tonight. Now it rubs me like a wool sweater that descendants of the founding families remain in leadership positions. Sure, they treat our coven as equals—allowing us into their inner circles, seeking advice for anything remotely mystical, and honoring us at the Founders' Day celebrations. But they still have the influence and—more important—the wealth we don't.

"We won't let that happen," Mercer tells me.

The street widens as we get to her subdivision. Mercer lives about a fifteen-minute walk from my house. Ximena lives in this neighborhood too, a few minutes south.

"I was thinking of asking Ximena to help me investigate," I say, since apparently I can't stop thinking about her.

"Oh really? Y'all finally made up?"

"We agreed to put the past behind us," I reply slowly.

"So she apologized for ghosting you?"

"Not exactly. I'm pretty sure she tried to earlier this year, but I wasn't ready to hear her out. You can't just come back to town after four years and expect me to be welcoming. Not after what she did."

Up until we were thirteen, I spent every single day with Ximena. I told her all my secrets and shared my biggest dreams. She was there for me when my parents died. I celebrated with her when she became a big sister. Then I mourned her for abandoning me.

"*Can* you forgive her?" Mercer asks.

"I don't know." There's got to be a good reason she ditched me four years ago, but I'm more scared than curious to hear the explanation.

"Well, you need to try. It's time the two of you reconcile. For real." I open my mouth to protest, but she continues, "If not for yourselves then for the sake of your rogue case. This is too important to let old issues get in the way. You know what would be nice? A proper sitdown. You were friends before you had that kiss. That's got to count for something."

"You sound like Nana."

"She's a smart woman. Squash your beef. It's time to move on."

"I plan to, as soon as I finish my heartache tonic."

Mercer shakes her head, her expression dangerously close to pity. I don't care. The truth is, it doesn't matter how much I missed Ximena in the last four years or how being near her in the store yesterday made my heart race. I don't have room in my head or my life for someone who chucked me aside like an invasive garden weed.

I don't know how long it'll take to finish my tonic, but teaming up means Ximena and I should at least be cordial. It's one thing to work together at Bishop Brews, where we have customers and chores to distract us and lo-fi hip-hop music to fill the silence for a few hours a week. Actively partnering on an unofficial investigation that could save or end Bishop Brews is a whole other beast.

"You okay to walk back? You could stay over," Mercer asks as we stand on her porch.

"I'm good. I'll see you tomorrow."

Mercer waves goodbye and goes inside. I linger for a while longer, trying to find it within myself to make the next move. It's so much easier said than done. When I've stalled long enough to annoy myself, I pull out my phone. It's infinitesimally less horrible to text her this time. Much to my surprise.

> If you really wanna fix this, meet me at Honey's after school tomorrow.

Three little dots pop up on my screen, taunting me. I glare at them as if I can make her text back with sheer willpower. I may or may not be holding my breath, but that's only because I want to get this over with.

**Ximena (Don't Fall For It) Reyes:**
i knew you'd come around. see u tmrw

# 7

Bishop Brews is closed. Deputies photographed the store this morning, and a locksmith is coming late this afternoon to put a new lock on the back door. My family's apothecary will remain dark until then.

The sheriff gave us the go-ahead to reopen tomorrow, which means back to work with Ximena, who I still haven't decided isn't involved. It doesn't help that she's so eager to assist in the investigation. The guilty always return to the scene of the crime.

Honey's is an old-fashioned diner, a block from Bishop Brews, that sells greasy burgers, milkshakes, and the best French fries in town. I haven't been here in years thanks to Ximena. This was our spot in middle school, and after she left, I couldn't bring myself to return. Everywhere I looked I saw her. Eventually, I wrote off the restaurant completely.

Since Ximena moved back to town and started haunting

my classes, working in my store, and generally being present in my life, returning to Honey's shouldn't be a big deal. I hope.

**Ximena (Don't Fall For It) Reyes:**

here!

She must've had an open period before this if she's already inside because I came right after school. According to Nana, the locksmith is coming around four. I want to take stock of the store before then. That gives me and Ximena an hour to sort out our differences and examine Bishop Brews.

As soon as I step through the door, the smell of butter, fresh apple pie, and general nostalgia drifts over me. Ugh. I've missed this greasy little place.

I walk past the long laminate lunch counter with twelve slippery red stools underneath it in search of her. When I make it to the rows of tables in the back, Ximena's tuft of black hair catches my attention. She's slotted into a booth next to a window.

Seeing her there brings me back to being thirteen, covered in grass stains and achy from a grueling soccer game. Ximena and I traded easy laughs over a large basket of fries and two vanilla milkshakes. It was right around the time I started noticing how wretchedly pretty she was, the way the light would capture flecks of gold in her eyes and hues of auburn in her hair. That day, my crush was raging rampant. I thought I'd suffocate under its weight.

I remember being so worried that she could tell, but Ximena seemed oblivious to my overt staring and nervous giggles.

Now, in this same dappled light with Ximena drumming her fingertips on the table and bobbing her head along to a beat only she can hear, I can almost pretend that no time has passed. Almost.

She stands as I approach, smoothing her oversize graphic T-shirt—*Hamilton* today—that she's tucked into a pair of loose cargo shorts. She looks different now than she does at school. More relaxed. More like her old self. It's weird and disarming.

"Hey."

"Hi."

There's an awkward moment where neither of us moves. Same as last night, Ximena breaks first, gesturing toward the seat across from her. I slide in, suddenly aware of myself in a way I haven't been in years. My Day 5 wash-n-go is pulled into a quick French braid that could be neater, and at the bottom of my boring gray crewneck is a hideous yellow stain from a failed tonic that refuses to come out. I totally forgot it was there until halfway through school.

"So, what's the game plan?" she asks.

I force my shoulders to drop from around my ears. "We're going to secretly investigate the break-in."

"Secretly?"

"Technically, the sheriff's investigating since it's a non-magical crime, but my coven is assisting because Leigh's memory loss was magic-induced. That makes the break-in within our coven's authority. Nana doesn't want me involved, but I can't let the coven do all the work and take the blame for my forgetfulness. I'm responsible for Leigh's condition. It was my tonic that she drank. I left it out and didn't dispose of it properly."

Ximena tilts her head. "The heartache tonic you mentioned?"

Blood rushes to my cheeks. Do I tell the person responsible for reigniting my feelings of heartbreak after four years about the tonic I created to make said feelings go away?

"It's slightly more complex than that," I say to save face. "The tonic is supposed to get rid of all the bad feelings that come with losing someone. It's for Bishop Brews."

An unreadable expression flickers across Ximena's face. "Sounds . . . lucrative. You couldn't have known someone would steal it, but I understand why they would."

"If I don't find who did this and soon, the sheriff could close the store because it's a liability. If that happens, I'll be out of a job. You'll be out of a job. And you can kiss your income goodbye."

Her neck muscles strain. "Noted."

I lean back, the stiff plastic of the booth digging into my shoulder blades. "But we're not partners," I say. "If anything, you're my sidekick. I'm in charge."

Ximena chuckles lightly. It's the first laugh she's given me in years, and my brain briefly short-circuits. "Whatever you say."

I clear my throat and try to find my footing. "Have you talked to Leigh today?"

She runs a hand through her short hair. "No. To be honest, it's been a few weeks since we've hung out. We've both been busy. I was serious when I said I can reach out to her friends, though. She'll be okay, right?"

"She should be. Nana is an expert brewer, no matter what the sheriff thinks."

"That's good." Ximena drums her nails some more. Silence.

I resist the urge to fidget, focusing instead on grounding myself in the moment and trying to come across as sincere as possible. "I'm sorry I fired you."

Ximena raises her eyebrows, as perfectly formed as calligraphy brushstrokes. She flashes me a smile that I think is supposed to be reassuring but instead makes me more nervous. "Apology accepted."

Officially having run out of things to say, we end up in a staring contest, which the server blissfully interrupts. She's familiar in the same way most people are in tiny towns. She pulls a notebook out of the blue apron tied around her waist. "What can I get you?" she asks, limp hair falling into her face.

"I'll have a vanilla milkshake," I reply. "And a basket of fries."

Ximena's eyes dart to mine before flicking back to our server. "Same. Extra whipped cream on the shake."

"Coming right up." The server tucks the shiny menus

neither of us touched under her arm and moves on to her next table.

I have to bite my bottom lip to stop myself from mentioning that we ordered exactly what we used to back when Honey's was our designated hangout a hundred years ago.

Ximena doesn't seem to get the "put the past behind us" memo. She purses her berry-colored lips before saying, "Remember when we used to chug vanilla milkshakes to give ourselves brain freezes?"

I tighten my hands around the hem of my shirt. She's extending an olive branch, one I need to take because Bishop Brews and my coven are counting on me. Us. "I do," I reply. "We'd be too full to eat our burgers."

Ximena laughs easily. "I miss those days."

I swallow hard and try not to let the disquiet her confession stirred up get the better of me. This is as good an opening as I'm going to get. "As I recall, *you* ended our friendship."

Ximena frowns. "That's not . . . It's complicated."

"I think it's pretty simple, actually," I reply through my teeth. "You were bored of me." Ximena leaving made it painfully clear that opening my heart to someone isn't worth the possibility of losing them. I'd rather my life stay the same so there's no chance of getting hurt if my new favorite things get taken away from me.

Ximena's eyes widen. "No. I—"

"It's fine. I just wanted to say you were right. Consider this our new start, all right? Everything else is old news."

The soft edge of her jaw tightens. "It's clear you're still upset about what happened."

"Ghosting your best friend was a pretty shitty thing to do."

Ximena flexes her hands. "I didn't know how to explain what was going on with me."

"And now?"

She shifts her weight. "I don't know what to say and I don't know how to make this better. I am sorry. I didn't want to hurt you."

My whole body is tense. "Right. Well, you did."

Ximena drops her gaze. I can breathe a little easier now that I've told her she hurt me. I'm still not okay. Maybe there will always be this ache in my chest when I'm around her, but that's a problem for the tonic to fix.

"For the sake of the investigation, let's make a pact not to bring up our history," I say. "It's the only way this will work."

The server chooses that exact moment to return with our food. I grab my shake and let the cold of the glass dissolve some of the heat burning in me.

Ximena's quiet and her food sits untouched. She works her mouth like she's trying to decide what to say. Eventually, her shoulders slump in defeat. "Fine. Whatever."

"Great."

There. Situation handled. I freeze out the voice in my head that begs to differ with three giant slurps of milkshake.

Ximena's confidence comes back in record time. She lifts her brow. "So, where do we start, boss?"

I grind my teeth at the moniker but manage to, at least, sound unaffected. "Bishop Brews."

Ximena nods. "Return to the scene of the crime. I like it. Any suspects? Aside from me, of course." She gives me a knowing look.

"At least you realize you're suspicious," I reply smoothly. "But I'm not focusing on you right now. You aren't the strongest suspect."

She bats her eyelashes. "Should I be flattered?"

"No. Now, considering whoever broke into the apothecary only stole tonics, I'd say this was a targeted attack done by someone who wanted our brews."

"That narrows it down." Ximena quirks her lips. "So this isn't just a random burglary, or they would've gone for the cash. They only wanted the tonics."

I plop a fry into my mouth and nod. "I don't see why someone would steal our tonics when Nana would readily give them out to those in need."

"Maybe the thief wanted to resell them," Ximena says.

"The way I see it, the thief might not have wanted to hurt anyone but wanted some free magic. Or they did and intentionally targeted Leigh, the founding families, me, the coven, and or Bishop Brews. The break-in was either random or very personal."

Ximena takes a giant swig of her milkshake. Some stays on her lips, making it very difficult to concentrate on what she's saying. "This is muddled as hell. Maybe it's best we treat everyone as a suspect for now? We shouldn't rule anyone out until we're certain they're in the clear, including your coven."

I shake my head. "I don't think a witch did this. No one would put themself in jeopardy over a few tonics."

"People can surprise you." She takes another long sip of her shake, the soft skin of her throat bobbing.

I need to stop staring.

"I'm curious," she continues. "Why am I off the hook for now? I know you called the customers, but are there any other reasons?"

"My magic heightens every property of the ingredients, including their pigments. That, on top of miscalculating how much magic I needed, is guaranteed to result in killer stains that aren't coming out with water and Tide. They'll dissipate from someone's skin on their own, but not for a week or two. Whoever stole the tonics spilled mine everywhere. I'm willing to bet it's on their hands and clothes too. Even Leigh had plum-colored stains on her chin and mouth, same color as my failed tonic. So unless you're hiding a very powerful magic stain remover, or you had an accomplice, I'd say you're in the clear for now. The coven too."

"How do you know I wasn't wearing gloves?"

"Do you *want* me to suspect you?"

"If you're into that sort of thing. Sure."

I choke, wheezing out pitiful spurts of air and barely managing to keep milk from shooting out my nose.

"Bad joke." Ximena hands me a napkin. She leans back

and smiles. "I'm impressed, although I guess I shouldn't be. You always were good at solving puzzles."

"So were you," I reply automatically. "And now you're good at . . . singing 'In the Heights'?"

Her face brightens. "You've seen it?"

"Googled the lyrics," I say, without realizing that makes me seem like I care, and I don't. "I didn't know you were a fan."

She nods. "I like pretending to be different characters for a couple of hours, living another life, someplace far away." She clears her throat. "A lot can change in four years."

I look her up and down, taking in her new short haircut with the sides and back shaved, the moon tattoo behind her ear, and the unexpected effortlessness of her appearance. It really is crazy what time and distance can do to a person.

"Clearly."

# Sage's Heartbreak Tonic

## Attempt Number Twenty-Three

### INGREDIENTS

⅓ cup Hemwood spring
   water

1.5 oz. crushed lavender

3 wild pansy petals

1 oz. crushed St. John's wort

As much honey as you want

Luck. How else is this
   going to work?

### DIRECTIONS

1. In a brewing pot, pour in the spring water, scatter the lavender, and drop in pansy petals one at a time. Let mixture simmer on low heat for 10 minutes. Think about anything other than how long it's taking.

2. Toss in the St. John's wort. Stir enthusiastically. Seriously, people should be concerned. Let steep for 2 minutes.

3. Close your eyes and focus your intentions on making a tonic to forget your heartache.

4. Carefully bind the properties of the herbs together with magic.

5. Add that honey. Live your best life.

6. Eagerly check the mixture to see if it's glowing.

**Pro Tip:** *Mental clarity required. Will not work if desperate, tired, or both.*

## 8

**B**ishop Brews looks exactly as it did yesterday. It'd be easy to pretend nothing happened. And yet, the hair on the back of my neck prickles as I move around the store, and the facade starts to crack like bad foundation. There's still a strange patch of dried elderberries by the front door and along the counter, though less of it since the police took samples as evidence. I file the observation away for later and head toward the kitchen.

Now that the adrenaline of first discovering the break-in has subsided a bit, the damage is obvious. Failed heartache remedy number twenty-two has spilled everywhere. It dried in dark streaks across the counter and the floor. The thief also knocked over the bird-of-paradise that's lived next to the back door for the last two years. The disrespect is a thorn between my ribs, sharp and insistent.

I inhale shakily and try to keep my cool, but my hands

tremble. Ximena's next to me a moment later. "I'm sorry about this. Again."

I refrain from rolling my eyes and reminding her that none of this would've happened if she'd paid better attention during her shift. I don't say it because there's no use being witchy if we've got at least a week of regular face-to-face interaction and sleuthing coming up.

The careful, thought-out aloofness I planned to exhibit during our work shifts might not hold up if we're going to bounce around ideas. And I'll admit, it's hard to hear anything happening in the back of the store when you're in the front, especially if you're chatting with customers. Who knows what a burglar would have done if Ximena *had* caught them. Blackclaw is a relatively crime-free town, and since it's so small, reputations have weight. Every now and then, a tourist will have their wallet or phone stolen, or a deputy will pick up a drunk driver, but burglaries rarely happen.

"See anything helpful? Clues?" Ximena asks. She picks up the overturned plant and carefully scoops its dirt with her hands. It's such a gentle act, I almost forget to answer. As she replaces the soil in the pot, the thorn releases from my side, and I can breathe easier.

"Aside from the remains of yet another failed tonic? Nothing." I wander in circles, pinching spilled herbs back into their jars, straightening out the mixing pot, and trying not to get worked up. On the counter is a spilled jar of Hemwood soil. With a snap of my fingers, the dirt rises into the air and dribbles back into its container.

Ximena jumps to her feet, closes her eyes, and creases her button nose.

"What are you doing?" I ask.

Ximena startles. "Oh. Uh, nothing. I—I thought I smelled something."

"Okaaay. If you're done sniffing around, I'm going to make a quick batch of FindIt. It's good for finding misplaced objects. Nana invented it for Tiva, who's constantly losing her phone. The police searched the store, but there's always a chance they missed something."

"You know how to make the tonic?"

I flip open the grimoire with a flourish. "The instructions are in here. I may be failing to make my tonic, but that's only because I'm trying to invent something new. FindIt is tried and true. All you need is a little poke root, because it's good for finding what's lost, and rosemary—good for clear thinking and seeing the bigger picture. Weave them together with Bishop magic, and you've got a pretty powerful tonic for finding stuff."

Ximena joins me at the counter, resting an arm against the wood. "How does it work?"

"Like all tonics, it targets pathways in your brain, particularly the ones for attentiveness."

She nods, and it's casual, but there is more behind her gesture. When we were younger, her facial expressions always gave her away. Over the last four years, she's gotten good at hiding how she really feels. But there's a part of me that still knows her, even if I hate that it does. Right now, based on her quirked lips, I'd say she's impressed.

Ximena has never seen me brew. I wasn't allowed to make my own tonics until I was thirteen, right after Ximena gave me the boot. I think it was Nana's way of bringing me out of my funk, to be honest. And, for the most part, it worked. I've made all the basic brews we keep stocked in the store: remedies to shorten the flu, courage elixirs, and memory boosters. But there's always room to experiment, which is how Nana made FindIt and how I hope to make my own tonic to fix the mess in my heart and everyone else's.

I move through the process as quickly as possible, cleaning out the brewing pot and then pouring in a batch of fresh spring water. I've never actually made this before, but with the grimoire as a guide, I'm not too worried about getting it right.

As I work, I'm acutely aware of how close Ximena is standing next to me. I can smell her shampoo and her earthy perfume, and beneath that, something warm and familiar I can't quite place. "Can you hand me the rosemary and the poke root?" I inch away, needing to concentrate.

Ximena arches a surprised eyebrow before moving to the spice rack. She finds the jars of herbs grown right in Nana's garden. "Was that some kind of test? I know what rosemary looks like, and there's a label on the poke root," she says, handing them to me.

"Not a test." I couldn't exactly ask for a second of breathing room. "It's just faster if you help. You *do* want to help me solve this, right?"

Ximena rolls her eyes. "Yes."

I take the herbs from her, careful not to let our fingers touch. Three pinches of rosemary and a dash of crushed poke root later, and the blend is finished and glowing a faint pearly white. I steady myself against the counter as fatigue engulfs me. Magic requires a delicate balancing act. Use too much, and you'll drain yourself. Small doses like what it takes to make a tonic aren't too exhausting, but the more often I do it, the hungrier I get. Other tasks, like manipulating plants for long periods of time, can cause chronic fatigue. Nana once came home so tired after helping my aunt redecorate a founder's yard, she fell asleep standing up.

My stomach makes a loud, monstrous noise. I ignore it, fill up my ladle with the FindIt mixture, and drink it straight down.

"How long will it last?" Ximena asks.

"Ten minutes, maybe? It's for the best. This stuff makes your vision weird."

And soon enough, the tonic begins to take effect. I blink hard as the world blurs into a smudged sketch, everything soft and fuzzy like Nana says the world looks without her glasses. I wish there was a tonic to reveal the culprit, but magic doesn't work like that. It shows you what you're missing from an equation. It doesn't give you the answer.

I scan the room, searching for something sharp and clear, but the fuzz stretches from one wall to the next.

"Anything?" Ximena asks.

"Just give me a second."

Nothing seems to be happening. I start a second lap

around the kitchen at a more sedate pace. I scan the shelves, the floor, the table, the kitchen counter, the window, the back door, the mini fridge—

Wait. The back door.

It's *slightly* sharper than everything else. I rush to it, carefully scanning for anything that might be out of place, but nothing aside from the frame is in focus.

"Do you smell something?" I ask Ximena, who's wrinkling her nose again as she spins around.

Ximena reaches for the door handle instead of answering. Before I can protest, she yanks it open with a determined expression that's quickly replaced with a grin.

I follow her line of sight and stop. There, as clear as the sky after a rainstorm, is a crumpled ball of yellow tissue stuck inside the doorjamb, like it fell after the door was pushed open. It wasn't there when I performed opening procedures yesterday. Nana's meeting the locksmith here in thirty minutes, so it can't be his. When deputies came to take pictures of the store this morning, they didn't touch anything. They must have missed the tissue because it's hidden between the hinge and the jamb. They clearly weren't as thorough as they should've been, which is even more reason to conduct my own investigation.

Whoever left this must be the same person who broke in. I crouch down to fish it out and give it to Ximena. Her hand brushes mine and my skin flares with heat.

Ximena unfolds the tissue, her forehead creasing. "It's a napkin. Something's written in the left-hand corner . . . *Annual Spring Harvest Festival*, and here's the town's symbol." She flips the napkin over. Aside from a green smudge in the corner that could be anything from salsa to a glaze, it's blank. Ximena turns her head and fixes those dark, sparkling eyes on me. "Did we just find a clue?"

I tear my gaze away. "Maybe. I'll call Mercer. She'll be able to tell us exactly where this came from."

"We don't really need her," Ximena says. "I mean, there can't be that many stores with custom napkins for the festival. We can ask around."

I tilt my head. "Is this about your 'everyone is a suspect' thing? Because Mercer didn't break in."

Ximena's lips twitch. "We don't know that. I know she's your friend, but my method is the best way to go about this."

"Okay, Agatha Christie. Well, I think going door-to-door would take too much time. It's not like we won't double-check Mercer's work by going to the store it came from."

Ximena grunts and I think she'll push back more, but she deflates. "Fine."

"Fine."

An hour in, and she's already being difficult. It's almost like she wants to drag out the mystery. The sooner we get this over with, the sooner I can shove all thoughts of Ximena Reyes back into the furthest depths of my mind. That day cannot come fast enough.

# 9

The Enchanted Emporium is a squat store with a
forest-green paint job and oversize windows that
resemble eyes. Someone told the owner, Henry, as
much, and ever since he's kept the blinds in one of the
windows half raised, so it looks like the store is winking
at you when you walk by. That's pretty much the sentiment of the entire shop: eccentric. It's a mash-up of a
magic store and a thrift store. You can find almost anything here. For the tourists, they sell mundane plastic
wands, crystal balls, picturesque postcards, decorative
spell books, and cauldrons. For everyone else, there are
typewriters, grandpa sweaters donated by actual grand-
pas, couches, and chessboards—everything with a story
and its own kind of magic. And because Henry's friends
with Nana, the inside of the store is covered in dozens of
vines and ever-blooming flowers.

The door jingles when we step inside, and as usual, I'm hit with the smell of old fabric and dust.

"You know, I can't remember the last time I was in here," Ximena says, eyes widening. The wonder on her face softens her features and makes her look more like the girl I remember.

Licorice, the old black cat that haunts the store, bounds down the aisle to greet us with a loud meow. Henry found him wandering behind the store last year. He's the friendliest cat you'll ever meet, round as a volleyball with striking golden eyes. He arches his back and rubs against my leg. Smiling, I give him a pat.

Ximena moves closer, and Licorice hisses and swats at her.

"Licorice! That's not nice!" I scold. "What a little diva."

Ximena rubs the back of her neck. "He can probably tell I'm a dog person."

Licorice beelines for his window perch, clearly done with us. He hisses when Ximena glances back at him.

We move deeper into the store, and Ximena stops at a glass cabinet filled with instruments. She leans in to read the sticker next to a shiny clarinet that reads "Ask Me About My History (I'm famous!)"

"Mercer's really turned the emporium into a special place," I tell Ximena. "It was her idea to give every item a backstory, and now they're a huge hit with customers."

"You're proud of her," she says.

"Well, yeah. She's my best friend."

I swear Ximena's face deflates a little, but that can't be right. She *had* the best friend title. More than that. She didn't want it. It feels like we're walking on a tightrope, toeing the line between dredging up our past and staying firmly rooted in the present.

A loud clang from deep within the store followed by a swear saves us from further conversation. We dart toward the noise and enter the back room to find Mercer hunched over a box nearly twice her size and a bowling ball charging toward an expensive-looking antique mirror poised against the back wall.

Vines outline the walls like fairy lights. I reach for my magic on instinct, urging a vine to unhook. I'm fast, but somehow Ximena's faster. She juts her foot out, knocking the ball off course. Her olive-colored Dr. Martens squeak against the shiny polyester surface. The bowling ball doesn't smash into the glass like intended, but it does bump the frame, sending the mirror wobbling forward. My vine loops around the top half, saving us from seven years of bad luck.

"Nice teamwork," Mercer says, turning her full attention to me and Ximena. "You would not believe where that ball has been. No way it's going on display." She brushes her hair out of her face, eyes gleaming as they flick between us. "So. This is a surprise."

She purses her lips, no doubt biting back a comment about Ximena and me being here together. "We need your expertise," I say.

Ximena, who's been standing off to the side, inches a

little closer. She tucks her hands in her pockets and keeps her chin high, but I get the sense, based on the subtle drumming of her foot, that this is as awkward for her as it is for me. Blackclaw is a small town with one high school. Mercer and Ximena obviously know of each other, but I don't think they've really talked.

"For your secret investigation?" Mercer asks with an exaggerated wink.

"Yes. For that."

Mercer cracks open the flaps of the box in front of her. "Okay. Let me finish this up. I'm almost done. Henry asked for the history of these donations an hour ago." The tips of her fingers emit a soft glow as she dips them inside the box. Her cheeks flush as she shuffles through the used items like a deck of cards.

Ximena leans forward in interest, but her shoulders and jaw remain rigid.

Mercer puts a book to the left of the box and an autographed baseball to the right. "When people think of witches, they picture the items we sell up front: wands and broomsticks, spells and hexes. Maybe that fits for some witches, but Blackclaw witches are really just a bunch of woodland fairies with forest magic. Did you know you can read a tree's whole life from its rings? That's what I'm doing here, except with objects."

She says it for Ximena's benefit, and yet, Ximena only frowns and touches her wrists. It's then I notice the gold permanent bracelet she's wearing. I've seen a few girls in my high school wearing similar pieces of jewelry, the metal welded closed around their wrists and necks. Ximena's is way more intricate. It has swirling blue gemstones filled with what might be plant shavings of some kind.

"Can you also read people's pasts or only . . ." Ximena motions to the box.

"Only objects. But that would be cool." Mercer puts the last item, a fancy crystal ball, off to the right. "Done!" She tucks her legs underneath herself and folds her hands in her lap. She's a little pale from the effort, but she keeps a stack of protein bars in her purse that will put some color back into her face in no time. "How can I help?" she asks.

If this were an official police inquiry, the napkin we found would be in a plastic baggie on its way to a lab. Instead, I pull it out of my pocket and dust off the lint. I hand it to Mercer with a sheepish smile.

I could give this or any other clue to the police, but with all the red tape, it'd take longer than the amount of time we have to save the store to figure out who the clue belonged to or how it relates to the break-in. It's easier to operate strictly on our own.

Mercer's fingers glow when she touches the napkin, and her eyes flutter closed. "I see the apothecary floor, the dark lining of a pocket, a glass food case . . . the counter of a crowded restaurant or store that starts with an 'N' or 'M.' I'm not seeing the sign from a good angle." She opens her eyes and hands back the napkin. "That's the best I got. Further back, and my vision is dark, which means it was probably in a box."

"Can I see it?" Ximena asks, holding out her hand. Mercer raises an eyebrow but gives her the napkin.

Ximena chews on her bottom lip as she trails her fingers across the green smudge in the corner. With only an ounce of hesitation, she brings the napkin to her face and inhales. A second later, she snaps her fingers. "Mystic Muffins!"

"What? Are you sure?" I ask.

"Positive. I knew I smelled something sweet. It was sugar."

"When did you get such a good nose?"

Ximena shrugs. "Born with it. You just never noticed."

Huh. I don't think it's that, but maybe some of my older memories have faded?

Mercer climbs to her feet. "Mystic Muffins does start with the letter 'M.'" She sizes Ximena up as if seeing her anew. "Nice catch."

"Thanks." Ximena gives Mercer a once-over. "Do you get a lot of free time at work? It seems quiet for a Monday."

"It's busier in the mornings and evenings during the week, at least until tourist season hits. Henry doesn't micromanage. As long as I get my work done, he's good. Yesterday was busy. I was stuck behind the register all morning." Mercer inclines her head. "Need to check the security footage?"

"I'm just being thorough," Ximena replies dully.

Licorice starts meowing before the silence can stretch on too long.

"Incoming customer. He's better than a doorbell," Mercer explains.

"We'll walk with you," I say. I take back the napkin and tuck it into my pocket. The three of us meander to the front of the store, where Mrs. Hart is petting Licorice. Parked outside is her van with the sliding door open to reveal three boxes piled in the back seat along with several bouquets of flowers. Deliveries, probably.

"Hi, girls! You must've heard Licorice calling." She scratches the cat's chin. "Do one of you mind grabbing those boxes for donations? My doctor said I'm not supposed to lift more than twenty pounds and those bad boys are *stuffed*."

Mercer steps forward, but Ximena beats her to the punch. "I'll get them," she announces before running outside. It's like she's trying to prove her usefulness. Mercer merely shrugs.

"The ginger ale worked wonders, of course," Mrs. Hart tells me. "Thank your grandma for me?"

"Totally." Mrs. Hart pats my shoulder, and then leaves to browse the store. With her gone, there is nothing to block my view of Ximena. She disappears into the van and reappears a moment later. Her arms flex as she hauls out all three boxes at once. She doesn't even break a sweat.

I try to swallow but all the saliva in my mouth has suddenly evaporated. I'll say this: she is much stronger than she was four years ago. Ximena smirks as she walks by us with the boxes, heading toward the back room.

Beside me, Mercer grins. "I see her appeal. You need some water? You're looking a little thirsty."

"Stop!"

Mercer laughs. "How long are you staying?"

"Not long. We should go to Mystic Muffins before they close," I manage to reply.

Ximena returns a moment later, not a single hair out of place. "I put the boxes next to the one you were looking through when we got here," she tells Mercer. To me, she says, "Ready?"

Mercer grabs a tiny notepad from her back pocket, scribbles on it, and rips off the sheet. She holds it out to Ximena. "Actually, can you give this to Mrs. Hart? It's in case she wants to claim the donations on her taxes."

Ximena looks between the two of us and rolls her eyes. She snatches the sheet from Mercer. "Fine. Meet me outside when you're done, Sage."

Mercer turns to me once she's gone. "So, did you make up at Honey's? I've been on the edge of my seat over here."

"She said she wants to make things right."

"I'm not surprised. Senior year has people feeling nostalgic. It's everyone's last chance to do the things they always wanted to do before college."

"I don't buy that."

Mercer shakes her head. "Despite Ximena's skepticism about me, I just want *you* to be happy. Would it be the end of the world if after the investigation, you two remain on speaking terms or, I don't know, are friendly?"

"Yes, the world would implode," I deadpan.

Friends don't hurt each other the way she hurt me. And if we're being honest, we were always more than friends anyway. I don't know what Ximena tells herself, but I still remember the way she used to ogle me, how her hand felt in mine, and how her lips tasted. Working with her wouldn't be so hard if I didn't.

"For what it's worth, she's putting in effort. She didn't have to come here with you, and she did help find where the napkin came from," Mercer says, straightening the picturesque postcards of Blackclaw on the souvenir rack next to us.

"That doesn't mean I want us to be friends again."

"Why not?"

*Because she broke my heart.* The confession sits on the tip of my tongue, as sharp and bitter as vinegar. Mercer is smart enough to suspect, but I never actually told anyone how much I liked Ximena. I wanted to keep the depth of what we had sealed tight. Too much air, and everything that brief but epic relationship meant to me might evaporate.

"Just leave it alone, Mercer. Please," I say instead.

She takes a while to reply but eventually says, "All right. Call me later?"

"I will. Thanks for the assist today."

Mercer waves me off. "Anytime."

)·)·)·)●(·(·(·(

Agnes Evergreen, the owner of Mystic Muffins, is not a witch, but she might as well be, with how bewitched all the residents of Blackclaw are by her baking skills. Seriously, the woman makes the most heavenly pastries in town.

When we enter, she bellows, "Welcome to Mystic Muffins, where dessert is always on the menu!" A red ribbon ties up her bleached blond hair, and her rolled-up sleeves show off a tapestry of colorful tattoos. She towers over the counter and grins when she spots us. "Hi, Sage! I don't remember you placing an order. Have I mixed up the days?"

I'm here once a month to curb Nana's sweet tooth. She'd order more than that if Tiva and I weren't so concerned about her blood sugar levels. "Not here for the pecan pie today. We're here for you." Before I can ask about the napkin, I spot a whole stack next to her on the counter. They're the same color with the same writing as the one we found in Bishop Brews. They weren't here last month. "Are those new?" I ask.

"Arrived last week! I figured the bakery could use a little bit of a refresh before the festival this year, but I completely forgot to add the shop name! Thankfully, the rest of the inventory says Mystic Muffins!" Her laugh is hearty.

I check out the cupcakes, pies, macaroons, cookies, and of course, every kind of muffin in the glass case next to the register. None of them have green icing like what's smeared across the napkin. They do make my mouth water and my post-magic hunger rear to life.

"Did anyone order custom desserts yesterday?" I ask.

Agnes shakes her head. "Not that I recall. Yesterday was mostly about the promotion."

"What promotion?"

"For the high school athletes. I always admired the graduating students raising funds for rising seniors. This year, I thought a little pre-fundraiser fun for participants would be motivating. If the athletes wore their team uniforms, they got a free cupcake. Mystic was packed with what must've been the entire basketball team and cheerleading squad. Even the mascot with her furry wolf costume came!"

Ximena shivers. "That suit gives me the creeps."

The cupcake promotion explains why I saw Poppy and Morris standing outside in their warmups. "What time was this?" I ask.

"From eleven-thirty to twelve on Sunday," Agnes replies. "They were my big rush for the day. I even made a special icing, white and green, the school's colors."

I tug the napkin out of my pocket and hold it out. "Could this have been from one of the cupcakes?"

Agnes leans over. "Yep. It's the right color. Do you want one? I think I have a few extras in the back. They won't be fresh, so I apologize, but I hate being wasteful."

"Yes, please," I say.

"Me too," Ximena adds.

As soon as Agnes is gone, Ximena turns to me. "You think an athlete at our school did this?" she asks.

I nod. "I doubt anyone would give away their cupcake,

because everything Agnes makes is divine, but we shouldn't discount the possibility. A jock or a cheerleader might've broken in. I wonder if the thief knew my tonic had been misbrewed."

Ximena rubs her chin, thinking. "Who knows about the side effects of misbrewed tonics?"

"Only you, my coven, and the founders."

"But I'm not an athlete."

I know what I said before about her not having any tonic stains on her clothes, but there's still a second option. "You could've partnered with one."

"Fair, but I didn't do this, remember?" Ximena seems more amused than annoyed that I'm reconsidering her as a suspect. She leans against the counter and counts out possible culprits on her hand. "Leigh, Morris, and Jason are founders' descendants and athletes. Poppy's a witch and an athlete. They all know the effects of misbrewed tonics, right? Leigh could've broken in herself. Or maybe Morris, Jason, or Poppy did. But why would one of them target Leigh? She's not exactly a ray of sunshine, but she's no Regina George either. Maybe Morris finally acted on his crush and gave Leigh the tonic so she'd forget about Jason? Bet you didn't know he's secretly liked her since fifth grade."

"Seriously? But he's dating Poppy! Then again, they were arguing on the day of the break-in. All right, your theory's promising. What about this? Poppy could have beef with Leigh I don't know about. No one wants to be the second choice. Another cheerleader could've stolen my tonic too. Poppy told the entire squad I was working on a heartache cure. Zero heartache equals better focus."

"Could Poppy also have told them about the side effects of a misbrewed tonic in passing? Maybe a cheerleader wanted to oust Leigh as captain." Ximena sags further against the counter, likely as overwhelmed as I am by the work we have cut out for us. "The way I see it, a witch or founder could've told anyone about the side effects."

"Then we need to narrow our scope. The timeline of the break-in is tight. I left the store around . . . twelve-ten? You called to tell me about the break-in at twelve-thirty. The fundraising rally started at one, so whoever broke in likely went straight to school to slip Leigh the tonic."

"Okay. Let's confirm no one but an athlete received a festival cupcake and go from there," Ximena says.

Agnes returns with two boxes and a grin. "Added some sprinkles too," she says, handing them over.

"Thanks, Agnes. Did you give these to anyone else in town yesterday morning?" I ask.

"Nope. Uniformed high school athletes only."

Then the thief was likely someone from BVH. Holy crap, we actually figured something out!

"That's really helpful, Agnes."

She beams. "Glad to be of assistance. Let me know if there's anything else I can do. I heard what happened at Bishop Brews and about Leigh Lawson's condition. I know I'm just a baker, but I'm here if you need anything." She pats my hand. "Enjoy your cupcakes."

I thank Agnes again then burst out of Mystic Muffins.

I hop onto the sidewalk and nearly knock into a woman who lives down the block from me, walking her cat on a leash. In her hand, she carries a bag with the words "Bottled Wonders" printed along the side. Et tu, Brute? Suddenly, I'm not sorry for almost bumping into her.

I take a huge bite out of the cupcake and sugary goodness fills my mouth. Ximena stays beside me, hands in her pockets and her silky hair tousled and twinkling in the afternoon sun. Her steps are slow.

"Come *on*," I say, riding the adrenaline high from what we just learned. It could also be the sugar rush. "We need to question the athletes who were at the rally yesterday."

Even though we traced the napkin back to the bakery, there's still the chance someone else is involved. A jock or cheerleader could be tag-teaming the situation, maybe even with a Bishop Brews rival. Knock out Leigh and the town witches in one fell swoop.

"Sage, hold on. We can't interrogate everyone in a single day. We should regroup and come up with a strategy. I'll ask around and see where some of the athletes are going to be this week."

I stop. She's got a point. "Okay. Call up your friends."

She props up her foot against the brick storefront. The tendons in her arms flex when she rubs the back of her neck. Her skin is practically glowing in the sun. "I'll text them, but how about we break for an early dinner first? Don't think I didn't notice you getting tired after making that tonic. It takes energy to brew, doesn't it?"

*She noticed?* "Not more than I can handle," I reply distractedly. "It makes me hungry." And okay, this time I was more fatigued than usual, probably because FindIt was a new recipe for me, but it's fine. And between all the early mornings and late nights trying to crack this stubborn heartache remedy, I've been pushing myself lately.

"Well, I'm starving," Ximena says. She thoroughly licks the green icing off her cupcake as if to prove a point.

I swallow hard. "We just got cupcakes." The sugar has helped some, but my stomach growls audibly. When I've used as much magic as I have today, I need at least two full meals to counteract the side effects and get my energy back.

"Do you still like pozole?" Ximena asks, ignoring me. "My mom said she was making some for dinner. I know it used to be your favorite. There will be plenty. If you're down."

I narrow my eyes. Growing up, Mrs. Reyes's cooking had me in a choke hold. Her flautas are to die for, and her Saturday morning chilaquiles need to be left on my grave instead of flowers. As for her pozole, I would eat it for every meal if I could. It's been a long four years without it.

The question isn't whether I want some, but why Ximena's inviting me over. She *wants* to spend time with me? And apparently, she still remembers how to get me to agree to do something I'd rather not do. She's even making that face, the one where she softens her stupidly pretty eyes, pouts her lips, and drops her chin. Unbelievable. I can feel it chipping away at my resolve right now.

When I still haven't responded, Ximena frowns before adding, "No pressure. I just thought I'd offer. I'll text my group chat with Leigh and her friends, but in the meantime, I'm going home."

Mercer's comment about Ximena seemingly trying to get along comes back to me. Regardless of her reasons, I can't deny that Ximena *is* trying. She was good with the few customers we had at Bishop Brews and has been helpful with the investigation. We make a decent team. We may never be friends again, but I suppose we can be a pinch more refined. If Ximena's putting in a little effort, I can too. An inch for an inch.

"Fine, I'll come over for dinner," I reply. "But only if I can get seconds."

# Sage's Investigation

## TIMELINE

11:30 a.m.–12:00 p.m.—cupcake promotion (those cupcakes were *fire*)

12:10 p.m.—I leave Bishop Brews and walk to Tea for Thought.

12:30 p.m.—Ximena calls to say there's been a break-in.

1:00 p.m.—The rally starts at BVH, where Leigh ingests my misbrewed heartache tonic.

## MOTIVES

1. To discredit or harm Bishop Brews or witches in general. Giving the tonic to Leigh: coincidental or accidental???

2. To harm Leigh or the founders in general. Use witches as scapegoats given town history. They would have to have known the tonic they gave Leigh was misbrewed—aka a witch, a founder, or a stalker (please no).

3. Money—probably about $200 cash for the premade tonics and way more if a buyer knew just how valuable my heartache brew was.

## SUSPECT PROFILES

- A disgruntled customer, a competitor, or someone with a grudge against a witch

- An enemy of Leigh's or someone with a grudge against a founding family

- Someone with intimate knowledge of misbrew side effects

- An athlete who stole the brews wanting to make extra cash

# 10

"You're kidding. Y-you didn't drive?" I stammer at the sight of the purple bike chained outside Honey's.

Ximena unlocks her bike with a grin. "Nope. Did you?"

"Carpooled with Mercer." Ximena and I walked from the diner to Bishop Brews, but I was so focused on the investigation, it never occurred to me that she didn't drive into the town center.

"Then it's settled. Biking will be faster than walking." Ximena swings her leg over the seat. "Hop on. I'll be careful, I promise," she adds with a wink.

She hands me her helmet. I climb onto the pegs attached to the back wheel and wrap my arms around her waist as she kicks off. Never in a million years did I think I'd be holding her again. Her body is so warm beneath my hands, my heart actually flutters. I should not have gotten on this bike. Now I have to spend the next ten minutes breathing in the comforting scents of sugar, coconut shampoo, and something earthy that is uniquely Ximena.

I try to focus on the ride, the streetlights blooming as the sky darkens and the cold wind nipping at my face.

Ximena brakes as we turn onto her street. The Reyeses live on a quiet block that's currently painted with streams of setting sunlight. Behind it, the Hemwood crests like a prickly dark wave. I'm less familiar with this portion of the woods compared to my own, but the trees still call to me.

Ximena parks her bike in the driveway leading to a little blue house with white shutters. The sight of it shakes loose long-lost memories of jumping off the porch and tumbling down the sloping front lawn. With my magic, I grew Ximena's favorite flowers in the backyard, black star calla lilies. We'd pluck them, stick them in our hair, and then pretend to be garden fairies. I spent half my childhood here playing and growing.

Following Ximena inside is easier than I thought it'd be. The smells of boiling chicken, vegetables, and a wealth of seasonings rush to greet us. Lively music—a blaring trumpet and a wildly plucked guitar—sails down the hall. The house is untouched by the rift between us. It's as homey and inviting as it's always been, much louder than my house but just as comforting.

"Hi, honey!" Mrs. Reyes calls out. "Dinner is almost ready. The boys are outside."

"Okay. Sage is here," Ximena replies.

As soon as the words leave her mouth, I hear a rapid shuffling of feet. A head of curly black hair pokes out from around the kitchen doorframe.

Mrs. Reyes is a stout woman with wrinkles around her eyes and an easy smile. She's wearing a pretty spring dress and a yellow apron that says "Kiss the Chef." Even though she looks sweet as honey, there's always been a fierceness in her only found in mothers who have a chancla at the ready.

Before I know it, I'm wrapped in her arms, inhaling freshly ground spices and floral perfume. "Sage, it's been too long! Tell me you're staying for dinner," she says.

"Hi, Mrs. Reyes," I reply once she's released me. "I am if you'll have me."

There's a raised scar on her face, from temple to chin. I've seen her around Blackclaw a few times over the years, but in passing only. The last time we had a real conversation was four years ago, and she didn't have the scar. It puckers when she grins.

"Of course! I'm glad you're here. Ximena rarely has anyone over, so this is a real treat," she says.

Ximena ducks her head. "Mom, please."

Mrs. Reyes waves her off and ushers us both into the kitchen, where dinner is warming on the stove. "How have things been, Sage? Ximena told me what happened at the store. Are you all right? Is Bishop Brews staying open?"

"We're reopening tomorrow."

"But you're taking precautions and keeping safe, right?"

I nod.

"Good. And Ximena told me you're working hard on something new? I hope no one was trying to steal it from you."

I told one customer, the man with the slicked-down hair and mustache, about my heartache brew, and Poppy told her whole cheerleading squad. It's not out of the realm of possibility that my tonic caught the wrong kind of attention.

"I was working on something, yes, but every recipe so far has failed." When I think about working on another one now, I just feel anxious and tense.

"You'll figure it out," Mrs. Reyes replies with a smile. "Mena says you're very determined."

"Oh my god." Ximena groans and hides her face behind her phone. It could be the light from the fading sun, but I swear I catch a hint of a blush creeping up her neck.

"All right, why don't you two go check on the boys? Dinner's nearly ready," Mrs. Reyes tells us with a quick glance out the window, where her twins are playing on the tire swing in their backyard.

Ximena's out the door before I can even respond. I hesitate only a moment before following. Ximena runs to her brother on the tire swing and gives him a solid push. Her other brother, wearing red-framed glasses, runs circles around them, trying to get as close to the tire as he can without being knocked down. A high-pitched giggle bursts from his mouth at every narrow miss. She scoops him up and spins him around. The boys were babies the last time I saw them. Now they're four. Tall, lean, and as bright as sunflowers.

Ximena seems so unburdened around them, different from how she is at school. Their joy is infectious, and pretty soon I'm laughing too.

Ximena turns at the sound. The light catches in her hair, making it appear almost metallic. "Adrian, Erik, do you remember Sage? Can you say hi?"

"Hi!" the boys squeal in tandem.

"I texted Jason," Ximena says, giving the swing another good push.

Jason Dunn is Leigh's boyfriend and the sheriff's son. I don't know him well, but Ximena seems to. She grins when her phone chimes.

"There's a bonfire tomorrow night," she says, reading the text. "Everyone from Blackclaw Valley High will be there. I figure we could go and question some jocks. And if we're lucky, the thief could forget to wear gloves. We can check if anyone has stained hands or clothes from the tonic. It did splash everywhere."

When you live in a small town surrounded by forest, most people our age attend bonfires. Someone's birthday? Bonfire. Graduation? Bonfire. A random slow Monday? Yep. Bonfire. And I've never been once. All those people make me nervous, and drinking and dancing in the sacred place where magic originates seems wrong. And okay, maybe I also feel too boring to go. I've never been cool, always stuck on the outside with my plants, my anxiety, and my magic. Parties always seemed out of my depth.

"Um . . ." It's not that I don't want to question BVH athletes, but doing so in front of everyone's curious eyes is daunting. No one minds their business here.

"Um? Where was all that spunk you had an hour ago? I could hardly get you to break for food. Now you don't want to chase down leads? The bonfire doesn't have to be a big deal. In fact, you might actually have fun. You do know what fun is, don't you? Outside of brewing, that is?"

I snort. "I know what fun is. I don't have to party in the woods to have it, though."

Ximena saunters forward, pulling the tire swing with her until we're standing close. She's always been a couple inches taller than me, so when we lock eyes, I have to tilt my head. I should step back but for some reason I don't.

"I promise, no fun will be had at this party," she says. "We'll be working on the case the entire time. Strictly business."

I search her face for any sign of duplicity and my brain for alternative options, but nothing comes. We've got to start narrowing down our suspects, and if I need to go to this party to do that, then so be it. Comfort be damned. "Okay. Let's go."

Ximena doesn't hide her smirk. She releases the tire swing, and it rocks to a stop. Her brother Erik tries to jump off while she's waving over Adrian, but instead of his feet, he lands right on his knees.

The shrill sound he makes has both of us rushing over to him. Ximena gets there first and scoops him up as fat tears threaten to fall down his cherub cheeks. She tries to calm him while frantically brushing grass off his legs. His knee is scraped. It's minor, but he's upset, and his twin is visibly worried now.

Ximena releases a frustrated groan while she rubs circles on her crying brother's back. And . . . I don't know. There's something about seeing her struggle to get her brother to calm down. Something about that blush in the kitchen. I want to help.

I close my eyes and reach for my magic, sitting just beneath the surface. I conjure it with happy thoughts, pushing themselves to the forefront of my mind. Bishop Brews in the summer, brimming with customers. My parents, when they were still alive, cuddling me with easy laughs and warm hugs. Nana teaching me to brew for the first time. I still vividly remember that day. We made morning glory elixir—a banishment tonic, good for getting rid of negative thoughts. I accidentally dumped in the crushed petals instead of sprinkling them and the entire brew went bubbling everywhere.

"Wow!" a tiny voice exclaims, followed by giggles.

When I open my eyes, the flower beds framing the back of the house have tripled in size. The petunias burst with color, and the pink roses are as tall and lean as the boys. There are no black star calla lilies like Ximena loves, and yet it's a stunning sight.

"You're a witch," Adrian says with a grin.

"I am."

"Do more magic!" Erik pleads.

Ximena steers him and Adrian by the shoulders toward the house. "Maybe after we eat," she suggests.

Adrian skips next to me. "You should come over more."

Ximena slows. She doesn't meet my gaze, but her response is as solid as a promise when she replies, "Yeah. We'd like that."

Though I smile, I still wonder why she shut me out four years ago only to try to rope me back in now. I don't get her. She talks about me to her mom and invites me over for pozole like we're thirteen again. You don't suddenly start hanging out and being nice to someone you ignored for years without a reason.

What's your endgame, Ximena Reyes?

# 11

"Keep making that face, and you're going to scare away the customers."

I flatten my lips and uncross my arms as our second customer of the day exits Bishop Brews with a premade Feverfew tonic to cure his chronic migraines. Ximena's behind the register, unraveling a fresh roll of 10-percent-off stickers. Since the Spring Harvest Festival brings an influx of customers and people are more likely to buy things on sale, Nana has us reducing the price of all our bestselling products today. She's positive the coven will figure out who broke in, restore Leigh's memories, and right our standing with the founders within the next week. I wish I had that kind of confidence.

"Any of these people could be the thief," I grumble.

"I promise we'll figure this out," Ximena tells me, putting freshly discounted organic perfumes on the top shelf behind the register. "The bonfire tonight should help narrow down suspects."

*We.* This is only her second shift, and yet she already sees herself as a member of team Bishop Brews. I am not above admitting that she fits in, charming the customers and expertly finessing the cranky old register.

When the next customers enter, Ximena is all smiles. "Welcome to Bishop Brews, where everything is brewed with love!"

"Hi! My sister and I need some help," the customer says. She's wearing a green Blackclaw College sweatshirt and cute floral Keds.

Blackclaw College is known for its stellar arts program and its very selective Practical Magic for Witches major, which attracts young witches with varying magic gifts from all over the country. Nana has always wanted me to go to college. She never went herself and has stressed the importance of school since the day I was born. Same for my dad, who ended up taking a few online classes but never got a degree. That I'm attending Blackclaw College this fall is a huge deal.

"This is probably a long shot, but do you have anything to make my silk press last longer than a week?" the college girl asks with a hopeful shrug. "I have a date next weekend."

"We have an antihumidity spray that works on all hair types and styles," I reply.

"Even 4c?"

"Yep. We got you." I turn to Ximena. "Can you show her? It's in the—"

"Body and hair care section," Ximena finishes for me with a grin. She leads the customer away, and I focus on the sister, who looks about twelve.

"What about you?" I ask her.

"I'm getting acne," she mumbles. "Do you have anything that can help? The drugstore stuff doesn't work."

"Oh, definitely." I lead her to the same section as her older sister and grab our blemish recovery paste. "This is made with magically enhanced calendula, which promotes healing and collagen production. The cream will take care of dark spots, pimples, and any other imperfections. Try some. It may tingle."

As soon as the mixture covers the acne bump on her face, it shrinks and the redness fades.

"Oh. My. God! Stop, it literally disappeared. This place is so much better than Bottled Wonders!" she squeals while she waits for Ximena to ring up her cream and her sister's hair spray.

"They don't have anything for the curly hair community and none of their products have any variation. Everything is made with the same three ingredients: chamomile, ginger, and elderberry. And it's always so busy, the workers barely have time to explain or demonstrate the products," the older girl adds.

"Sounds charming," Ximena replies sarcastically as she bags the girls' products and slips in a coupon for their next purchase. "I saw their ad on the highway. It's giving corporate superstore calling itself a cozy apothecary."

"Exactly that! Bottled Wonders is nothing but bright fluorescent lights and sterile linoleum. A beauty supply store infused with some one-size-fits-all magic," the girl says, taking the bag. "Anyway, thanks for the help. We'll be back."

The customers leave with smiles on their faces, reminding me exactly why I love working here. Still, it's hard hearing how well Bottled Wonders is doing, despite being generic. I'm not as optimistic as Nana that Bishop Brews will survive the rise of Bottled Wonders.

Ximena must sense my shifting mood, because she says, "I think it's time we size up the competition. You heard Bottled Wonders uses elderberry, right? Didn't you find some the day of the break-in? One of your theories is that an athlete stole your tonic to resell to a competitor. The closest one is Bottled Wonders. Let's determine exactly what they have and what the employees know about Bishop Brews. Even if they aren't involved, the more information we have on them the better. This store has been in your family for generations. No way some corporate megastore is threatening to put you out of business."

My heart swells at her declaration. "I'm in."

She beams. "Good."

I slide off my chair and make my way around the counter. "I'm taking my break. This tonic isn't going to create itself." As I turn for the kitchen, I swear Ximena's face falls. Maybe she's just bored?

During my break, I try to perfect my heartache tonic. I lay out all my ingredients and start the process of mixing in each herb, being sure to concentrate on my intentions to forget the pain of losing someone. When I think of my own heartbreak now, it doesn't hurt as much as it did when Ximena first moved back to town.

It's harder than usual to add my magic to the brew this time, like there's less to draw from. I stir the mixture, waiting for the contents to glow, telling me it worked, but the change never comes. A foul smell escapes instead, filling the entire room.

"Yuck." I cover my nose and yank open the window, breathing in sweet fresh air.

Ximena pokes her head into the kitchen a few moments later. "Everything okay back here? You've been gone awhile."

I drop my head into my hands. "No," I mumble.

"Yeah, it smells rancid. Need help?"

I raise my head just enough to scowl at her. "Shouldn't you be on the register?"

She leans against the doorframe. "No one has come in for the last ten minutes. I think I can spare a few back here." She grabs a pink apron hanging on the hooks by the door and ties it around her waist. "Plus, we've got that bell now, so I'll know when someone enters."

"Okay, well, did you finish—"

"Discounting items? Yep. I also dusted the display shelves and checked the till." She grins.

"You seriously want to help me with this?"

Letting Ximena in, even to help on a personal project, notably one she inspired, isn't something I ever thought I'd do. Is she trying to get back in my good graces? Because, not gonna lie, it might be working.

She brings her chair from the register and puts it next to mine, close enough that I can feel her body heat. "I'm here, aren't I? Just tell me what to do."

I drag the brewing pot toward us. "Hand me the spring water from the mini fridge."

Ximena practically skips to the far side of the room. Memories of us playing here during the summers flood my mind. We were so small the aprons hung down to our ankles. We'd mix everything we could find in the brewing pot and create imaginary tonics that would fix all the world's problems in a single dose. Part of the magic of playing pretend is making your dreams come true. Even better if you're doing it with someone you love.

"What's next?"

Ximena's voice is grounding, serving to shake off the memory. "Let's try mint for healing and allspice for relieving aches," I tell her.

She moves around the kitchen like she's been working here her whole life. She collects the herbs, and I reach for the jar of flowers on the windowsill. The roses haven't bloomed yet, so I twist my wrist and the buds unfurl, revealing perfect crimson petals. Roses happen to be good at curing heartbreak and at declaring one's love.

"Can I ask you something?"

"Shoot," Ximena replies.

"Why don't you invite friends over?" I've been curious since I left Ximena's house yesterday.

"We usually only go to Morris's house or Jason's. Mine is too loud, and honestly, I like keeping my space separate and just for me."

"But you brought me there. I'd stay over all the time when we were younger."

"You don't count. I always want you around." Ximena ducks her head and grabs the measuring cup. "Anyway, they're cool. Jason's a musician, Leigh wants to be president, and Morris cares more about most things than he lets on. But my friendships with them aren't like how ours was, or I guess like yours and Mercer's is now."

I pour the spring water into the brewing pot and then pinch off two mint leaves and chuck them in. "My friendship with Mercer isn't exactly the same as mine was with you."

Ximena fidgets with the container of allspice. "You seem pretty close."

"We are, but it's different. She's like a sister to me."

There's a hopeful lift to Ximena's expression. I could throttle her. She doesn't get to be jealous of Mercer, not after she ghosted me for years. When she left, I was a mess. I begged Nana to ask Ximena's parents to bring her back, and all Mr. Reyes would say is that Ximena was with family and needed time away. But I want answers. I deserve as much.

I push the brewing pot aside. "Where have you been?"

She pauses before answering. "I was in Los Angeles with my aunt and cousins."

"Why?"

"I needed to get away from Blackclaw for a while."

"Cryptic much?" It's infuriating how she's simultaneously the girl I used to know and a total stranger.

"It's the best I can do. If you want, I *can* tell you about LA?"

She waits to see if I'll shut her down. I don't. Maybe I'm a masochist, but I want to know about the place she left me for.

"The arts were huge at my high school. That's where I got into music. I even learned to play the piano."

"Really?" I can picture her now, both hands fluidly moving about the keys, her bottom lip between her teeth as she concentrates on the song. "I'd like to see that," I say.

"Done." Ximena grins. "And there are tons of fun outdoorsy things to do around LA, like hiking, surfing, even skiing in the mountains. I have a suspicion there's a special kind of magic in the Angeles National Forest."

"You can keep the skiing and surfing. I like my feet firmly planted on the ground, thank you. I can watch people fall off boards in Blackclaw. The beach is rocky, but it's there. And tourists love the hiking trails. If not for the werewolf legend, we'd get even more hikers."

Ximena shakes her head. "Fear of werewolves is a perfect example of how this town never changes and how people who are different can be labeled monsters." She gestures to the window. "There's so much more out there: new experiences and chances to grow. Exploring brings me a special kind of freedom I don't have in Blackclaw."

"Where else have you been?" I ask, because I don't want her to stop talking. I drag the brewing pot back toward me.

"Ensenada. That's where my dad's family is from in Mexico. The seafood there is so fresh it's practically still swimming, and nothing compares to how blue the ocean is. I want to see everything the world has to offer."

I'm quiet as I shake in the allspice and drop in four rose petals.

"Do you want to travel?" she asks.

"I'd like to see new places, but I don't think I could live anywhere but Blackclaw. I have roots here that go back generations. My magic is here, and my coven."

"You don't have to be afraid to leave your magic. There's so much to do, I bet you'd hardly miss it."

"You don't know that. You don't know me anymore," I snap.

Suddenly, the rapport we were building is gone.

Ximena pulls off her apron with a sigh and tosses it onto the chair.

She heads for the swinging door leading to the rest of the shop. She turns slightly. "You're right, I don't know you anymore. But can't you see I'm trying to change that?"

Before I can reply, the door slams shut behind her.

I hang back and pluck at a loose string on my apron.

It's easy for Ximena to want to explore new places. She doesn't have magic to give up. There's nothing tethering her to Blackclaw. And I need to remember that the next time she's inviting me over for dinner or offering to help me with my brew. I can't fall for her again, because our new friendship—if having one is even possible—is going to end the same way our last one did, with her running away and me standing alone in her wake.

# 12

Ever since Ximena came back from an extended break, she's been quiet, which sounds ideal but leaves my stomach in knots. I didn't mean to upset her when we've just started to get along again.

"Can you say something, please?" I ask.

A beat passes.

"Do you want to take a quick trip to Crimson Grove?" Ximena asks as she clocks out for the day. "We can visit Bottled Wonders. I don't want to go home yet."

My hope rises despite my flaring nerves. Saying no would make me a hypocrite after telling her not an hour ago that I wanted to see new places and wasn't afraid to leave town.

We only have a week to find who poisoned Leigh before the council decides Bishop Brews is more a liability than a benefit. Bottled Wonders is a suspect we still need to clear, and now is as good a time as any.

I inhale deeply. "Okay."

Ximena nods. "Okay."

She leaves first, and I lock the door behind us. Her truck is parked at the curb. She opens the passenger-side door and waits for me to climb in, a gentle expression on her face. Maybe she's not as upset as I thought.

I hop in, and Ximena does the same soon after. Jack Harlow bumps through the speakers as she drives toward the edge of town. The narrow streets stretch into a two-lane road. The Hemwood rises on our right, and the Pacific Ocean swells on our left. Waves break against the rocky shoreline, and the surface sparkles as sunlight dances across it like crystal ballerinas on a bed of baby blue eyes. The luscious foliage and colorful buildings fade from view and then we pass the town sign reading "Welcome to Blackclaw Valley." The red bricks are decorated with festive neon garlands for the Spring Harvest Festival.

I clench my hands together to stop them from trembling. Leaving town is *way* outside my comfort zone. The only memory I have of leaving is when my parents took me to Thrill Zone in nearby San Francisco when I was six. I didn't have control over my magic then, nor did I feel as strong a connection to it as I do now. I always imagined that as soon as I crossed the town line, I'd feel my magic ebb away, sucked back into the Hemwood like a receding tide. I thought I'd be left with an empty space like the one I had when my parents died. Only, there is no such fanfare. And while my magic is less full, it's still flickering with the Hemwood so close.

Ximena briefly shifts her attention to me. She stretches her hand across the console and rests it atop mine. She knows this is my first time leaving Blackclaw since having magic. That I'm doing it with her feels ironic, and yet, I let her confident presence steady me.

A plain white sign appears in front of us with stiff metal letters forming the name Crimson Grove. We pass pristine subdivisions—the homes and condos all painted the same tan color.

After driving a few more minutes, we enter what I assume is downtown Crimson Grove. Even the streets here lack the festive feel of home. No decorations are strung on streetlights; no flowers wave at us from the windows. Residents and tourists walking the streets lack the same kind of pep in their steps and the ease commonly found in Blackclaw. It's scary how little joy I find.

Google Maps navigates us to a plain white building with large empty windows. The only evidence that the store is an apothecary is the decal of a giant tonic and the crisp black lettering spelling "Bottled Wonders."

We enter through double glass doors, and a sterile smell clings to the air, so different from the herbal scent of Bishop Brews. Blinding fluorescent lights illuminate rows upon rows of tonics, each one in a slender glass vial that makes it appear medicinal. At Bishop Brews, we keep our tonics in rounder bottles to give them a more homegrown flair.

Dozens of people cram inside, trying on charm necklaces, examining premade tonics, and asking for samples. I pretend to browse while Ximena takes pictures of everything. All the workers are practically carbon copies of each other—young, thin, and expressionless. They wear matching blue polo shirts with "Bottled Wonders" printed across the front pocket and crisp white tennis shoes. Their eyes are framed with bags and their skin is pale.

Aside from the amount of customers, the number of tonics lining the shelves is also shocking. There must be one hundred in the front room alone. It's definitely giving mega beauty supply store. No wonder the workers look exhausted. Since tonics are made with perishable ingredients, they typically don't last longer than five days. A week, tops. Bottled Wonders must be regularly brewing to keep the shelves stocked.

"Do you recognize any of the tonics as the stolen ones?" Ximena whispers.

"No. I doubt I'd be able to tell." I rub my forehead with a stifled sigh. "Then again, I can hardly see anything beyond all these customers. Bishop Brews has never been this packed."

Ximena rests her hand on my shoulder. "Bishop Brews values quality over quantity of tonics. That's why our customers always leave satisfied. They get personalized products."

Her response reduces some of my worry, and I find myself wanting to apologize for snapping at her during our shift.

Before I can say anything, an employee approaches us. Not even her concealer can hide the dark circles under her eyes. "Can I help you find anything?" she asks.

"Um. Yes. What are your bestsellers?" I ask.

The employee points to a floor-to-ceiling shelving unit lined with dozens of purple tonics. "Those would be our infamous elderberry elixirs for general wellness. They can help lower your blood pressure, boost your immune system, and even lower stress and inflammation in the body."

Elderberry is the same herb I found in Bishop Brews the day of the break-in. Could it have come from here? Someone certainly could have bought an elixir before coming to Bishop Brews for something more custom, but who?

"Impressive. They don't have these at Bishop Brews," Ximena says with a subtle lift to her voice that lets me know she's fishing.

The employee chuckles. "Too bad the owner isn't here to hear you say that."

"What do you mean?" I ask.

"He wants to grow Bottled Wonders nationwide. But first, we have to surpass the local competition."

"How is he planning to do that?" I ask.

The employee cants her head at my lack of subtlety.

"I know I'm being nosy, but we're witches too and want to know more about the job before we apply," I lie.

"Oh, I didn't realize we were hiring. Makes sense. We need all the help we can get." Her shoulders drop as some of her tension drains. She lowers her voice. "The job has solid pay but is a ton of work. We've been trying to invent new tonics, which is tough, considering how busy we are already. The witch with the best tonic gets a bonus."

"Any success?" I ask.

"Nothing good enough to sell. Yet." She smooths down her shirt as an automated bell announces new arrivals. "If there's nothing else, I need to help these customers."

She leaves us standing by the elderberry elixirs. "Sounds like motive," I tell Ximena once the employee is out of earshot.

"True. If these employees are desperate enough to deprive themselves of sleep for that bonus, I wouldn't put it past one of them to come to Bishop Brews to do a little espionage of their own. But what does Leigh have to do with any of it? Or Mystic Muffins?"

"Maybe they teamed up with someone in Blackclaw to split the bonus? It seems like a lot of Bottled Wonders employees are around our age. It's not far-fetched that one of them might know people in Blackclaw who need extra cash."

A pleased glint ignites Ximena's face. "Let's question every athlete we can at the bonfire later tonight."

"I'm down." I start toward the exit until a warm hand on my forearm draws me up short.

"Speaking of athletes," Ximena whispers. She nudges me toward the door, where a familiar shock of brown hair immediately snags my attention.

Morris Brown, Poppy's boyfriend, walks into Bottled Wonders with his shoulders hunched and his head slightly bowed. He approaches the first employee he sees. The pair are too far away for us to hear their discussion. Even if we were closer, there are so many people in the store, and their conversations are all overlapping, making individual exchanges practically indiscernible.

The pimply teen in an ill-fitting polo shakes his head in response to Morris's question. He then points at a narrow glass case of different-colored tonics before turning to the next customer.

Ximena and I don't even have to talk, already on the same page to rush over and question him. Morris startles when he sees us. His eyes double in size, and he nearly drops the glass vials in his hand. Traitor.

"What are you doing here?" I ask.

He regains his composure quickly, straightening his back and tightening his lips into a thin line. I don't miss the way he covers the labels of the tonics he's holding with his thumb. "I could ask you the same. Don't you have your own apothecary to run?"

"We're scoping out the competition. What are you buying from here that Bishop Brews doesn't have?"

He shakes his head amusedly, likely picking up on my bitter tone. "None of your business."

"Morris, come on," Ximena presses.

"I'm serious. It's personal." He crosses his arms, effectively hiding the tonics.

It doesn't matter. I've already glimpsed the glowing green and blue liquid inside, and easily matched the coloring to ones on the shelf behind him. Morris groans as I step around him to read the labels. He's picked up a pain management tonic and a self-improvement tonic.

Morris raises his shoulders. "My, uh, knee has been

acting up. I just need something to get me through basket-ball season, and maybe help me out on some tests. My parents are riding me to do better."

"You could've come to Bishop Brews for that."

"Maybe I didn't want people knowing I'm not at my best. Besides, Bottled Wonders is supposed to have great tonics."

Is he purposefully trying to annoy me? "So, this is your first time here?" I ask, thinking of the elderberry shavings I found in Bishop Brews.

"As a matter of fact, it is," he replies. "And to think I came here to escape your judgment." He sighs. "Now that I'm sufficiently embarrassed, can I go?"

"I guess."

He skirts around us and beelines for the cash register. Ximena watches him leave, her brows lifting. Seems like we're thinking the same thing.

"Could he be lying about not coming here before?" I ask her.

"I don't know," Ximena replies. "Something's off, though."

I follow her outside and to her truck. "Going to the bonfire is sounding more and more appealing."

"Most definitely." Ximena turns to me, a mischievous gleam in her eyes. "This is gonna be enlightening."

# 13

When I get home, I find Nana and Tiva sorting through the herbs in the kitchen. Shaye Thorn, my covenmate, is in the living room making a list of what appears to be different tonic ingredients. I hand them the grimoire I brought home from the store, and they immediately start flipping through it and calling out various herbs, to which Nana replies yes or no.

"Sage, you're just the person I need," Nana says. "What ingredients did you use for your brew? Please tell me you've been documenting your attempts?"

"Don't worry. You taught me well." I turn to attempt number twenty-two and hand over my notebook. Counter brews are essentially the reverse of the original tonic, so Nana needs to know exactly what herbs I used and how I used them.

Nana pushes up her bifocals and reads. The bags under

her eyes are deep and her shoulders wilt. "How long have you been working on this?" I ask.

"Too long. I don't want us coming close to that one-week cutoff for the counter brew. The founders only have so much patience. Mrs. Carver questioned the basketball team yesterday. Seems they all went to Mystic Muffins before the rally. Of course, they denied having anything to do with the break-in."

Nana grabs the gingko, an herb good for boosting memory, and scatters some into the massive brewing pot we keep at home. I feel awful for putting us in this situation and even more motivated to go to tonight's bonfire. It's time to make some serious progress on this investigation.

)·)·)·)●(·(·(·(

I spend an ungodly amount of time styling my hair. I shouldn't care this much. I *don't*. And yet I can't help but nitpick every little thing, like that one curl that just won't sit with the others. I've smoothed and twisted my hair within an inch of its life by the time I finally put on my nicest pair of jeans and a crop top Mercer picked out. I asked her to come with us, but her parents need her to babysit her little sister.

"You look *niiice*. I still can't believe you're going to a non-coven-related party," she says, her face popping in and out of the phone screen as she paints her toenails.

I tug at my shirt. "We need to question suspects."

"Is that what the kids are calling dates nowadays?"

She leans back against her couch so I can see her satisfied smirk.

"This is *not* a date." There was a time when this might've been one, back when the lingering glances, hand-holding, and whispered secrets meant something. Not now. My crush on Ximena has totally mummified.

Mercer makes kissing noises like a middle schooler, which, of course, causes my face to flame.

"I hate you."

"You love me." Mercer positions herself directly in the phone frame. "Listen, I know everything seems dire, but enjoy tonight. This is our senior year! Do something you normally wouldn't."

"Doing things I normally wouldn't is literally one of my triggers. If I deviated from my routine, I wouldn't be Sage Bishop. I'd be Ximena Reyes, carefree and completely unbothered."

"Just try to have some fun," Mercer amends. "But not *too* much. Don't make me use Find My Friends to track you."

"Ugh, I can't believe I let you talk me into adding you."

"Safety first. Now go before you bypass fashionably late and jump straight to rude."

I roll my eyes and hang up, her words urging me to step outside my comfort zone lingering in my ears. I did just that today by going to Crimson Grove. Sure, it wasn't far enough to lose total access to my magic, but it was a big step, and I'm proud of myself.

I put on a dash of Nana's eyeliner and spray two squirts

of Tiva's perfume that's magically enhanced to highlight your best scent. As I admire my handiwork in the downstairs mirror, I worry I've overdone it. *This is not a date.*

The parlor palm reaches toward me, nudging my arm. Twining my fingers through its leaves calms me, and before I can second-guess myself, I head out.

Rising above the horizon is the Hemwood, an endless crop of gentle giants standing with limbs outstretched like waiting friends. The official entrance is walking distance from my house. The forest is preserved by witches and regularly explored and hiked by tourists and residents of Blackclaw.

A wooden sign is lodged in a mound of earth, marking the start of a dirt trail. I've walked this path many times, but tonight feels different. The trees seem twice as big. The ground is swathed in shadows, save for the speckles of moonlight dotting the forest floor and illuminating the path.

Ximena texted me to meet her at the bonfire, but I'm currently wishing I hadn't come alone. After about ten minutes, I hear the faint sound of laughter on my left. I step off the trail and trudge over a patch of prickly bramble and overgrown ferns. My steps sink into the ground as I head toward the noise.

I spot the glow of the fire a moment later. Bright flecks of light sprinkle through the trees, and the rhythmic thump of feet stomping around the glade to blaring music fills the air. When I finally make it to the clearing, there are several dozen people from my high school milling around and laughing as they drink from red Solo cups. A group of girls in tiny denim shorts and glittery tank tops sway slightly off-beat to a catchy pop song blaring from a portable speaker. Across from them, two band boys make out on a picnic blanket. Behind them, a group of freshmen are sitting on a fallen log while a senior makes his hands into claws and flashes his teeth. He's probably telling them the wolf legend.

I move about the party. A girl I recognize from environmental science downs a tonic. I immediately clock the familiar green ribbon and label. By her glowing skin and shiny hair, I'd say it was our Glo-Up mixture. Seeing someone I know using products from Bishop Brews boosts my drive to save the store.

Nearly the entire BVH basketball team and a few cheerleaders are here. I should start asking questions, but nerves have me spiraling, a barrage of *what ifs* attacking me from all sides. What if they ignore me? What if they accuse me of hurting their friend? I'm not afraid of them, but sometimes my brain likes to make things more complicated than they really are.

I wander away from the crowd, checking my phone every so often, but there's no text from Ximena. Just as I start to worry she isn't coming, I hear her laughter. I swivel toward the sound and find her standing to the right of the fire ring wearing black cutoffs that complement her geometric-patterned button-up. My pulse flutters as the flames from the fire catch the highlights in her hair and accentuate the warm hue of her light-brown skin. It's only when her head tilts and she waves me over with a confused frown that I realize I'm staring.

My feet carry me to her on their own.

Ximena says goodbye to her friend, who leaves to join the group of dancers behind us, and then she turns to me. A hint of wonder lurks in her expression. "You came," she says.

I nod. "Nice party." *Smooth, Sage.*

Ximena's lips twitch like she wants to smile. "It's okay. The dance floor seems promising."

I scrunch my nose. "You mean the patch of dried fir needles underneath those sweaty, drunk teenagers wearing too much cologne?"

She laughs, a sound as bright as firelight. "Yes, that dance floor."

I shove my hands into my pockets just to give myself something to do. I don't know why I'm so nervous. "You look nice."

Ximena leans in, her eyes glimmering, and tucks a wayward curl behind my shoulder. "You look better."

I can hardly think beyond the heat that lingers on my skin from her touch. "Thanks," I whisper. I try to find my footing by turning my attention to the semi-crowded party happening around us. "Any suggestions on how we play this?"

"Let's just see what people might know and not raise too much suspicion."

Olivia Byrd, the person who wears our school mascot costume, flips her hair over her shoulder and waves enthusiastically at Ximena. Olivia has that same interested

kick lately. Last week, she thought she saw a giant wolf in the woods with colored claws," Jason adds.

Ximena shifts her weight. "A wolf?"

"Weird, I know, but she swore she wasn't lying. It was probably just a stray dog," he replies.

"Several people have seen giant wolves near the trails recently," I offer.

Jason shrugs. "We done with this episode of *Criminal Minds*?"

I stop myself from laughing. "For now."

"Cool." He turns to Ximena. "You coming to the pickup game tomorrow night? I need to regain some clout after you wiped the floor with me in music theory."

Ximena grins. "I'll try to make it. If you think of anything else, text me."

He nods before joining Morris and a few other athletes Ximena was talking to before she found me with Jason. Olivia takes the opening she's been waiting for and comes dancing over. She sweeps her hair across her shoulders and wiggles next to Ximena.

"Is this about Leigh? We all want her to get better," Olivia says.

"She will. My grandmother is the best brewer on the West Coast, and she has been working on a counter brew practically nonstop. In the meantime, we need to know who stole from us and why. Were you at Mystic Muffins for the free cupcakes?" I ask.

"Yep. Showed up in my costume and got there early to avoid the line."

"What time did you get to school?" Ximena asks.

"I can't remember exactly. Maybe twelve-forty? I annoyed the cheerleaders because everyone was supposed to be in the gym at noon. It's not my fault my car was acting up again. It needs a new alternator, and the auto shop wants to charge three hundred and fifty dollars. I don't have that kind of money."

Interesting. Olivia fits our theory that someone could've stolen the tonics to resell for cash. "Did anything unusual happen during the rally?" I ask.

"Um . . . The cheerleaders wanted me in one of their routines, which doesn't happen often. Oh! And I overheard Poppy ask her coach if she could be captain for the remainder of the year. She said Leigh missed a lot of practices and acts above the team. Now that Leigh lost her memory and can't remember any routines, Poppy's likely to take over. You don't think she did something to Leigh, do you?"

Since when did Poppy want to be cheer captain? She only joined the squad last year, and that was to diversify her college resume. Granted, she's a quick study and determined, but captain is a reach, even for her. And yet, with Leigh's memory loss, Poppy is perfectly positioned to be captain. It's still hard to believe Poppy would do this. I guess people can surprise you. Ximena sure has.

"I don't know," I reply honestly.

The song changes to one with a deep bass, and I can't help but tap my foot along to it. The playlist is good, I'll give the party that.

Ximena is seemingly oblivious to the way Olivia's eyes not-so-subtly trail up and down her frame. She's practically drooling over her. If my shirt was longer, I'd offer her a corner to mop up.

"Has Leigh said anything in the last week or two that seemed odd?" I ask.

Olivia huffs. "I don't know. . . . Uh, at the last bonfire she was worried Jason was going to break up with her. It could be why she was late for practices and preoccupied."

With that, Leigh dosing herself doesn't seem totally implausible.

"Ximena, you finally decided to come join us. I've been basically begging you to attend a bonfire for months," Olivia says, clearly over my questioning. She dances closer to Ximena.

I know I'm like a desperate reporter with a notepad out here, but I can't help that I'm motivated. Time is of the essence.

Ximena chuckles nervously and rubs the back of her neck. "I'm not really the partying type."

Olivia nods eagerly. "I gathered. I guess partying can get old after a while, but there's not much else to do in this town."

"Work and family stuff keeps me plenty busy, though I do like to have a little fun every now and then," Ximena says lightly.

"I've heard you in the music room at school. You can really sing." Olivia shifts even closer, rocking her hips to the music and running a long pink manicured fingernail along Ximena's arm. "What *else* are you good at?"

Something fiery rockets through me. Is Olivia really flirting with Ximena like I'm not here? And why does it feel like Ximena's entertaining it? She can talk to whoever she wants. Obviously. It's none of my business. But don't act like I'm invisible.

"We should get going. There are other people we need to talk to before the night's over," I say, sounding like a total buzzkill, but honestly, we're here to work.

Ximena frowns. "Sage, it's fine. We have time."

"You're all work and no play, huh?" Olivia says to me. "Loosen up."

Ximena doesn't say anything in my defense this time, probably because she agrees, which only irks me more.

Mercer's words come to mind. *Do something you normally wouldn't.* Normally, I'd walk away. When I think of doing that now, it seems cowardly. Maybe it's the music or the crowd or nighttime shielding me like a well-loved coat, but I feel bold. I want Ximena to know that I've changed too.

I flick my wrist and a root beneath us juts out of the earth as Olivia tries to move further into Ximena's space. All her flirting and seductive dancing comes to an abrupt halt as she tips forward. Ximena doesn't let her fall, catching her effortlessly around the middle. Once Olivia's upright, Ximena steps back, and I waste no time grabbing her hand. I steer us to the other side of the dance floor and yell, "Bye, Olivia!" over my shoulder.

"What are you doing?" Ximena asks as we merge into the crowd of people throwing themselves around to the music.

"Enjoying myself." Away from Olivia, I can breathe easier. Except now I'm left standing awkwardly in front of Ximena with no idea what to do with my hands or the annoying fluttering in my stomach.

Ximena tucks her elbows in as the crowd undulates around us. "If I didn't know any better, I'd think you were jealous," she says with a raised eyebrow.

"I wasn't *jealous*. I was getting secondhand embarrassment from watching Olivia awkwardly flirt with you." Saying it out loud sounds very jealous, so I add, "We have a better view of the party from here anyway."

Ximena narrows her gaze, and once again, I feel transparent. After a quick glance at the swarm of bodies next to us, she lets me off the hook. "I guess you're right. We should blend in a little, though, don't you think? Show me some of your dance moves."

As soon as the words leave her mouth, the song changes to one I recognize. Ximena sways from side to side. She pokes her tongue out in the same way she used to when we were kids and I was anxious about something. I hate that the gesture calms me.

I let the music move me, the melody thrumming in my veins like a second pulse. I raise my hands and the buds of redwood sorrels speckling the bushes nearest us burst into full bloom, the bonfire catching their bright white petals and illuminating them like lightning bugs. Ximena laughs.

And it's so *easy*. I forgot how nice it is to be around her. Even as I grow dizzy from the magic and the twirling, I hold on to the carefree feeling flowering between my ribs. Keep it tucked in close.

Ximena closes the space between us, and my stomach dips. The wind sweeps dark strands of hair into her perfect face. I can't stop staring at her, and a familiar warmth blossoms low in my chest. I'm supposed to loathe her for breaking my heart. I shouldn't be tongue-tied and useless like I'm thirteen again realizing I have a crush on my best friend. I should not be thinking about our hovering bodies while we're trying to catch a thief. I should be as focused as I told Ximena to be. I should . . . say something. About the investigation. Or, absurdly, tell her how nice she looks again, especially with the eerie way her irises seem to shift from their usual walnut brown to a shocking amber color.

I'm probably making a weird face, because Ximena tilts her head in question. "In this light, it almost seems like your eyes are amber or gold," I murmur.

She misses a step, her heel smashing my toes. "Sorry," she mutters. She checks her phone and frowns. "We should go. I have a curfew."

It takes me longer than I'd like to catch up. Eventually, I climb out of whatever wormhole I fell into and try for a response. "Okay. Sure."

"Cool." She gestures weakly at the opening in the tree line. "I'll walk you home."

# 14

Ximena says goodbye to her friends before we leave the party. Instead of watching her hug Olivia, I do a final once-over of the crowd. Two girls spill the liquid in their cups as they laugh uncontrollably. A boy from my Honors English class furiously texts someone while the people next to him jump around as the bass flares.

Jason and Morris talk by the makeshift bar, a plastic folding table with Solo cups and two bottles of alcohol. Based on their stiff stance and the way Jason is balling his fist, I'd say they're having an intense conversation. Ximena's still busy with Olivia, and I really need to not think about them flirting, so I inch closer to the bar, pretending to be preoccupied with something on my phone.

"I messed up, bro. I should've waited, and now Leigh's *hurt*," Jason is saying.

"You did what you had to do. Don't worry. Leigh will be fine," Morris tells him.

I move closer, snapping a branch. They glance up at the sound.

Morris's nostrils flare. "Damn, Sage. You're everywhere. Can't you see this is a private conversation?"

My shoulders rise toward my ears. "I wasn't trying to eavesdrop."

"Yeah, you were," Jason replies. "Want to ask me more questions? You could at least buy me dinner first."

Morris laughs. I ignore them both.

"What do you feel horrible about?" I ask.

Jason crosses his arms. "Nothing for you to worry about. It's not related to your shop's break-in."

"It might be. Did you know Leigh was missing cheer practices? Maybe Leigh stole my tonic because you broke her heart and now you feel guilty because she can't remember you. Or did you steal it because you wanted Leigh to forget something you did?"

Jason grimaces. "I didn't steal from you."

"Then prove it. What time did you get to the rally?"

"Jason and I got there at the same time," Morris says quickly. "It was around twelve-twenty, right, bro?"

Jason glances at him. "Uh, yeah."

The timeline doesn't add up. Morris and Poppy were arguing outside Tea for Thought at 12:10 and that lasted a few minutes. BVH is ten minutes away from the apothecary. It's possible to do the drive in less time if traffic is light and you speed, but not by much. Someone's lying.

A warm hand brushes against the back of my arm as Ximena slides in next to me. She takes in a scowling Morris and a jittery Jason. "What did I miss?"

"Nothing," Morris grumbles at the same time I reply, "Timeline issue."

Ximena pivots between us, partly amused and partly troubled. "We'll work it out later. Ready?"

Her hand is too warm against my skin as she leads me away. I fill her in on my conversation with Morris and Jason. It's not long before the roar of music dims, and the quiet hush of rustling leaves and the scuttle of forest creatures engulfs us. I follow closely behind her, half surprised she knows her way through the knotted woods and back to the trail considering she never comes to bonfire parties. Like on the dance floor, I have the uncharacteristic urge to break the silence between us.

"So that was an infamous bonfire party," I say.

"Not too bad with the right company."

"Like Olivia? She was charming."

Ximena shakes her head with a smirk. "She was a little drunk, but she can be fun."

"Unlike me?"

"You're more than fun. You're creative and determined and know what you want out of life, which is inspiring. I'm sure I'm missing some key qualities, but I want to learn them. That's all I was trying to do at Bishop Brews earlier today."

At Honey's Diner, I told her that our past was not up for discussion, but here I go breaking my own rule. "Why?"

Ximena's steps falter. She rubs her undercut as if it'll lend her courage. "I miss you. I've missed you every day for the last four years."

I suck in a harsh breath through my teeth. The sound is louder than anything else out here. "Ximena, *you* ghosted *me*."

She stops completely and throws her hands up. "I didn't want to, but I didn't know what else to do!"

"That doesn't even make sense!" No one held her down and stopped her from texting me back. There must be cell reception in Los Angeles.

She rubs at the creases in her forehead, then takes a deep, steadying breath. "It's not . . . I was dealing with a lot. I *had* to get out of here."

"You could have talked to me about it. I thought . . ." It's my turn to fumble for the right words. "I thought we were closer than ever when you left. Is this . . . is this because we kissed?"

I'd rather be launched into space than hear her answer yes to that, but I *need* to know. That summer before freshman year was the first time I realized the way I felt about Ximena was different from the way I felt about Mercer and Poppy. Those emotions took up my whole chest. What we had ended before anything could really begin, but my love for her was real. Where I'm usually filled with doubt, there was nothing but certainty around her. I thought she felt the same. She *said* she did, but maybe . . . Maybe she couldn't handle it. We were young, I guess.

Ximena narrows the space between us in a single step. "No! Of course not. That kiss meant so much to me."

I drop my head and scrape my Converse across the ground. "Okay, then what happened?"

Ximena gets a faraway look in her eyes as she stares out into the forest. "I changed," she replies, then shakes her head. "No, that's not right. I . . . I realized something about myself that was always there, but I hadn't noticed before."

"Vague."

The muscles in her jaw twitch. "I don't know what you want me to say."

"I want you to let me in. You're making it really hard to trust you."

She shakes her head. "I know, and I'm sorry, Sage. I never meant to hurt you. I was trying to prevent that. But I promise, I'll never hurt you again."

I deflate a little. I've had this anger in my heart toward her, as toxic as black mold, I couldn't get rid of. I had resigned myself to it spreading unless I found a way to stop it with my heartbreak tonic. And yet, Ximena found a way to kill it with a single phrase.

"Is there any way we can fix this?" she asks, gesturing between us. "I want us to be actual friends again," she offers, followed by a lopsided grin that makes my insides swoop.

"Fine."

Ximena perks up. "Really?"

I nod slowly, allowing a languid smile to spread across my face. Ximena relaxes. There's a visible lightness in her steps as we make our way down the trail. The forest fills the quiet between us. The moon sits just above the tree-tops as evening bleeds into night. The bonfire will rage on for another hour at least, but my curfew is ten. Hers must be too, given her abrupt desire to leave.

The arboretum pops into view through a break in the tree line. Lush green bushes clustered with rose-red berries frame the wooden welcome sign. Sitting at the end of a winding drive is the house that's been in my family for generations. Ximena walks me to the start of the driveway. Her hands flex in her pockets as she chews on her bottom lip.

"Thanks for walking me home," I say.

"Anytime."

"Do you need a ride?"

She shakes her head.

We're standing a few feet apart just watching each other. What's the protocol for saying goodbye to an old crush–turned–new friend? Do I hug her? High-five? Casual thumbs-up?

Ximena puts me out of my misery like the well-adjusted person she is with a small wave. "See you tomorrow, Sage," she says, and then heads back the way she came. She grins over her shoulder before disappearing into the trees.

Our friendship, shiny and newly renovated, is a spark

# Sage's Investigation

## REVISED TIMELINE

11:30 a.m.–12:00 p.m.—cupcake promotion (still thinking about that red velvet!)

12:00 p.m.—Cheerleaders arrive at the rally, minus Poppy and Leigh.

12:10 p.m.—I leave Bishop Brews and walk to Tea for Thought.

12:20 p.m.—Morris and Jason arrive at the rally???

12:30 p.m.—Ximena calls to say there's been a break-in.

12:30 p.m.—Poppy arrives at the rally.

12:35 p.m.(?)—Leigh arrives at the rally.

1:00 p.m.—The rally starts at BVH, where Leigh ingests my misbrewed heartache tonic.

## MOTIVES

1. To discredit or harm Bishop Brews or witches in general. Giving the tonic to Leigh: coincidental or accidental???

2. To harm Leigh or the founders in general. Use witches as scapegoats given town history. They would have to have known the tonic they gave Leigh was misbrewed—aka a witch, a founder, or a stalker (please no).

3. Money—probably about $200 cash for the premade tonics and way more if a buyer knew just how valuable my heartache brew was (had it not been misbrewed, of course).

## SUSPECT PROFILES

- A disgruntled customer, a competitor, or someone with a grudge against a witch

- Big Business Buttheads, Bottled Wonders

- An enemy of Leigh's or someone with a grudge against a founding family

- Poppy

- Someone with intimate knowledge of misbrew side effects, most likely Poppy, Jason, Morris, or, dare I say, Ximena?

- An athlete who stole the brews wanting to make extra cash, like Little Miss Flirty, aka Olivia, the BVH wolf mascot

# 15

My brain has decided to hyperfocus on a certain ex-crush-turned-coworker-turned-friend. I'm currently seeking out a familiar shock of dark hair among the mass of students loitering at their lockers in between classes. Instead of Ximena, I lock eyes with Olivia as she rushes up the stairs, a bike helmet under one arm and sweat dripping down her face. Maybe her car finally gave out?

I open my messages with Ximena and debate texting her. It's not really unusual that I haven't seen her today. Ximena and I are in different homerooms and have different schedules, but apparently my brain finds that explanation unacceptable. I wait for Mercer to switch out her books and reapply her lipstick, and then she loops her arm through mine and we're off, swallowed by the wave of students also heading for the cafeteria.

"How about some gossip to ease the pains of secondary education?" Mercer asks as we enter the lunchroom.

We bypass the line of students wrapping around the hot food bar and beeline for our usual table in the back. It's directly across from Ximena's lunch table, and when I glance over, her friends are there. Ximena's absent. They open their lunches or pick at the school's rubbery pizza without her. Despite the knot that forms in my belly, I tell myself it's not a big deal. I'll see her later for our shift.

"Let's hear it," I reply lightly, plopping into the seat next to Mercer. The plastic chair squeaks.

"Poppy's pissed at Morris. Apparently, he's been distant," she says, barely able to contain the lift in her voice.

"And let me guess, you're going to offer her a shoulder to cry on?"

"No. I'm going to be supportive and helpful like a good covenmate should, but I've always thought she could do better."

I pause midway through taking out my lunch—a plain turkey sandwich and chips. Ximena did say Morris has had a crush on Leigh since forever, giving him motive to dose her with a misbrewed tonic to forget about Jason. Especially if he believed it'd only target feelings of the heart. Or maybe Poppy found out that Morris was still into Leigh?

"I should tell you, Morris and Poppy are suspects in the investigation."

Mercer crosses her arms. "Poppy didn't do this."

"Can you prove it? Have you magically read any of her stuff lately?"

"You know I don't like doing that to covenmates. I finally have my Sight under control, and I'm not using it unless I have to."

Mercer spent a long time learning how to only use her Sight when she wants. Before then, she was always inadvertently reading things, causing *a lot* of drama in her family. She touched her uncle's bag once and saw that instead of being in Chicago on a business trip, like he told his wife he would be, he'd been in San Francisco with another woman. That was not a good day.

"Fine. She's an athlete and was standing outside Mystic Muffins on the day of the break-in. She knows the side effects of misbrewed tonics include memory loss. She has a reason for not wanting Leigh to have her memories: she wants to be cheer captain. And she was late to the fundraising rally." I pull open my bag of chips and pop one into my mouth.

"And your other suspects, Miss Marple?" Mercer asks. At my pause, she adds, "What? I read those Agatha Christie books *with you*, remember?"

"How could I forget your two a.m. calls to compare suspects?" I take out my notebook, the one I've been using to keep track of different tonic recipes. It's quickly turned into an investigative journal. I flip to the page where I have my updated list of clues and suspects. Laying out the facts makes it easier to parse out what we've missed and come up with next steps.

Mercer nods as she reads. "Not bad."

"You think so? The search is coming along better than the counter brew for Leigh," I reply.

Mercer cracks open her bento box and bites into a slice of melon. "Your grandma's struggling with a counter brew? Man, I thought my magic was the only one out of whack. I had trouble reading some of the new donations for the emporium."

"And I haven't been able to figure out my heartache tonic to save my life. Granted, I knew it'd be hard, but twenty-five failed tonics seems excessive."

"Yikes. You think there's a problem with the magic?"

"There hasn't been before. I don't see why there would be one now, but I'll check the grimoire or ask Nana when I get home."

As I finish off my bag of chips, my mind drifts to Ximena—another troubling puzzle I'm trying to solve.

Mercer leans her elbows on the table. "I know that face. What else is going on? It wouldn't happen to be about a certain dark-eyed brunette, would it?" she asks in a singsong voice.

"No," I reply too quickly, practically giving myself away. "We're fine. Friends now, actually."

Mercer rolls her eyes so hard I fear for her ocular health. "Sage, you've been not-so-subtly searching for her all day. Since when do friends do that?"

"I look for you when you're not here."

"Because I'm your best friend, not your ex who you're still crushing on."

"I'm not! She's not—"

Mercer shakes her head. "All I'm saying is that your relationship may be past tense, but are your feelings?"

"They are," I say, even though I lack conviction.

"Believe me or don't, but I think you owe it to yourself to tell her that you want out of the friend zone."

"You make it sound so easy."

"No. Putting yourself out there is hard. And scary and uncomfortable. But none of that outweighs the chance that Ximena might actually like you back."

"If you're so wise, why haven't you told Poppy how you really feel?"

"She has a boyfriend. And I don't think they want a third. Ximena, however, is blessedly single."

"That doesn't mean she likes me. You should've seen her with Olivia last night."

"Of course you have competition! It doesn't mean Ximena feels differently about you."

Even if Ximena returned my feelings, we can be nothing more than friends. The bonfire may have been exciting, but I can't get used to her sticking around. Leaving is not just a dream for her. Once she has enough money to cover what her scholarship can't, she'll be gone. And I'd rather not have her at all than lose her twice.

)·)·)·)●(·(·(·(

I may or may not be more eager than usual when I enter Bishop Brews, the bell above the door singing its welcome and thick rays of late sunlight edging across the hard-wood floor.

Ximena is already inside, clocking in on Nana's old laptop behind the counter. I'm surprised to see her here before me, considering I practically made Mercer speed over as soon as the final bell rang.

"When we were younger, you hit your snooze button like fifteen times," I say instead of a proper greeting.

A genuine smile tugs her lips. "I'm punctual now."

Ximena and I swapped shifts with Nana and Tiva today so they can work on another counter brew at home without customers distracting them.

"Were you at school today?" I try to sound casual and fail if Ximena's wince is anything to go by. She raises her arm to brush a tuft of hair from her face, and an angry pink scratch peeks out from beneath her shirtsleeve. I make a mental note to offer her some honey ointment before the day's over.

"No, I had a headache this morning. It's gone now, though." She shoots a teasing grin my way. "Why? Miss me?"

"Ha. Please." I turn my head before she can see the smile threatening to form.

The day moves faster than usual. Ximena is a natural. She knows the store better than our last employee, who was with us for sixteen years. Even more shocking, the discomfort I used to have around her is mostly gone. We move around each other with a familiar ease, and the time flies by rather than drags.

Mayor Brown, Morris's dad, enters around four. He's one of our regulars, coming in for his custom hair growth serum made of rosemary, green tea, and ginseng, the properties of each heightened with Nana's magic.

"Hello, Sage. It's always nice to see you," he greets me. "I was shocked to hear about the break-in. I hope it's straightened out soon." He pats his thinning hair. "You know I need my serum."

"I have it ready for you." I grab the glass vial from beneath the counter, where we keep custom products for our regulars. "What's new with you this week?" I ask while I pack up his hair serum.

Nana says the mayor loves to gossip, but really, he's just complaining. Last week it was the stock market, and before that it was his in-laws.

"Same ole stuff. Morris is still doing his own thing despite all the guidance his mother and I give him. I practically had to bribe him to intern with me this year to help boost his college apps, and don't get me started on basketball. Coach hardly puts him in the game."

I chuckle awkwardly and hand over his product. "Sounds like he has a lot on his plate."

Mayor Brown straightens his tie. "Not more than me when I was his age. Oh, before I forget, I was wondering if you have anything for managing chronic pain?"

"We have a pain-reducing balm you can rub on sore muscles and a tonic for migraines. If you want something stronger, I can tell my grandmother, and she can make a custom brew." Maybe Morris wasn't totally lying, and his pains from basketball are real.

"That would be great. Do let me know if there's anything I can do about the robbery. I take crime very seriously. Once we find the culprit, they'll be dealt with swiftly."

*Even if it's your son, Mayor?*

"I will," I tell him instead.

Once he's gone, I make gift boxes while my mind strays to the investigation, the dodgy magic, and mastering my heartache tonic. Tiva taught me that when my anxiety flares up, I should try to separate all my problems into more manageable pieces. *How do you eat an elephant? You don't. But if you* had *to, one bite at a time.* The problem is the number of bites is doubling by the day.

"Oof, I'd hate to be that tissue paper right about now," Ximena says from behind me. At my confused frown, she points at the shreds of fine yellow paper on the table. I'm supposed to be folding it into threes so it's easy to insert into the boxes. Instead, I've been shredding it.

I lean back against the chair. "I've got a lot on my mind."

Ximena moves closer. "Care to share with the class?"

She has this exasperating habit of seeing right through me and plucking out the hidden truths. Always has.

"You know I've dreamed of taking over Bishop Brews since we were kids. I'm worried there won't be a store left to inherit. And I think there's something off with the magic."

"Wait. Run that back. What's wrong with the magic?"

"Mercer's having trouble reading donations at work. Nana's struggling with the counter brews, and I can't crack this heartache tonic."

She rubs a hand down her face. "Shit."

"Even if we find out who broke in, how are we supposed to save Leigh and run the apothecary without magic?"

Ximena leaves her spot from behind the register and joins me on the other side of the counter. "What did your grandmother say?"

"I haven't talked to her yet."

A warm thumb traces circles across my knuckles. "Then let's worry about the magic after you talk to her. Right now, we need to focus on the investigation. We'll get to the bottom of this."

She releases my hand, and I tell myself I don't miss her touch. She picks up the drawstring bag of crystals nearby. Inside are clear quartz for clarity, fluorite for concentration and decision-making, and amethyst for calming nerves. It was my idea to group different stones together as a gift set.

"How can you be so certain?" I ask.

She moves closer. Too close. I can count the freckles on her nose—eleven—and see the muscles of her throat ripple as she swallows. She smells lovely, like coconut and vanilla and something that reminds me of the Hemwood after fresh rain.

"Because you're running point, and you're the most stubborn and imaginative person I know," she says without a lick of indecision. Like it's the most obvious thing in the world. I pull a face, and she laughs. "Don't believe me? Remember when—"

She stops. Concentrates on her hands.

"Tell me."

She jerks her head up, eyes wide and bright. "Remember when I got stung by a wasp while we were playing near Willow Creek? I was so scared to go back home and tell my mom after she nearly went hoarse from telling us not to play there unsupervised because of the wasp nest."

"I took you back to the cottage and created a makeshift poultice out of plantain leaf to draw the stinger out and used lemon balm to reduce inflammation."

"Worked like a charm! My mom was never the wiser. You're innovative, especially under pressure. There's no problem you can't solve."

I missed this, and not just how she nurtures my self-confidence. I missed *her*. It's then I realize how little space there is between us. I clear my throat and step back. "Do you want to help me with my tonic?"

"Hell yes!"

In the kitchen, I lay out the mixing pot, the herbs, and my notebook. Ximena's the only non-witch I've ever brewed with. She's good about handing me ingredients while I keep a steady rhythm stirring them together.

She rests her hand on my arm. "Hold on, have you tried using motherwort? It sounds like this tonic is based in comfort, right? Well, ginger is great for those, but also a lot of other things. Maybe a specific herb like motherwort will be more helpful."

I stare at her stunned, my mouth catching flies.

"What? I've been listening!" she says around a belly laugh.

"Motherwort could work," I reply. "Or yarrow flower. I've been switching out different ingredients every time, but I haven't tried either of those yet. Nice suggestion."

Ximena takes my praise with grace. She hands me ground motherwort. The green flakes have a leafy sharp smell and are bitter as hell despite the herb being in the mint family. It eases anxiety and helps regulate hormones. It really might be more beneficial in this mix than ginger.

According to the grimoire open on my right, motherwort should be spread in. I do as the instructions say, concentrating on my intentions of healing heartbreak while Ximena watches quietly on my left. Not a moment later does the brew emit a faint glow.

"Oh my god," I gasp. My hands tremble as I lean over the rim of the pot, my whole body featherlight. "It's working!"

"Yes!" Ximena squeals as the glow grows stronger.

She wraps her arms around my waist and squeezes. Our first hug in years feels like falling into bed after a long day. I let myself sink into her embrace. She must feel how fast my heart is beating. She releases me but doesn't step away.

Another glance at the brew has my shoulders sagging. The mixture is dimming. "I don't think it's going to hold," I whisper, because talking normally while we're standing this close seems wrong. "I mean, finally, we're one step closer. But what if I never get this to work?"

Ximena bites her bottom lip, and my brain short-circuits.

"You will, Sage. You're going to make the perfect tonic. It'll beat out anything Bottled Wonders can come up with. I'm sure of it."

Ximena's belief in me is enough for both of us. She always seemed so sure of my abilities, especially when I was first learning to control my magic. What does it mean that she still has such faith in me after all these years?

Ximena has yet to step back, and for some reason, I'm looking at her lips—perfectly plump and probably softer than I remember. Back when we first acknowledged our feelings for each other, we'd get milkshakes after soccer practice, and after an hour of pretending not to be obsessed with each other, we'd hold hands under the table. And then one Saturday while we were alone in my backyard, Ximena licked her lips, darted forward, and pressed her mouth to mine. Half a second later she was nervously bunching her hands at her sides and fumbling for something to say. I laced our fingers together. Hers were calloused. Mine were sweaty. I leaned in and stilled her nerves with a quick kiss of my own.

I should not be thinking about that moment right now, not after Ximena and I agreed to be friends. We were a thirty-second middle school fling and nothing more.

I try desperately not to think about how the curious tilt of Ximena's head sends a flurry of excitement from my scalp to my toes or how the arc of her mouth forms a soft, genuine smile.

God, I really want to kiss her.

Mercer was right. I'm crushing on Ximena.

Again.

# Sage's Heartbreak Tonic

## <u>Attempt Number Twenty-Six</u>

### INGREDIENTS

½ cup Hemwood spring
    water

4 oz. crushed motherwort

3 roses

3 oz. cut yarrow flower

1 tsp. ground cinnamon

Honey, honey, honey

### DIRECTIONS

1. In a brewing pot, pour in the spring water, spread in the crushed motherwort, and scatter rose petals one at a time. Try not to have an existential crisis while the mixture simmers on low heat for 8 minutes.

2. Throw in the yarrow flower. Stir like your life depends on it. Let steep for 3 minutes.

3. Close your eyes and focus your intentions on making a tonic to forget your heartache. If it fails, you can always try Carrie Underwood's method.

4. Shake in 1 tsp. ground cinnamon.

5. Add however much honey you want. You know the drill.

6. Carefully bind the properties of the herbs together with magic.

7. Wait for the mixture to glow.

Warning: *If possible, do not fall for your assistant!*

# 16

I basically ogle Ximena for the rest of our shift. If she notices—she must—she doesn't say anything. She goes about helping customers, assembling boxes, and checking the till. All the while, I try to figure out how the hell I got myself into this predicament. I can't like her again. Been there, done that, donated the T-shirt. We didn't work the first time because she shut me out. What's keeping her from doing the same thing again, especially when she has bigger and better things on the horizon, like a whole life outside our tiny coastal town?

Instead of trying to figure *that* out, I throw myself into work, losing track of time in day-to-day tasks. I tie twine around dried herbs and stick logos on hand-poured candles with crystals and crushed petals. I check the thank-you cards to make sure they have the right address and phone number of the shop.

And then I peek at Bottled Wonder's Instagram for the

millionth time. All their posts look the same—stale photos of their shelves stocked with the same plainly labeled tonics. If Bishop Brews had an Instagram, I'd post colorful shots of our custom charms, the storefront decorated with red-and-green wreaths, or welcoming candles burning in the windows.

Maybe I should create a social media account for the store. It could help with foot traffic and, coupled with the website, could bring in a flood of new customers from outside Blackclaw Valley. I've been wanting to do it for a while but never got around to actually posting.

Ximena pauses her duties behind the register to crush peppermint and saffron, which we use in lots of products since they're high in antioxidants.

I actively try not to watch her, but I never was able to ignore her completely, even when we were furthest apart. Now, knowing how much I still like her, it's nearly impossible to keep from glancing her way. I'm barely concentrating.

She catches my eye, and before I can turn away, she says, "Need another break? We've only got twenty minutes left."

I smile. "That obvious?"

"Only a little." She nods at the mess I've made of labeling items, stickers that say "Brewed with Love" half stuck to glass vials and twine unraveling. I glance at the clock. "Can you help me make an Instagram account? We desperately need more customers." Ximena is a cool girl now; maybe she can use some of her coolness for good?

"Oh, absolutely."

I hand her my phone, and she starts taking pictures of our shelves while I help customers. Most are regulars, but we do get two new visitors, including my English teacher, Mr. Parker. He's been teaching at Blackclaw Valley High for thirty years and even taught my dad when he was my age. He nervously asks for silver charms for his grandson and his friends, who are camping this weekend. I scribble a reminder on the notepad we keep next to the register to ask Nana how to make the silver charms. At this rate, we're going to sell out before the month's over.

Ximena slides in next to me. Our arms brush as she leans over to show me what she's captured. "What do you think?"

I scroll through the photos, more than a little impressed. "These are awesome. Do you think they're flashy enough?"

I stop on a candid of me. My head is thrown back, eyes closed, and mouth open mid-laugh. Ximena was being goofy, pulling funny faces while exaggerating her stance.

"They're perfect," she says, and taps my phone. "This one most of all." My cheeks warm, even though she's just being nice. "I think we should post them and take pictures of your grandmother working here too. Customers like seeing the face behind the products," she adds. "Can I text these to myself? I can edit a few before we post them. I can also get a few of my friends to amplify."

I hand Ximena back my phone. As she navigates to my text messages, her eyebrows shoot to her hairline.

"Ximena (Don't Fall For It) Reyes, huh? What does *that* mean?"

My stomach drops to my ankles. Rookie mistake not to scrub my phone for embarrassing content before handing it over. "Uh . . . It means don't fall for your . . . tricks."

"What *tricks*?"

"You know. You're"—I wave my hand around and try not to die of shame—"charismatic."

The corner of her mouth slowly lifts. "Am I?"

I'm making a mess of this. Bury me.

"Forget you saw it." I snatch my phone back. My fingers fly across the keyboard and change Ximena's contact name to "Ximena." "Matter of fact, I just changed it."

I drop my phone onto the counter followed by my head and pride. Ximena chuckles but doesn't tease me further.

We perform closing procedures in easy silence as I count the till. Ximena sweeps and closes the blinds, and we both clock out.

I linger by the front door, not ready to let the day end completely. Doing something concrete like working the investigation will take my mind off my resurfaced feelings for Ximena. Working with her at Bishop Brews is inevitable, but all this extra time we spend together is the reason my heart keeps skipping. The faster we find who broke in, the sooner I can put some distance between us and cool off this crush.

"Do you have plans after work?" I ask. "I want to ask Poppy about usurping Leigh for cheer captain and confirm what time she got to the rally."

"You're in luck. I'm completely free." Ximena unties her apron and hangs it up on the rack near the kitchen door. Her scratch peeks out as a reminder.

"Let me get you some ointment for that first." I nod to the cut on her arm. "What happened, anyway?"

The first aid kit is in the storage closet. Tiva stocked it with all her homemade creams while Nana added gauze and Band-Aids. I pry open the metal box and grab a jar of honey, which is a good antiseptic and protectant for small scratches like Ximena's.

"I got it playing with the twins," she replies a little too quickly. Although it's entirely plausible, I sense it's a lie. Does she not trust me? I don't know if this crush will go away anytime soon, but trust is something we're going to need as coworkers, friends, and partners in this investigation. Though, to be fair, I did cut the "don't fall for it" part from her moniker only two seconds ago.

Using a cotton swab, I rub the honey on her arm as softly as I can. She flinches a little. "Does it hurt?"

She shakes her head. I try my hardest not to get lost in the deep brown of her eyes. It's useless. I clear my throat and lean back. "All done." I close the lid of the first aid kit and shove it aside. "Let's go."

Ximena drove to work, which is great for me because I don't have to pretend she has no effect on me while I'm pressed against her during another bike ride.

It's an unusually hot day, even in the evening, and the inside of Ximena's truck is a furnace. Stale air rushes out of the vents as she fiddles with the AC before ultimately deciding to roll down the windows. Her silver earrings sparkle in the setting sun, and her winged black eyeliner cuts into the soft brown of her skin, accentuating her eyes.

Shit. I'm staring again.

I turn around. The familiarity of the clutter in the back seat makes me smile. She may be punctual now, but she's still messy. Among the wreckage, I spot a half-open gym bag full of clothes, a full case of bottled water, and a pack of glittery eyeshadow. Against the door is a shredded T-shirt; the only visible lettering is the word "hades" plus part of a bright red rose.

When Ximena follows my gaze, she's quick to toss it under the seat. I chalk it up to being self-conscious about her car. I get that way with my room. No one wants all their private habits on display.

We wind north along Main Street with the Hemwood on the right. The center of town, where all the shops and restaurants are, sits directly in the middle of two residential neighborhoods. The neighborhood to the south, where Mercer, Ximena, and I live, is thinly populated and heavily wooded. Poppy, Morris, and the other rich kids live on the north end. Cawing birds circle the lumpy treetops, and the scent of sap and lilies fills the air. The houses in northern Blackclaw are cookie-cutter, same picture windows and neutral paint. Every house on the block is a replica of the other. Within five minutes, you go from nothing to something. From overgrown grass and no sidewalks to manicured lawns and evenly spaced flowers planted along cobblestone walkways. From Toyotas to BMWs.

Still, magic thrums through the soil here like it does all throughout Blackclaw and Crimson Grove. I use it to calm my nerves. As we barrel down the road, I reach my arm out. My lips tug into a smile as I brush my fingers along the sharp magenta petals of the purple owl's clover ringing someone's mailbox. They stretch to greet me like eager kittens.

Ximena hangs her arm out the window too, her hand riding the wind and the sun glinting off her pink, orange, and purple nail polish. The cool breeze kicks up her dark hair and reddens her cheeks. She's beautiful.

Not ten minutes later, we turn down Poppy's street. The Carvers live at the end of a cul-de-sac in a large house with pale yellow siding and a fancy white door. Seeing her house makes me wonder, not for the first time, whether Poppy really did steal my tonic. Criminal implications aside, she'd have gone against our coven and put us all at risk. And for what? To be cheer captain?

Ximena parks in the driveway. "What's our plan of attack, boss?"

"I'll do the talking while you search for clues."

"Clues being . . . tonic residue?"

"Obviously that or, like, a lock-picking kit, gloves—"

"Ski masks?" Ximena laughs.

"I'm just being thorough!"

"It's cute—uh, *cool*." Ximena shakes her head and leaps out of the car. "Ready?"

*What the hell was that?* Obviously, she meant *cute* in an endearing way, like how her brothers are cute when they start singing at the dinner table. I don't take it the way I want to. I know we're just friends.

And then Ximena loops her arm through mine, making me second-guess myself. Mercer and I walk arm in arm all the time, but with Ximena, I nearly miss a step. She's warm and solid against me, emitting a kind of magic all her own. A dangerous, addicting kind I can't let myself feed into because she's going to leave and grow in ways I might not and forget all about me. Again.

I jam my finger against the doorbell. Mrs. Carver answers a moment later. She's dressed in casual clothes with glasses perched high up on her nose.

"Hi, Mrs. Carver. Sorry to bother you. Is Poppy here?" I ask.

"Hi, Sage," Mrs. Carver says. "Poppy isn't home yet but she should be soon. Do you want to come in? You're welcome to wait for her."

She steps aside and gestures to a light-gray couch. The inside of their home is all sharp lines, clean wood tables, and abstract art. Mrs. Carver is an interior designer and started a lucrative design business, Spellbinding Spaces, with her late husband. Her work is good, but I always think she should incorporate more plants.

There's a small wicker wastebasket next to the couch. Among the tissues and gum wrappers are two empty glass vials. I'd know that green twine anywhere, so I'm not surprised to see the Bishop Brews label stuck on the glass.

"I have some work to finish up in the den. You know where everything is, right?" Mrs. Carver asks, dragging my attention away from a possible clue.

"Yep. Thanks," I reply.

As soon as she's out of sight, I'm on my feet and digging through the trash. Is this what my life has come to?

The labels of the tonics read "Courage" and "Clear Communication" with a bottled date of last Saturday—the day before the break-in. Both are popular premade tonics like the ones that were stolen.

I'm not proud of what I'm going to do, but we need to move this investigation along, and I have an inkling Poppy might not be forthcoming if she feels cornered. I creep toward the stairs, making sure to keep my steps light as I ascend to the second floor.

"Sage!" Ximena whisper-shouts after me. "What are you doing?"

The soft shuffling behind me lets me know she's following me. "Sleuthing!"

"This is such a bad idea," she whispers.

"I know."

Poppy's room is the first one off the landing. The door

is ajar. The floorboards screech when I step inside. My ears strain to hear if Mrs. Carver is coming, but there's only silence. I blow out a puff of air and continue.

Poppy's room is huge and messy. The desk is covered in books and papers, and clothes are strewn over the swivel chair. Ximena and I divide and conquer, moving swiftly since Poppy will be home soon. I don't find much, just schoolwork, lost socks, and some dust bunnies.

"*Psst!*" Ximena waves me over to the closet.

She moves aside but not far enough. I still have to lean over her shoulder to get a glimpse at what she found, which, of course, causes my heart to kick wildly against my ribs. On the floor are a few clothing items, a pair of headphones, and a phone charger.

Ximena wiggles her nose like she smells something weird, but to me, it all smells like expensive perfume mixed with sweat and laundry detergent. She points at an oversized BVH hoodie.

I grab the sweatshirt. It's a little worn, and someone has sewn a patch on the front that reads "Sunday Scaries." There's a dark purple stain on the sleeve. I drag my fingers across the rough dry patch. It's the right color and the right consistency of my tonic. I start to bring it to my nose, hoping for an herbal scent, when the sharp crack of a floorboard startles me into dropping it.

I whirl around. Surprise weakens my muscles, but I get my hands to push at Ximena's shoulder and my feet to stagger out of the closet.

Too late.

Poppy enters her room, a white leather purse strung over her shoulder and an annoyed expression plastered on her face.

Morris, who's trailing a few steps behind her, spots us first. His face morphs from bland disinterest to fury in two point five seconds. "What the hell are you two doing in here?"

Poppy and I lock eyes, both of us surprised to see the other. "Your mom told us we could wait for you," I mumble.

Poppy blinks. "In my *room*?"

"Well . . ."

She spots the hoodie on the ground, and her expression hardens. "Were you *snooping*? This is low, Sage, even for you." She snatches the hoodie and throws it in the closet.

"I'm sorry, but you weren't here and—"

"What do you want?" she asks bitterly. Seeing Poppy disappointed in me cuts deeper than I thought it would. Everything is already so muddled between us, and I just mucked it up further.

"Did you give Leigh a misbrewed tonic so she'd lose her memories and you could become cheer captain?" I ask in a single breath.

Poppy is quiet for a long moment, and then she starts to laugh—and not in an amused way. "Incredible. How did you come up with that one?"

"That's not an answer."

"No, Sage. I wanted to be cheer captain because Leigh wasn't taking the squad seriously anymore."

"Okay, then why are there empty courage and communication tonics downstairs?"

"I needed them before the rally because I get nervous before a performance, and I knew I was going to talk to Coach about being captain. My mom keeps a bunch of your grandmother's tonics in our kitchen. I didn't hurt Leigh, and I didn't break into your store. Happy now?"

Oh. Well, now I feel bad. Ximena and Morris share a tense look.

"Want me to call someone, babe? Your mom? Sheriff Dunn?" Morris sneers.

Poppy rolls her eyes. "Don't be dramatic." She turns to me and Ximena. "Can y'all leave?"

I grab Ximena's forearm and make for the hallway. We rush down the stairs and out the front door. Mrs. Carver is none the wiser. If I'm lucky, Poppy won't tell her mom about this. She might hate me for real now, though, and that stings.

"Were you able to confirm what that stain was?" Ximena asks when we're on the sidewalk. The sun has officially set, taking with it some of the heat.

"It looked like it could've been a tonic stain, but I can't know for sure."

"I thought I smelled something herbal," she replies. She opens the passenger door of her truck for me.

"You have a pretty strong nose, then, because all I smelled was sweat." I'm anticipating a laugh, but it doesn't come. Her forehead is creased like she's deep in thought.

Ximena climbs into the truck and starts the engine.

"Did you notice that logo on the front that said 'Sunday Scaries'? It's the name of Jason's band."

"The sweatshirt is Jason's?" At least something came of this.

"Or one of his bandmates'. I doubt the band is popular enough for anyone else to have its name on their clothes," Ximena replies.

"So a member of Sunday Scaries could be involved?"

"They'd also have to be an athlete or adjacent like Olivia. Otherwise the cupcake doesn't make sense. Plus, we'd need to tie them to Leigh and give them motive, but maybe," Ximena replies as she reverses out of the driveway. "Did you know Poppy had a party last weekend?"

"I heard her accusing Morris of acting weird at a kickback outside Tea for Thought on the day of the break-in," I reply.

Ximena nods. "That party was Saturday night, the day *before* the break-in. If Jason wasn't wearing his sweatshirt during the robbery, he must've left it at Poppy's sometime before Sunday. On the other hand, if he robbed Bishop Brews while wearing it, that means Jason was at Poppy's house this week."

When she's stopped at a light, Ximena pulls up a text thread between half a dozen people and starts to scroll. "Okay. Morris, Jason, and Olivia stopped by Poppy's Sunday morning to pick up pregame supplies."

"Is it possible Olivia wore Jason's sweatshirt to break into Bishop Brews? Maybe she wanted to throw off the cops," I suggest.

"She does need the money. She still hasn't gotten her car fixed and I saw her biking to school a couple times this week," Ximena replies.

"If someone was wearing that hoodie when the store was robbed, we'll need concrete evidence. The thief could be anyone who went to Poppy's kickback or pregame, which leaves Jason, Morris, Olivia, or Poppy herself. Let's talk to Jason first since it *is* most likely his sweatshirt."

The light turns green, and Ximena hits the gas. "A bunch of basketball players host a pickup game at the public courts tonight. Jason said he'd be there."

"Yeah, he invited you while we were at the bonfire," I reply.

Ximena nods. "Let's confirm Jason left his sweatshirt at Poppy's and that the stain on it is from your tonic before we mention it to anyone."

"Agreed."

"What happens if he is the thief?" Ximena asks.

"Seeing as he's the sheriff's son, I doubt there will be any serious consequences."

Ximena pulls onto my street and slows down. "And us? Will things go back to how they were before?"

"I—"

"I want us to stay friends," she clarifies quickly. She glances at me, and her eyes are infinite orbs that snag my attention and cause my heart to flutter.

Air rushes from my chest as I reply hoarsely, "Okay."

But as I reply, a snake slithers between my ribs and coils

around my lungs. I don't want to stay friends. Friends is never going to be enough. It never was.

"Do you want to come inside?" I ask.

Ximena bites her lip and nods. She parks the truck at the start of my driveway and gets out. As we walk side by side down the gravel path, she parts her mouth like she wants to say something. Her eyes flash amber just like they did at the store and the bonfire before that. It wasn't the light.

"I've never seen someone's eyes change colors like yours do," I tell her. "They've done it before, I think. They never used to, though." A wild expression flashes across her face at my words. Her jaw tightens, and she backs away, each step a physical blow. "What's wrong?"

"Nothing. Sorry. I need to go, but we can meet at the basketball courts in an hour." Her hands tremble as she fishes her car keys out of the pocket of her flannel.

I reach out to touch her arm. "Hang on. Tell me what's wrong." She runs to her car. I can't get to her fast enough. "Ximena, wait!"

She jumps inside and starts the engine as I race after her. From a few feet away, I notice her knuckles are white against the steering wheel. "I'll see you at the basketball courts. I just . . . I need to go. I'm sorry, Sage."

And then she's driving away, leaving me standing in the middle of the driveway wondering what the hell just happened.

# 17

The basketball courts are lively as a pickup game ensues. It's not only high schoolers here, but anyone wanting to play an early-evening game. I don't see Jason—just a lot of people in basketball shorts, Jordans, and Golden State tees.

Ximena is also MIA. Sitting alone on a park bench watching sweaty athletes dribble a basketball may sound appealing to some, but it is not how I want to spend my night. I'd thought I'd at least be with Ximena. Instead, it's been an hour and fifteen minutes since she sped away from my house.

I text her again, then stare at the unread messages.

Where are you??

Hello?

Someone build a funeral pyre for my dignity. I've officially been stood up. I don't get it. Why would she invite me here only to bail? What was so important that she practically ran from my house?

"Hey! Are you playing or what?" Enzo, a short boy in my grade wearing a BVH jersey, points at me. "We need another player."

My leg bounces as I try to decide what to do. All this excess energy needs to go somewhere and sitting around doesn't help anyone. "I'm playing!" Have I ever played a pickup game before? No. But is making a fool of myself on the court better than waiting around for Ximena? Yes.

The game starts with a ball toss, and my team takes first possession. I run down the court, passing a girl with blue locs and guitar picks for earrings. Her bright-blue nail polish winks in the sunlight. She sits at the same lunch table as Jason. "Is Jason coming?" I ask between breaths.

She lunges sideways and tries to swipe the ball from the other team but fails. "Nah."

I gesture toward her earrings. "Are you in his band, Sunday Scaries?"

"It's *our* band," she replies hotly.

"Right. Sorry. Was the rest of the band at the fundraising rally?"

She eyes me like I'm a mosquito buzzing in her ear. "No. Just Jason. Sam and I had a gig." She runs to the other side of the court before I can ask more questions.

The other team's point guard is Enzo. He drives hard

down the court and right toward me. I do my best to guard him, but he sidesteps me easily, charges for the hoop, and makes a layup. My teammate is there to grab the rebound, and everyone runs to the other side of the court.

"Do you know when Jason got to the fundraiser? Was it after twelve?" I ask Enzo, trying not to wheeze from all the running.

He frowns. "Jason Dunn?" I can only nod. "We both got there around noon," he replies.

"Was he at Mystic Muffins with you?"

"Nope. He's gluten intolerant. His mom brought the driest cookies to practice last year." Enzo chuckles to himself at the memory, and then he's gone, charging after the ball. His steal is clean, and before I can catch my breath, we're all running toward the hoop. He passes to an open teammate who takes the shot from the three-point line. The ball swishes into the net, and the spectators cheer.

After the game, though I did not score a single point, I'm lighter and much less on edge. I survived my first pickup game *and* got new information. Ximena is the first person I think to tell, but thoughts of her throw me back into reality. I did the thing I told myself I wasn't going to do. I fell for her, and she's already pushing me away.

I'm torn between storming over to her house to demand an apology and hiding in my room for the next millennium until I recover from being stood up. Well into my walk home, I still haven't decided.

When I pass my great-aunt's landscaping business, the Garden Genie, I draw up short. Outside, a man with a handlebar mustache and slicked-back hair is talking to my aunt. He was a customer at Bishop Brews on the morning of the break-in. I told him about my heartbreak tonic. Could he have gone around back and stolen it? But no, that doesn't add up with the Mystic Muffin napkin unless he knows an athlete who gave him a cupcake. And I've never seen him at a parent-teacher conference or school function.

Today, instead of dressing like a first-time hiker, he's wearing slacks and a crisp button-down shirt. As if that isn't odd enough, he hands my aunt a small card before climbing into his Ferrari and speeding off.

I cross the street and find my aunt on the phone. She gives me a quick hug and flits about the shop, clearly too busy to talk.

"Who was that man you were talking to, Aunt Genie?" I ask.

My aunt falters for a split second. "A client," she whispers, "like the one on the phone." She makes a shooing motion with her hands before turning her attention to her planner.

I don't really believe her, because no one in town drives a car that fancy. I let her get back to work. Still, I can't shake the feeling that Mustache Man is suspect.

Once I'm home and showered, I plop onto my bed with a groan just as my phone starts buzzing in my pocket.

Mercer.

"Why haven't you been responding to my texts?" she asks by way of greeting.

"I was playing basketball. And you know who was supposed to be there with me but never showed? Yep, Ximena. Who does that? I thought we were past the pettiness." Contempt scorches through me at the memory.

"Maybe she had an emergency?"

"She could've said that! She's keeping secrets."

"She'll tell you when she's ready. If she doesn't, I could always try to read her bracelet at school tomorrow to see where she's been—"

"Yes!"

"*Or*," Mercer continues with a light chuckle, "you could ask her outright."

"I'm less excited about that option," I reply dully.

"At least you'd have an answer," Mercer replies. She pauses and then asks, "What's up with you?"

I roll onto my stomach and string my fingers through the morning glory weaving through my headboard. The vines twist and stretch. Their petals gently nudge my hand. "What do you mean?"

"I mean Ximena has been elusive for years, but all of a sudden, it's bothering you? Last week you wouldn't even have carpooled with her, and now you're mad she didn't drive you home. Come on, Sage."

"Driving me home is common decency, Mercer."

"Fair, but I think there's another reason you're upset," she presses, because she doesn't know how to let anything go.

"I don't know what you expect me to say."

"Oh, I don't know, how about confess to that massive crush you've been harboring since forever?"

Mercer continues to allude to my feelings for Ximena, and usually I ignore her because she's wrong. But it just so happens that this time she's right. Within a few days, Ximena has managed to burrow herself so deep under my skin I have no chance of fishing her out.

"Okay. Fine. I have a crush on her."

"Wait. Holy shit, seriously?"

"As serious as ingesting poison hemlock. Isn't this what you've been wanting to hear?"

"Yes. Obviously. But I didn't think you'd admit to it. This is so exciting! When are you telling Ximena?"

"I wasn't planning on telling her. She just wants to be friends."

Mercer scoffs. "You can't believe that."

"I'm only relaying what she said right before she stormed off. I can't tell her how I feel and have her reject me."

"Girl, that's a risk you have to take if you ever want to have a chance with her again or anyone ever."

"Says who? I haven't thought that far ahead. I only started to like her again today."

I can practically hear Mercer recalculating her approach in the pause that follows. "Your denial is worse than expected. No matter. I'll get you there." She inhales audibly. "Sage, you've always liked her. Full stop."

"That's not—"

"It's true. You know how every time she's in the room, it's an adrenaline rush? You feel nervous and sweaty and stressed? Your stomach is all tight, and you have to actively try not to look at her? I've been paying attention, but have you? Your heart's been trying to tell you the truth for years. You're only now just starting to listen."

My lungs feel overstretched. My skin too tight. Mercer's right. I haven't been listening, but it's all I hear now. I can't get Ximena out of my brain. I want to text her funny videos and hear her opinion on a certain movie everyone's watching.

"What do I do?"

"Exactly what I've been saying to do: talk to her. She might surprise you," Mercer replies.

Talking rather than avoiding hard stuff out of fear has never been my strong suit. I'm usually content for everything to stay the same. When it comes to Ximena, though, I don't know if I can.

My slow, simmering embarrassment from earlier fades, and all that's left is a need for an explanation. I'm owed that, especially after she practically begged for us to be friends again. And I'm not above copping to the fact that a part of me *is* a little worried about her.

"Thanks, Mercer."

"Anytime."

As soon as I hang up, I swing my legs over the side of my bed, snatch my house keys from my dresser, and rush outside. We only have one car, which Nana and Tiva took to run errands, so I'm stuck with my bike. It's not ideal, but I could use the ride to figure out what I'm going to say.

My legs burn as I pedal out of the arboretum and toward the Reyeses'.

*What's your problem? You* invited *me to the courts, remember?* Hmm. That's a little aggressive.

*Ximena, I was really looking forward to hanging out with you and you stood me up. Not cool.* Better.

I glide down her block, slowing to a creep when I spot her truck parked crooked in the driveway. The lights are on in the house. If Ximena's in there, chilling with her little brothers and not even bothering to text me back, I will lose it.

I start for the door, ready to demand an apology. Only a low, threatening sound echoing from the forest behind the house stops me from ringing the doorbell. There are all kinds of animals in Hemwood, but the only things large enough to have such a deep growl are big and dangerous.

I poke my head around the side of the house to see if there's anything lurking in the backyard so I can warn Mrs. Reyes. Instead of a black bear, cougar, or even a bobcat, I spot a single olive Dr. Marten boot. And a foot from that is the flannel Ximena was wearing today.

My lungs expand, but no air gets in. I'm moving without thought, disappearing into the woods, Ximena's name on my lips. I have to find her.

I shine my phone flashlight over the ground so I don't trip as I make my way further into the Hemwood.

Between a patch of trees, I spot a flicker of movement.

My head swivels toward the sound. Fractured moonlight streams through the canopy, illuminating a long snout and tufts of thick gray fur peeking between tree trunks. Everything else is swathed in shadow.

If the animal attacks, I could tug on tree roots to trip it or trap it with obedient vines, but I've never used magic defensively before, and I don't want to start now if there is an issue with the magic. I could wind up overexerting myself and passing out.

The creature creeps closer. I jump back. My hand tightens around my phone as I hold it out. The trembling pale light reveals round, focused eyes and huge paws with long pink, orange, and purple claws.

A wolf.

Not just any kind, though. A massive gray wolf.

It throws its head back and howls. That sound is familiar in a primal way, like knowing your mother's voice in a crowded room. When it spots me, it freezes like a deer at the sound of a snapped twig. Cold alarm trails down my arms, leaving goose bumps in its wake. I can't move.

Is this what Leigh told Jason she saw in the woods and the reason we're nearly sold out of silver charms? Could the legend be true?

My breath sputters out when the wolf moves closer. In the glow of the flashlight, I see its eyes, huge amber orbs that pin me in place.

Its head thrashes from side to side, the bones cracking and then shrinking. I startle back, tripping over a snake-root vine bursting from the dirt beneath my feet. I land in the darkened sky. A second chance I didn't know I wanted until Ximena bulldozed her way back into my life. Even as I tell myself not to let her in too much, I can't help but let myself hope that whatever's between us now grows.

hard on my butt. The pain doesn't register. I can hardly hear anything over my own loud breathing. And yet, I can't look away. Thick gray fur recedes and vanishes beneath sweaty skin. Colorful claws retract into an enormous paw that thins and softens into a hand with pink, orange, and purple nail polish.

In a blink, the wolf is gone and in its place is a person, stark naked and folded over, the muscles of their back rippling like disturbed water. They raise their head and walnut-brown eyes lock with mine. The world churns as my brain tries to translate what I'm seeing. Not a wolf, but a girl.

Ximena.

# 18

My legs refuse to move, even though my brain screams for me to run. I'm stuck facing the very real truth that Ximena Reyes, First Crush & Heartbreaker, is a wolf. Blink once, I see gray fur and claws long and sharp enough to cut through flesh. Blink again, and there's a girl slumped over on the ground, shivering.

Despite my fear, I run to her. Her skin is pale and damp. Hoisting her to her feet is harder than I anticipated. Averting my gaze while simultaneously trying to maneuver her back into the house is harder still. Fresh scratches mark her arms. She's going to need her own jar of ointment.

The back door of her house is unlocked. There's a laundry room on our left, and inside a plastic hamper is a folded checkered blanket. I wrap it around Ximena's trembling frame. At my touch, she tenses.

She doesn't meet my eye when she mumbles a quiet "Thanks. You can't tell anyone about what you saw."

"I won't," I answer easily. As if anyone would believe me.

I have a million questions. I know Hemwood magic manifests in different ways for each family, but I thought only witches had magic, and that the story of wolves protecting the forest was local lore we capitalize on for tourists. Of course, I've seen the commemorating statue of the partnership in the town square enough times to re-create it from memory, but there really are shape-shifting wolves in Blackclaw—at least one—and she's been hiding under the guise of being human. Ximena has the extraordinary ability to turn into someone—some*thing*—new without anyone realizing.

"I'm sorry," Ximena whispers.

"Don't be. Seeing you transform from a wolf was terrifying but also *so* badass." I take her hand in mine. Her skin is soft, no hint of the fur or claws from ten minutes ago, simply a pretty girl with a deep blush creeping into her cheeks. "Should I get your mom?"

"No. It'll only worry her if she finds out it happened unexpectedly again. I've been having trouble controlling when I change lately. And then you mentioned the Hemwood magic being dodgy. I think the two things might be connected."

"Makes sense." I squeeze her hand as she leads us down the hall.

While she gets dressed, I take in her room. The space is nearly the same as it was four years ago. I assumed it'd be different, like her clothes and her friends, another extension of the new girl she morphed into, but nope. I helped her pick out the tapestry draped across the back wall and hang the black-and-white picture of Frida Kahlo next to an original 1998 *Buffy the Vampire Slayer* poster (a gift from her dad). The faded world map with pins stuck in the places she wants to visit is new. The overflowing white bookcase is not, but the novels and manga displayed are. I long to trace my fingers along their spines and peek at Ximena's tastes, trying to decide which ones are her favorites. There will be time for that later.

Ximena clears her throat once she's dressed. We stand facing each other on opposite ends of her room as I grapple with something to say. "I was worried," I blurt out. "I found your stuff in the backyard and thought for sure a bear got to you. I didn't know what I was going to do."

"I could probably take a bear," she says lightly.

I snort. "Always so smug."

She shrugs. "I've had a hairy day. Forgive me."

"Ugh, stop. That was horrible," I say around a laugh.

Ximena smiles toothily, and the tension between us dissipates like morning frost in the sun. She gestures toward her bed, and I plop down on her comforter. Everything in Ximena's room smells earthy and sweet, just like her.

"So . . . you're a werewolf? A shape-shifter? I don't know the appropriate terms," I tell her.

"A loba. Wolf. Everyone in my family is, except my dad." Ximena folds the blanket I wrapped around her and tosses it onto a fuzzy purple saucer chair.

*Loba.* As the word circles my brain, it weaves together clues until they form an understanding. "The moon tattoo behind your ear is a little on the nose, no?"

She snorts. "My cousin's idea. Got it right before I moved back to Blackclaw. My parents were furious."

Now her random scratches, the shredded T-shirt in the back seat of her car, her impressive sense of smell, her her eyes shifting colors, and her missing class make sense. So does her pulling away and the increase in demand for silver charms. Even Licorice's reaction to her mere presence. All this time, the signs were there. My whole life, I thought my coven was alone in our differences, but Ximena has magic too.

She throws a pair of ripped jeans and the geometric top she wore at the bonfire into a hamper and kicks a frayed sports bra under the bed. It's odd to see her trying to tidy up a room I've been in many times while in disarray. Usually, she's so charming and confident. But that was clearly an act, at least partially. She's been hiding a part of herself, and now I'm finally seeing the complete picture.

"So those wolf sightings near the hiking trail . . ."

She nods. "Me. I think Leigh saw me last week when I was just about to change. I can only shift in Blackclaw or Crimson Grove, but it's easiest in the forest. Legend has it, my ancestors were gifted magic as protectors of—"

"The Hemwood," I finish for her, because it's the same story Nana would tell me. Only, instead of the gift to shape-shift, it was to manipulate plants.

Ximena leans against the desk across from me and crosses her ankles. Divine favor is the only plausible explanation for why she appears effortlessly cool in a rumpled oversize sleep shirt and faded basketball shorts. I think about how while I was playing a pickup game and stewing, she was struggling to control her magic.

"Two centuries ago, this part of California was just forest," she starts. "Redwoods the size of skyscrapers spanned hundreds of miles from the mountains to the coast. The trees were magic, and the people who lived on the land revered them. When the foreigners came, cutting down most of the forest to make room for towns, they unknowingly ridded the land of most of its magic. Only one patch of redwoods remained, and the forest spirits gifted its inhabitants a portion of magic in exchange for protecting the trees from further harm. My ancestors were given the ability to shape-shift to scare off threats."

"We're all connected."

"Yeah, I suppose so." Her shoulders relax minutely before she adds, "You're the only person outside my family who knows."

"You can trust me," I tell her honestly. "And not just with this."

I pat the open space on the bed next to me and Ximena flings herself down, leaving barely an inch of space between us. The mattress springs protest weakly.

She peers at me over her shoulder. "I wanted to tell you four years ago. I tried so many times."

"Why didn't you?" I don't mean for my voice to get scratchy, but it does. When we were friends, I would've done anything for her. I wouldn't have seen her any differently for being a wolf. In fact, I'd probably like her even more. It's one of the coolest things about her. She never gave me the chance to tell her that.

She wraps a loose thread of her comforter around her finger. "I didn't know how to, and I wasn't sure how you'd react. Our family doesn't trust anyone. We see how scared people are of us. They call us hellhounds. For centuries, people thought we were attack dogs for witches. Good for nothing but violence." The words rush out, cold and spiked with hurt.

"But that isn't me."

She softens her face. "I know, Sage."

The Reyeses have been hiding their authentic selves because it's not safe to be open. Present-day, the wolves of Blackclaw's legend have always been seen as monsters under the bed.

"You must have questions," Ximena says.

"Only several hundred."

She gets comfortable by tucking her legs underneath herself. "Okay, let's see. I can usually shift at will," she begins. "My hearing, sense of smell, and even taste are heightened. That full moon stuff is a myth, and so is an aversion to silver, but the wolfsbane inside the charms we sell at the shop weakens my senses."

"That's why you let that group of customers grab the charms themselves. And why you've been sniffing all the clues."

Her nose wrinkles adorably. "I wasn't very subtle."

I lean back on my hands and stretch out. My feet brush against her leg and she leans in. "Have you always been able to shape-shift?"

She runs a hand through her hair, the roots curling with sweat. "No. I couldn't for a long time, and when it first starts happening, you don't have control. That only comes with practice."

We're quiet for a moment. I don't blame her for wanting to keep this part of herself quiet, but I don't understand why she completely cut me out of her life. If anyone knows what it's like to be different it's me. I'm a witch, and there are only four other families in town like me. I'm also a lesbian, an identity that swings between novelty or villainy depending on the day in this country.

"Why'd you push me away, Ximena?" I ask.

She pauses and swallows hard. "You know that scar on my mom's face?" Her eyes shine with unshed tears I long to wipe. "I did that. It was an accident. I couldn't control my wolf self. She got too close trying to help me, and I hurt her. When my parents told me I couldn't tell anyone, I knew things would change between you and me because I'd have to hide this part of myself. Even if we had stayed friends, I'd always want to tell you the truth, and I couldn't. So I pushed you away. That summer, I went to LA to stay with my aunt on my dad's side until I was ready to try to manage my wolf. I didn't want to leave. But eventually, my parents thought it'd be okay if I came back to Blackclaw. When I did, I figured it'd be easier to just start over with people who I felt I didn't owe my secret to."

I know that fear and the lengthy process of rediscovering yourself. The slow-budding worry bursting into stark realization that you are not like the others. At the same time Ximena was dealing with being a wolf, I was realizing the extent of my feelings for her. Admitting it to yourself is one thing. *Accepting* it is another. I had to learn to weave that truth into the fabric of my being like the forest wove its magic into my bones.

"I get it," I tell her quickly. "But you still hurt me. And if I hadn't come searching for you, would you ever have told me?"

She swallows hard. "I don't know. I'd like to think I would've. I'm glad we can talk about it now."

She twines her fingers through mine, and like before, our hands mold perfectly together. Her skin is soft and so warm. I'm supposed to be angry about her pushing me away and shutting me out, but I can't when she's watching me like I'm the only other person in the world.

"I'm sorry I never said anything. I couldn't be this close to you and hide something so big. I thought it'd be easier to let you go." She shrugs, a hopelessness crossing her face. "I was wrong. I ruined us."

I shake my head. "We're not ruined."

With my heart in my throat, I tug her closer still and

lean in. I swear I hear the call of blackbirds echoing in my ears. I picture them fluttering through giant redwoods as I breathe in her scent. My eyes slip closed. Her breath ghosts across my cheek. My mouth. Her fingers brush my neck and—

A loud knock on the door sends me hurtling back so hard I roll right off the edge of the bed. The carpet cushions my fall but does nothing to lessen my humiliation as the door creaks open and Ximena's mom pokes her head into the room.

"Honey, are you all right? I didn't hear you come in," she says, concern written on her face.

Aside from her reddening cheeks, Ximena manages to remain cool. "It happened again. I hardly made it to the woods this time."

Mrs. Reyes's fingers tighten on the doorframe. "Then we need to revisit our earlier conversation, including the one about having company over without telling me first."

*What? Can she even see me back here?* I raise my head above the mattress. Mrs. Reyes locks eyes with me. *Welp.* My legs are still wobbly from that almost-kiss when I stand and wave awkwardly.

"She knows your scent," Ximena clarifies when I shoot her a questioning look.

Mrs. Reyes takes in my awkward stance and wrinkled shirt, and then Ximena's flushed face and tangled hair.

"We weren't—" I begin before Ximena cuts me off.

"Sage knows," Ximena says. "She saw me shift."

There's a sudden stillness about Mrs. Reyes that makes me nervous.

"I found out by accident. I won't tell a soul. Not even my grandma. You can trust me. Promise," I tell her.

Mrs. Reyes drums her fingers against the doorframe. "It's not your grandmother or your coven I'm worried about."

"Everyone else?"

"Our family has always tried to do what's best for our pack. Telling certain people about our gifts has not always aligned in our favor. There was an incident a few generations back where a hunter saw my great-grandfather change. He managed to convince the man he saw wrong, but it was a close call. He almost went to the papers. I don't want to endanger my kids."

"I understand," I reply quickly.

"Good." She turns back to Ximena. "I'll call your aunt."

"What? I have school and work. I can't go to LA right now."

"School isn't a good idea if you can't control when you shift. And the sheriff is probably going to have more questions for you about the break-in. What if you shift in front of him?"

"Mom—" Ximena starts, but Mrs. Reyes cuts her off with a raised hand.

"When you're done talking, come downstairs." Her lips pinch into a narrow line.

Ximena groans. "Fine."

Mrs. Reyes nods in my direction. "Sage, it's always nice to see you."

Alone again, Ximena stretches, spine popping and toes flexing. She looks tired.

"I should go," I say.

"You don't have to."

"I know, but you need rest. And if I don't leave soon, my grandmother's going to wonder where I am," I say, crossing to the other side of the bed.

Ximena catches my wrist. "Do you want to go to the Magic Cauldron tomorrow?"

"What?" I try to keep my face neutral, and yet she can probably hear how fast my heart is beating.

"We were supposed to talk to Jason before the whole wolf thing got in the way. His band plays at the Magic Cauldron on Thursdays."

"Oh." For a second there, it almost sounded like she was asking me out. It's for the investigation. Of course. "Sure. He wasn't at the basketball courts, but I did learn he skipped Mystic Muffins because he's gluten intolerant, and none of his bandmates were at the rally. Once we find out why Jason told Morris he messed up, we can probably discount him as a suspect."

Ximena nods and keeps her eyes steady on me. "I'm sorry I stood you up."

I rest my hand against hers. "It's okay. I had fun playing basketball." I give her a small smile. "I'll see you tomorrow."

"Okay." She collapses back onto her elbows. The over-size shirt she hastily threw on inches down her shoulder. "Good night, Sage."

"Good night."

My insides are mushy, and my legs are putty as I stumble out of her room.

Ximena almost kissed me.

I shouldn't read into it. She'd just gone through a very emotional ordeal. Anyone would seek comfort after that. And yet, I'm still desperately hoping the almost-kiss wasn't a fluke.

# 19

The Magic Cauldron, Blackclaw's local bar and grill, haunts a narrow street off the main road. Monday is karaoke night, Tuesday is stand-up comedy, and on Thursdays, there's a live band.

I've eaten here for special occasions, on weekdays when no one wants to cook and we're bored to tears with take-out, or when Mercer is craving their breadsticks. Since that happens often, I've been to the Magic Cauldron a hundred times. The food is mildly overpriced and mid. The wait time on the weekends is over an hour, but the events are fun and so is the ambiance. Tourists love it because the restaurant has a witchy theme, and it's the only place that serves decently priced drinks—from what Nana's said, of course.

The atmosphere feels different tonight. It sparks with a fresh energy that zings along my fingertips. There's no reason to be nervous, and yet, there's something new and exciting about being here with Ximena.

I check my phone and find a text from her.

**Ximena:**

here! i got us a table in the back near the stage.

Funny, I figured we'd just stand in the shadows like a couple of inconspicuous detectives. I guess that's too obvious?

I head to the back, winding through empty clusters of tables and brushing past people at the crowded bar drinking from green and black goblets. Broomsticks and fake spiderwebs decorate the walls. Repurposed crystal orbs for lights hang above each booth.

It doesn't take long to spot Ximena perched on the edge of her stool at a high-top table near the stage. As soon as I see her, I feel underdressed. She's rocking a tight-fitting tan dress with her signature olive-green Dr. Martens. Even in the purple light from the stage, her makeup looks impeccable—subtle highlighter, nude eyeshadow, and pearly lip gloss. I love that she wears whatever she wants. Whether it's feminine, masculine, or somewhere in between, she seems comfortable in everything.

"You look great," I say once I'm in front of her.

A warm blush crawls up her neck. Although I like her

unrestrained wolf side, it's nice to see this softer side of her too.

"So do you," she replies.

"Please. I look like the Before picture."

Ximena laughs while I shrug off my grandpa cardigan and sit across from her at the table. At least the black off-the-shoulder top I'm wearing is cute.

"How'd you know Jason's band was playing tonight?" I ask.

She flips open the menu with an exaggerated flourish then leans in conspiratorially. I anticipate something elaborate but all she says is, "I checked his Instagram." She leans back with a grin. "And he may have mentioned it once or twice at lunch. Told you I'm useful."

I resist the urge to tell her she's much more than that. Thankfully, the server saves me from having to think of a response that isn't an impromptu confession of my feelings. Like all the waitstaff, she's wearing a garish black pointed hat and a white apron with little black cats on it. Staying true to the theme of the restaurant, she's supposed to be a witch. The first time I came here, I was mildly offended. Witches don't wear pointed hats and ride broomsticks. But the festiveness and the staff's enthusiasm at serving real witches mollified me.

Ximena orders the chicken sandwich and a milkshake (her kryptonite). The server writes down the order on a notepad in the shape of a scroll. She can't be more than a few years older than us.

"I'll just have a Diet Coke," I tell her.

She glances up. "No food?"

"Get whatever you want. It's on me," Ximena says.

"I . . . Really? Okay. Then I'll take spaghetti and breadsticks."

Our server nods approvingly between us. "That's so cute. My partner never offers to pay for anything. I can pay for myself, but it's nice to be taken out every once in a while, you know? Y'all are doing it right."

I visibly tense and stare wide-eyed at Ximena. "Oh, um—"

"We're just friends," Ximena says. "But you should totally tell your partner you want to go on a date some-time."

My skin feels cold. *Just friends*. Reminder: That near-kiss was an accident.

"Sorry, I shouldn't have assumed." The server quickly grabs the menus from the table. "Be back in a minute," she mumbles before disappearing down the aisle.

I shake off my sudden disappointment and try to inject some lightness into my tone. "You don't have to pay for me. I know you're trying to save money for college."

Ximena waves her hand. "It's fine. One dinner isn't going to break the bank. I know we're here on a stakeout, but we can also enjoy the vibes." She smiles.

The vibes. We can have a good time *and* work. Al-though, with Ximena as dressed up as she is, offering to pay for my meal, and talking about vibes, it's almost like this is a date, which it isn't, because she said we were friends. She's not wrong. We are. I . . . didn't realize hearing it would sting, though.

Her mouth opens, and her fingertips drum on the table like she's going to say something more, but then a mic clicks on and three familiar faces step onto the stage. I jump at the opportunity to break the awkwardness between us. "There's Jason."

He's wearing black skinny jeans and his band T-shirt. It's odd seeing him without his basketball buddies. He appears more natural and at ease.

Tact is all but forgotten as I rush toward him. I'm not nearly as worried about what he'll say as I was at the bonfire.

He rolls his eyes when he sees me and then plugs in his electric guitar to his amp with an annoyed sigh. "I see you more than my mom these days," Jason says by way of greeting. "I already told you, your grandma, and the police everything I know."

"I have follow-up questions. After this, I'll leave you alone. I promise."

Jason ignores me in favor of Ximena. "And *you*—I've invited you to see us play how many times? When you finally come, it's only so you and Sage can play detective."

Ximena's cheeks redden. She keeps her friends at arm's length but found it within herself to let me in, at least a little. That's got to mean she cares about our rekindled friendship.

"We'll be quick," I tell Jason. "Were you at Poppy's house last weekend?"

Jason grunts before he answers. "Yeah, I was there. We watched the game."

"Did you leave your Blackclaw Valley High sweatshirt at her house?"

"Is that where it is?" Jason asks.

"You didn't know?" Ximena counters.

"Nope. I wasn't too worried. I'm always leaving it somewhere." Jason tests the sound on his amp by strumming a chord on his guitar. The crisp note rings out across the restaurant.

"That party at Poppy's was before the fundraising rally, right?" Ximena asks.

"Yeah, the day before. Are we done here? I really need to finish setting up," Jason says.

"Dude, let's go! We're on in five," the girl with blue locs and guitar picks for earrings says. She was at the pickup game. She adjusts the mic while the other bandmate, a tall gangly boy, sets up his drums.

"Two more questions. Why'd you lie about what time you got to the rally?" I ask.

Jason stops. "I . . ."

"Morris said you both got there at twelve-twenty, but that's not true. Enzo told me yesterday you arrived earlier than that."

Jason runs a hand through his hair. "I don't know why Morris said we got there at the same time. We didn't. He came at maybe twelve-thirty, twelve-forty-five? I wasn't really paying attention. Coach was mad Morris cut it so close to game time, but it's not unusual for him since he never starts. He had Leigh with him. Could be why he was late."

Ximena and I share a look. His coming at 12:30 or later fits with when the store was robbed. "Does he usually give Leigh rides to games?"

"Nah. *I* do. That day, she didn't answer my call."

Why wouldn't Morris mention he drove Leigh to the fundraiser? Were they late because they were robbing Bishop Brews? Or are they seeing each other behind Poppy's and Jason's backs?

"Why'd you tell Morris you messed up?" Ximena asks.

"Will you leave me alone if I tell you?" Jason asks.

"Probably," I reply.

Jason sighs heavily. "Fine. Leigh asked if I would try a long-distance relationship with her for college. The morning of the fundraising rally, I told her no because we'd never see each other. Our schools are on opposite ends of the country." He runs a hand through his floppy brown hair. "The next time I saw her, she couldn't remember me. Happy?"

He shakes his head and joins his bandmates.

"He's telling the truth," Ximena whispers. "His heartbeat was steady the entire time."

"Wolf trait?" I whisper back, and she nods.

Okay, if Jason is telling the truth, that leaves me with two questions: *Is* the stain on his sweatshirt from my tonic? If so, who wore it the day of the break-in—Poppy, Morris, or our school mascot, Olivia?

Ximena and I head back to our own table to find the food has come. Around us, the high tops framing the stage have started to fill with customers.

"What are you thinking?" Ximena asks around a mouthful of chicken sandwich. There's a dribble of hot sauce on the corner of her mouth. I wring my hands in my napkin to stop myself from wiping it off.

"That Jason really did leave his sweatshirt at Poppy's the day before the rally, so he couldn't have been wearing it to rob Bishop Brews. We need that sweatshirt so Mercer can track it." I pick at my spaghetti.

Without faltering, Ximena reaches across the table and takes my hand. "We'll figure this out."

Any chance of a response dies when she sits back and winks.

I can pretend not to notice my crush but not forever. It's growing by the day. "You have got to stop doing that if we're going to be friends. I'm only human."

"Doing what?"

"All of it! The winking, being charming—"

She rests her chin in her hands and bats her eyelashes. "I seem to remember you calling me charismatic as well. Aren't those words synonymous?"

I glare at her. "Unbelievable."

"Not sorry." Ximena grins before returning to her food.

Do I tell her how I feel even though she plans to leave

once again? What if her mom makes her leave next week because she can't control her wolf? I'm not ready for another heartbreak, especially not without a heartbreak tonic to cure it.

)·)·)·)·●·●·●·(·(·(

"Where have you been?"

It's late. Nana is in the living room with her brewing journal open. Notes are scribbled across the page. I take it as a bad sign that she's still working on a counter brew. Our deadline is three days away. At this rate, we aren't going to have a cure to give Leigh before her memory loss becomes permanent.

I take a seat next to Nana on the sofa and pull up my feet. "I was with Ximena."

It's like she can tell just from the tone of my voice that things have shifted between us, because Nana glances up from her notes, a curious expression on her face. "I'm glad you've reconciled," she begins.

"We're investigating the break-in."

I'm expecting a lecture, not the snort that leaves Nana. "I know. I wasn't born yesterday. You've hardly been at home all week. Plus, you left your little investigative notebook open on the table the other day."

"You're not mad?" This is a shocking turn of events.

"You're going against my explicit wishes," Nana says sternly, and then her face slackens. "But you're doing it for the right reasons. Based on what I read briefly, you've uncovered more than the coven elders. You created a time-line, discovered that Leigh drank your tonic and not one of mine, and narrowed the thief to an athlete at your school. I'm *proud*, Sage."

My face flushes. I didn't know how much I needed to hear her say that.

"I never have been able to change your mind once it's set, so if you keep digging into this, which you will, please be careful. And I hope you know what you're doing with Ximena."

I rest my chin on my knees. "Didn't you want us to make up? Isn't that the reason you hired her?"

Nana closes her journal. "Partially. I know how happy you were when the two of you were friends. I also remember how hurt you were when things ended. I don't want to see that happen again. Not with so much at stake."

"You mean Bishop Brews? We'll keep the store afloat. I'm close to cracking my new tonic. I even got it to temporarily glow. Bottled Wonders won't know what hit them."

"I meant your heart, Sage. With every new bruise, it takes longer to heal."

"Don't worry, Nana."

"That's my job, honey."

I hug her, and the soothing smells of rose oil and lemon-grass wash over me. When we separate, I ask, "How's the counter brew coming?"

"I think we finally have something to try. It's been glow-ing for hours. We were going to give it to Leigh tomorrow.

Her family's been patient to an extent, but they're hoping to see her make a full recovery."

"You didn't notice anything weird about brewing it, did you?" I ask.

Nana frowns. "Only that getting the combination right took a little longer than anticipated."

I don't want to worry her if it turns out I'm wrong about the Hemwood magic being off. The counter brew *is* glowing. "I can take the tonic to her. I need to ask her a few questions anyway. I hope it works, because solving the break-in will be way easier if Leigh can tell us who gave her the tonic."

"From your lips," Nana says. "Let the Lawsons know the tonic was brewed by me. Go tomorrow straight after school."

"I will."

"Are you thinking about taking Ximena?" she asks.

"She's been helping me with the investigation. Her job is on the line too," I say. And if the magic is wonky, and this is all connected, Ximena's supernatural gifts are also in danger.

Nana hums and leaves it at that.

> Hey, meet at Leigh's house tomorrow after school? I have a counter brew for her.

Ximena:

> perfect. i'll drive us.

No need. I can bike it.

**Ximena:**

i want to ☺

I tell myself not to read too much into her offer or the smiley face. We're friends, right?

Ok. See you tomorrow 😊

# Sage's Investigation

## RE-REVISED TIMELINE

10:30 a.m.—pregame supply pickup at Poppy's

11:30 a.m.–12:00 p.m.—cupcake promotion (figure out what was in that icing?)

12:00 p.m.—Cheerleaders arrive at the rally, minus Poppy and Leigh. Jason arrives at the rally.

12:10 p.m.—I leave Bishop Brews and walk to Tea for Thought.

12:20 p.m.—Morris and Jason DID NOT arrive at the rally (I knew one of them was lying!)

12:30 p.m.—Ximena calls to say there's been a break-in.

12:30 p.m.—Poppy arrives at the rally.

12:30–12:40 p.m.—Morris and Leigh arrive at the rally late (shameful).

1:00 p.m.—The rally starts at BVH, where Leigh ingests my misbrewed heartache tonic.

## MOTIVES

1. To discredit or harm Bishop Brews or witches in general. Giving the tonic to Leigh: coincidental or accidental???

2. To harm Leigh or the founders in general. Use witches as scapegoats given town history. They would have to have known the tonic they gave Leigh was misbrewed—aka a witch, a founder, or a stalker (please no).

3. Money—probably about $200 cash for the premade tonics and way more if a buyer knew just how valuable my heartache brew was (had it not been misbrewed, of course).

## SUSPECT PROFILES

- A disgruntled customer, a competitor, or someone with a grudge against a witch

- Big Business Buttheads, Bottled Wonders

- An enemy of Leigh's or someone with a grudge against a founding family

- Poppy???

- Someone with intimate knowledge of misbrew side effects, most likely Poppy, Morris, NOT Jason, or, dare I say, Ximena? (It can't be her. I'd know, right?)

- An athlete who stole the brews wanting to make extra cash, like Little Miss Flirty, aka Olivia, the BVH wolf mascot

# 20

On Friday, after school, Ximena and I head straight to the Marigold Inn, a B&B owned by the Lawsons but managed by my covenmate Shaye Thorn. It's a central hub for tourists and residents alike because of the huge welcome room, which doubles as a community center with art and music classes. The tables are always lined with fresh pastries, and the couches are topped with warm throws. Shaye uses their cloning gift to be everywhere at once to make sure the inn runs smoothly, especially during peak seasons like now.

The house is a massive, beautifully preserved, salmon-colored Victorian only a block from downtown Black-claw. Today, three tourists are on the front lawn taking pictures with the hand-painted inn sign. Shaye is outside hanging lights on the bay windows, tying ribbons to the railing of the steps, and trimming the hedges. You can tell they're all clones by their semitransparent shine.

Mrs. Lawson surveys this with her hands on her hips, her pencil skirt and heels out of place among Shaye's jeans and sneakers. Mrs. Lawson strides over as soon as she spots me and Ximena. She's been waiting for a miracle, and with any luck, we might have it. She leads us to the backyard, where Leigh is making paper lanterns on a long white folding table. Her hair is tied into a messy bun, bangs falling into her face as she concentrates on painting the perfect petal onto the side of a pink lantern.

"Leigh, there's a counter brew for you to try," Mrs. Lawson tells her daughter.

Leigh smiles, but real recognition shifts her features when she sees Ximena. "I've seen you on my Instagram. What's your name again?"

"Ximena."

Leigh nods. "Right." She pulls up a photo on her phone to show us. Ximena, Leigh, and Olivia pose at the winter formal. In the picture, Ximena's smile doesn't quite reach her eyes, not like the ones she's been giving me over the last week. Now that I know she's a wolf, the restraint she has around her friends, and even pushing me away, make sense. It kind of—I don't know—also makes me a little sad for her.

If she could be so strong, what's stopping me from doing the same? Mercer's right. I need to find the courage to tell Ximena how I feel about her.

When Ximena catches me staring, she nudges my shoulder.

Mrs. Lawson clears her throat. "Are there any side effects with this counter brew?"

"There shouldn't be. My grandmother said it might taste bad, but it won't hurt her. Properly brewed tonics glow." I grab the vial from my messenger bag and shake it so Mrs. Lawson can see the brew's shimmery light.

"Once I drink it, will my memories be restored?" Leigh asks.

"Hopefully. Counter brews are mostly trial and error." Just because it's properly brewed doesn't mean it's the correct antidote for my misbrewed tonic. Drinking it won't cause any side effects.

Mrs. Lawson sighs heavily and pinches the bridge of her nose. "It's always something."

Leigh seems hopeful when I hand it to her, her eyes lighting up. We collectively hold our breath as she brings the vial to her lips and drinks the contents. Within seconds, her eyes snap closed, and she exhales audibly. I wait for the narrowed gaze I'm used to receiving from her.

All that comes is the same blank stare without an ounce of recognition. That alone makes me tense, but then Mrs. Lawson scoffs and she draws her lips together. Her words are laced with disapproval when she says, "What is this? What's the point of having witches when they can't even fix their own mistakes?"

The accusation bristles against my skin like needles. "I don't know why this tonic didn't work, but alienating Leigh's only chance of getting better isn't helpful."

Mrs. Lawson shakes her head. "I'm going to have a word with the council," she says, ignoring my very valid point, which only tells me she knows I'm right. She storms into the B&B without another word.

"Sorry about her. She's really stressed about this whole situation," Leigh says, returning to her paper lantern.

"Makes sense," Ximena replies. "How are you holding up?"

"Honestly? I feel useless. I wish I could remember who I am. The sheriff keeps asking me the same questions as if the tenth time he does will magically unlock the answers."

"I'm really sorry," I tell her.

I twist my wrist and coax a handful of dandelions from their perch in the grass next to us. They weave through the strings inside Leigh's paper lantern. A little extra décor can't hurt. If she remembered me, we'd totally be competing over who makes the best lantern. As is, all I want to do is lend a hand.

Leigh takes the lantern and hands me another one. "Thanks. Am I going to stay like this forever?"

"Not if I can help it," I reply.

"But there are only two more days before the effects are permanent," she presses.

I secure more dandelions inside the second lantern while I struggle to find a response. Two days is hardly enough time, even with the entire coven pitching in. The more time that passes without concrete evidence, the more I worry the founders on the council will have their way and close the apothecary. The relationship between Blackclaw and witches could dissolve faster than salt in warm water.

"Plenty of time," Ximena says with all the confidence I wish I had.

Leigh rolls her eyes in a familiar gesture. She may have lost her memory but not her entire personality. "How can you be so sure?" she asks.

This time the words come easily for me. "Failing isn't an option."

)·)·)·)◐●◑·(·(·(

I check in with Shaye before we leave to see how the coven's private investigation is going. Their clones are still outside decorating, but the real Shaye is inside at their desk. It took me a long time to be able to tell the clones apart from the real deal, but there is a permanence to the person in front of me that the other Shayes lack.

"We've pretty much established an alibi for everyone during the time of the break-in. The police checked the security camera in the alley behind Bishop Brews. Whoever broke in wore a hoodie and kept their face hidden," Shaye tells us.

"That tracks. We found a sweatshirt that might've been worn by the thief, but we're going to have Mercer read its history before we tell the rest of the coven," I say.

"Great." Shaye organizes the papers on their desk. At the top of the pile, I spot a name in big bold letters: **Olivia Byrd.**

"Wait. Why do you have Olivia's resume?"

"I interviewed her for a job. I've been having trouble

keeping the clones active for more than a few hours lately. The inn could use a seasonal worker."

I've never known Shaye to have problems with their clones. Plus, the counter brew should have worked. The Hemwood magic is waning for everyone. Time to tell Nana.

"When was the interview?" I ask.

Shaye frowns. "Sunday at noon."

"How long did it last?"

"About thirty minutes. Why all the questions? Is she a suspect?"

"Not anymore," I reply, relieved. Olivia was with Shaye in a job interview during the break-in, so unless she had an accomplice, which I doubt because we've pretty much interviewed all the athletes who could've left that napkin, she isn't the hoodie-wearing thief.

"We've got to go," I tell Shaye. "See you soon!"

I'm bounding down the steps a minute later, Ximena hot on my heels. "The only people who fit the timeline now are Morris and Poppy, but Poppy would've had to be speeding to get to school in under ten minutes," I tell Ximena.

"Olivia might still be a suspect. She could have partnered with Poppy to steal the tonics. She might've kept the premade ones for herself to resell to fix her car and given Poppy the misbrewed tonic to give to Leigh so Poppy could be cheer captain," Ximena theorizes.

"Or Jason could've partnered with Poppy. Olivia would have to have known my tonic was misbrewed, which is highly unlikely since she's not a witch or a descendant of a founding family. And I don't think she and Poppy are close enough to be partners in crime. Plus, I doubt the pre-made tonics would cover the cost of fixing Olivia's car. It's my heartbreak tonic that would be worth money because of its novelty, which is why Bottled Wonders is on the list. I think it's safe to scratch her off our suspect list. It's time we pay the competition another visit and get that sweatshirt from Poppy," I say, heading for the car.

"Agreed. But I was hoping we'd take a quick break before we do?" Ximena rubs the back of her neck. "We don't have a shift today, and I could use some fresh air. How about a short hike?"

"There are two days left until Leigh's memory loss becomes permanent and the council closes the store. Nana's tonics aren't working. Mine definitely aren't. Mrs. Lawson is probably on the phone with the sheriff and the mayor as we speak, and you want to go *hiking*?"

Ximena props her arm on the hood of her car. "I want a clear head before we question the last of our suspects. I also need to show you something that might explain why the magic has been funny," she says.

I cross my arms and study her. "You just like spending time with me. Admit it."

She laughs and holds up her hands. "Caught."

My belly swoops.

"What do I need to see that's a thousand feet in the air?" Unlike every other Californian, I don't hike. In fact, I'm a teeny, tiny bit afraid of heights.

"You'll see." Ximena slides in close and runs her fingers along the back of my hand, the motion somehow sending tingles down my spine. "Don't worry, I'll be next to you the entire time."

My mouth is desert dry. "You better be."

# 21

One of the draws of Blackclaw Valley, aside from the magic shops and the Spring Harvest Festival, is the hiking. Blackclaw sits in the crook of a mountain range, with the coast to the west and the mountains on the east. There are several trails along the range, each varying in difficulty.

The route Ximena chooses is supposedly not a difficult one—tell that to my lungs, which feel like they're going to burst with each step.

I don't like voluntary exercise. If I work out, it's on flat ground. I'm a witch who spends her time in the Hemwood harvesting for the store, playing with the foliage, or sunbathing near the creek. I don't mess with heights. I'm already sweating through my shirt, though that might be the nerves. This, like much of what I've done the past week, is way outside my comfort zone. But Ximena is right where she promised to be, by my side, helping me over rocks and holding my hand when I get a glimpse of the ground below us. She knows, of course she knows, that I'm nervous.

We pass several hikers on our way up, some in fancy gear and others dressed like they've come from running errands. They pop up along the slowly inclining trail and give us a wave or a thumbs-up.

After about fifty minutes, we veer off the path and break through a wall of trees. We've reached the summit. It takes me a long time of feeling like I'm breathing through a straw before I'm able to take in my surroundings.

Ximena is perfect as usual, not a single strand of hair out of place and only a few drops of sweat on her brow. She's always been more active—energized by physical exertion and accomplishing a challenge. I'm pretty sure that's why she loved soccer when we were kids. Her exaltation shows in the way her skin glows, rivaling the sun.

She nudges my arm, encouraging me to check out the view. With a steady breath, I do. And it's . . . *amazing*.

From up here, the redwoods look like broccoli florets, so small I could pluck them. Birds pepper the horizon, and the fluffy clouds shade the sun. To my right is a dark patch of forest where it appears several trees have died. The bark is gunmetal black, the branches bare and thin. A prickle of unease crawls up my back.

"What happened there?" I ask.

"That's what I wanted to show you. I did a little exploring as my wolf-self. That area of the forest is twisted and dead. I thought maybe there was a fire, but the soil is dry, not scorched. I'm not sure what's happening, but whatever it is, it's spreading."

I make a mental note to explore that area to see if I can feel anything off about the trees or the soil. The dead patch is right on the edge of Crimson Grove. Even from here, I can see wide streets littered with ads and plain, identical metal buildings. It's nothing like the wood, brick, and mortar of Blackclaw. The town is the opposite of ours in most ways except its magic.

"It's really been built up over the last few years. That might be the road Blackclaw is headed down," Ximena says.

"Like hell it is. No boring business execs are coming in and changing us."

"I hope not, but Blackclaw basically runs on tourism. We can't compete if everything here is old and all of Crimson Grove is new."

"People value tradition." Even as I say it, Bishop Brews's slowly dwindling customers versus Bottled Wonders's long checkout line comes to mind.

"If a businessman or developer from Crimson Grove is offering enough money, it's going to be hard for people to turn them down," Ximena says.

I rub my hands together, processing. "Then we'll have to show Crimson Grove that indie businesses can still be lucrative," I declare, and Ximena laughs. "What? It's true!"

"It is. You're so adamant, is all. It's cute."

"Cute, huh? Not cool?" I tease, remembering the last time she called me cute and got weird.

Ximena leans against a boulder, soaking up the afternoon sun with a lazy grin. "Both. And a little stubborn."

I force an exaggerated scoff that makes her laugh. I don't hide my own amusement as I admire the treetops dotting the horizon, a peaceful ocean of greens and browns. "I can see why you like it here."

"The view is incredible, right? Totally worth the hike. I could spend hours in the music room at school, but when I need to clear my mind and get fresh air, I race here. It reminds me that there's so much more out in the world. Sometimes Blackclaw makes me feel like I'm constantly walking on eggshells, waiting for someone to find out what I am."

"That's why you want to leave? I understand not wanting to stay in a small town forever, but doesn't running from the thing that makes you most unique feel . . . wrong?" I ask.

Ximena turns her head. "The wolf is only one part of me. It isn't all of who I am. Going beyond these town borders and experiencing life is more important to me. I don't want to be stagnant. I want to keep evolving and growing."

Even though I know she's being honest, I can't help but feel a twinge of discomfort. "I don't feel stagnant here. I'm always learning something new and changing, even when it scares me."

Ximena herself is a testament to that. She pushes me to think more about my life here, like how having residents who support witches affords me a kind of freedom Ximena lacks.

"There is so much to experience in Blackclaw; you just have to know where to look," I add. Ximena needs to see how much I love this place. "You've shown me your favorite spot to reenergize, now let me show you mine."

"Willow Creek?" she guesses. "That's been your favorite place since forever."

I purse my lips. "Somewhere else. A place I haven't taken you."

"If it's in the Hemwood, I know of it," she says.

I smirk. "You don't. C'mon."

We start our descent down the hill. It doesn't take nearly as long to get down as it took to get up. Once we're close enough to the base that I know the area again, I step off the path. Ximena follows with a single raised eyebrow. I trail the gurgling sounds of water sloshing over rocks and stretching toward the muddy banks of Willow Creek. Ximena may know these woods like the back of her hand, but she doesn't know all of what they can do.

After she stopped talking to me, I spent a lot of time alone in this part of the woods. Nana taught me different tricks to get my mind off things. One thing I learned is that magic is strongest at its source, and Willow Creek happens to run right through the heart of the Hemwood.

I can tell we're nearby when I feel magic's feather-like caress along my arms and smell the sweet scent of honey and sap.

"We *are* going to Willow Creek," Ximena says when she sees water moving through the trees.

"Nope."

I turn north, following the water's edge. My palms are sweaty with nerves. I've never taken anybody here before.

When I spot the crooked old redwood with pretty sorrels ringing its base and moss painting the bark green, I stop. Ximena turns to me with a confused little frown. That's when I reach for my magic, and whisper, "Watch."

All plants have memories from environmental stimuli, and since I've done this many times in the last four years, they know exactly how to move when I ask.

The tops of the trees sway and bend as if attached to strings. Branches interlace like fingers to form a canopy that blocks out the sun. Last year, I planted moonflowers. Without the light, they glow, illuminating the entire space. We could be in a fairy tale with how the creek trickles along the edge of our tunneled sanctuary and the glowing flowers bloom around our feet. The Hemwood is in total harmony here. This is my happy place, being surrounded by nature, magic streaming beneath my feet and its sweet tang in the air.

Fatigue immediately weighs down my limbs, and I waver on my feet from the effort. Ximena's fast. Her arms snake around my waist and hold me close. Her eyes are wide and shining with awe. In the space of a breath, her gaze drops to my lips.

That moment in her room comes barreling back to me. I need to know if what I'm feeling is one-sided, even if it means being rejected. "Did you only bring me to the overlook to show me dead trees?" I ask, my voice so low it's barely audible over the faint sounds of the forest around us. "Or was there another reason?"

Ximena tilts her head. "I guess I also wanted to share something I find special with you."

She's still holding my waist. Either the heat of her hands or the enormous amount of magic I used makes my head spin. Probably both. I don't know how to phrase my question without completely making a fool of myself. I try anyway. "Because you . . . like me?"

She chuckles lowly, the sound sending shivers down my spine. She seems to consider her response before replying, "Yes. I like you." Some of the tension visibly leaves her body, and she rolls her eyes. "I thought that much was obvious, at least." She releases her hold of me, not going far to make sure I remain steady on my feet. She rubs her undercut with a sheepish shrug. "I've been trying to let you set the pace because I know I hurt you last time, and I don't want that to happen again. But I like you, Sage. I always have."

"Oh." Somehow, I both did and didn't see that coming. Ximena invited me over to her house for pozole, asked me to the bonfire, the Magic Cauldron, and hiking. I thought all of it was just out of necessity or her way of rebuilding our friendship. Wow, was I wrong.

"I like you too." The whispered confession ties itself around my heart like a promise.

Ximena grins so bright it rivals the moonflowers blooming around us. Her eyes sweep across my face, drinking me in like beads of water in a desert storm. They drop back to my mouth, and my brain empties.

We're close enough that we can breathe in each other's scents. Ximena smells like coconuts, wildflowers, and endless summer. I wonder what I smell like to her and if her heart is beating as fast as mine.

When she leans in this time, there's no hesitation. I close my eyes, and my heart skips at the sudden but soft press of her lips against mine. Goose bumps sweep across my skin as a burst of something sweet, like honied sap, fills my mouth when our tongues meet. The distant call of birds, swaying trees, and falling leaves mix with the blood roaring in my ears. It's everything I love about the Hemwood—about magic—in a kiss. And it's far too short.

I chase after her when she pulls away, needing more, more, *more*. She chuckles against my mouth, the vibrations tickling, then tucks a chunk of curls behind my ear with deft fingers.

This moment is all I've wanted for so long. And it is much better than I could've ever imagined. I don't want to ruin it, but my brain never shuts up. "You said you want to be friends, but I can't go back to that. I want more."

She grins, and hope rises like a tide. "I only said that because I thought that's what *you'd* want. I want more too. The past four years have been ridiculously hard without you. I don't want to go back to that or friends."

I tug her to me this time, and when our mouths meet, I sink into her. Ximena kisses me sweetly, like she wants to savor it. And I indulge her until my lips tingle and my lungs beg for air and my legs turn to jelly. She slides her arm around my waist again to keep me upright. When we finally part, I drop my head onto her shoulder and breathe in the best smell in the world. She tightens her hold of me and does the same.

I let Ximena's easy presence fill me. I wish I could bottle this feeling in a tonic and drink it when I need a boost.

"So, you like me?" I ask again, just to hear her say it. It feels like we're thirteen again, holding hands under the table at Honey's, the whole world contained in a single moment. I chew my bottom lip and squeeze her hips. "And not Olivia?"

She barks out a surprised laugh. "I knew you were jealous!"

"You were jealous of Mercer!"

She sucks her teeth. "She took my place as your best friend."

"You gave up the title," I counter.

She tugs me closer still until our noses touch. "It's okay. I got something better in return."

We stay in the canopy until the sun starts to dip below the horizon, painting our sanctuary in hues of purple and orange. Reluctantly, we agree it's time to go. The sun is setting, and Nana will be expecting me home soon.

We didn't veer too far from the trail and eventually merge with a group of hikers wearing silver charms that gleam. I squeeze Ximena's hand. We're about ten minutes from the arboretum when she jerks to a stop, her arm slinging around her stomach and the tendons in her neck

jumping as her muscles tighten. She hunches over and releases a low, full growl.

"Ximena, what's wrong? Are you okay?"

"No, no, no. Not *now*," she groans. "Sage, you need
to go."

"What's going on?"

She raises her head enough for me to see her eyes. In a
blink, they lighten from deep brown to amber. She's about
to shift.

And we're in public.

# 22

"Tell me what to do," I plead as her skin ripples, the wolf inside desperate to escape.

I follow her as she staggers back off the trail, winding into a clearing some yards away. A smear of orange sky pours through the tangled mass of dark leaves overhead.

With a sharp shake of her head, she grits out a single word. "Go."

But that's the thing. I'm in too deep. Even if I wanted to, I couldn't leave her.

She strips down to her underwear, tossing aside her clothes as her skin dissolves. Instead of muscle and sinew, there's shiny gray fur. The change is swift, violent, and beautiful at the same time.

The wolf shakes out its new silky coat, then belts a deep, low howl. Its claws are sharp as knives, the tips sinking into the earth as it moves closer, huffing. I brace myself against the nearest redwood tree, breathing hard.

When Ximena the wolf leaps toward me, I trip over my own feet. Rocks and twigs dig into my back, but I manage to get my arms to work enough to push myself upright.

The uneasy stare of a wolf greets me. The long snout and rippling gray fur would scare anyone, but I know this creature. Seeing her again is different from the first time—less animalistic and more curious, like the first taste of something forbidden.

I extend my hand, palm up, to show I am not a threat. The wolf snarls at my gesture.

Ximena said when she's like this, everything is stripped down to bare needs. Does her wolf side recognize me?

The wolf springs forward. A heavy paw connects with my sternum and pins me to the ground. All the air rushes from my lungs on impact. One false move, one swipe, and that's it. I could call on the Hemwood for help, draw magic from the source, but if I do, I could hurt Ximena. Worse, I could overuse my magic and end up harming both of us.

The wolf flashes me a row of teeth as long as my fingers. I don't turn away. I can't. A wet snout drags along my cheek. I reach forward without thinking, not for my magic but something easily as grounding. The fur is softer than I expected when I run my fingers through it. A breath of air hits my face.

I rub my thumb over the paw like I would the back of her hand. "Ximena."

A spark builds in the amber depths of the wolf's eyes. She moves, calculated and slow. She doesn't swing at my throat. She hops off, backing away from me. The shift is swift. Ximena shrinks. The fur fades into warm skin. The claws compress into fingernails. The wolf's long snout shortens into a button nose. The same worried eyes stare at me.

I sink into the dirt, relief making my limbs heavy.

Above us, the treetops dot the sky like sponged clouds on a blue canvas. The sunset speckles the canopy in hues of gold. A tiny, incredulous laugh escapes me.

I crawl across the ground to Ximena, grabbing her clothes as I go. She's folded over and shivering when I tug her shirt over her head as quickly as I can.

"Are you okay?" I ask.

She nods, finishes getting dressed, then drops her head against my shoulder. Her hair smells like coconut, and her skin carries hints of vanilla and the woods. I wrap my arm around her back and pull her closer while she adjusts to her human form, rubbing her ears, working her jaw, and flexing her fingers.

"I should be asking you that. I'm so sorry, Sage. This is exactly why I can't wait to leave this place. I won't have to worry about hurting the people I care about."

"You didn't hurt me," I offer.

She balls her fist, the tendons in her forearm flexing. "I could have. That's what I'm afraid of. But I don't want to be away from you either." She raises her right arm and shakes the metal permanent bracelet hanging around her wrist. "See this? It's supposed to help from changing against my will. It's been in my family for generations, passed down from the time when wolves and witches were partners in protecting the Hemwood. Inside the gems is wolfsbane to keep the wolf at bay, but it's not working anymore. Maybe my mom is right, and I should finish off senior year with my cousins in Los Angeles until the magic is no longer iffy."

A cold sensation overcomes me. The last thing I want is for Ximena to leave, not after we've started something new. I school my features so the panic doesn't appear, but my words are strangled with it. "We'll figure this out. I can check the family grimoire. It dates back to the eighteen hundreds, when Blackclaw was founded. And if there's nothing in there, I can always ask Nana or Tiva. I know you don't want me telling anyone, but we can trust them. They both know the history of our town and might have some solutions to improving your bracelet."

"Thanks, but even if my mom agrees to rope them in, I don't think I can stay here much longer. What if someone finds out? The charms selling out and the history of curfews during full moons scream *leave*. In Blackclaw, wolves are monsters." She grinds her jaw in an attempt to calm down.

As much as I love this town, people do fear wolves. As kids, we'd all tell stories about wolves, not ghosts. "You are anything but monstrous, Ximena. I'll change this town for you, brick by brick, if I have to. And I'll throw out those silver charms tonight."

Ximena tucks a loose curl behind my right ear. "So chivalrous. I could also work at my tia's salon for a few months. She's always complaining about needing more help." Ximena kneads her hands together. "You could . . . come with me. After graduation. She has plenty of extra space. We could explore LA, and maybe go to a show?" There's a hopeful lift of her brows.

My stomach coils instead of leaps. I'm needed here, now more than ever, with Bishop Brews in danger. I manage to force a smile. "I'll think about it." It's only April. Who knows what could happen in a month?

Ximena picks up on my hesitation. She tries to hide her disappointment, but her face falls slightly.

I wish I could just say yes to her and mean it. I wish I wasn't so reluctant to leave, and she wasn't so afraid to stay.

# 23

Ximena insists on giving me a ride home or at least walking with me, but I manage to convince her I can get there on my own and that she should go home and rest.

I take the long way, staying on the major streets instead of cutting through the arboretum. Decorations for the Spring Harvest Festival have started to go up everywhere. Pennants drape from streetlights and streamers and floral wreaths hang on lampposts.

Mr. Lawson is standing outside his office and talking to the blond-haired customer I clocked at Bishop Brews and the Garden Genie. This time, I make it across the street before Mustache Man drives off.

"If you can come up with a cure for my daughter, I'll talk to Hazel about selling Bishop Brews," Mr. Lawson is saying.

"Hey!" I yell.

Mr. Lawson flinches but quickly tames his surprise as I approach. "Sage, we were—"

"Discussing selling my family apothecary?"

Mustache Man has the nerve to chuckle. "I made your grandmother a good offer. It's still on the table should she want to reconsider."

"Sorry. Who are you?" I demand.

"Someone interested in expanding into Blackclaw," the man replies coolly. He turns to Mr. Lawson. "Bill, always a pleasure." He ends the conversation by getting into his car and speeding off. Rude.

"Who was that?" I ask Mr. Lawson as he locks up his office.

He's slow to respond and even slower to face me. "John Winters, the owner of Bottled Wonders."

Understanding washes over me. He was pretending to be a customer to ask about Bishop Brews just moments before the break-in. He was scoping us out because he wants to expand.

"My grandma will *never* sell," I grit out.

Mr. Lawson rubs the bridge of his nose. "Then she'd better have a good plan on how to outlast Bottled Wonders, because John won't stop until he gets what he wants, and he doesn't care who's standing in his way."

) · ) · ) ● ( · ( · ( · ( (

When I get home, I find Nana in her herb garden. Sparkling tree lights illuminate the mostly dark earth. Her hands are deep in the dirt and her gaze is distant. She grows all our herbs for Bishop Brews in Hemwood soil to give them an extra boost. Tiva built her wooden planters two summers ago, and I made tags so it's easy to tell the plants apart—not that she needs labels. Nana knows her herbs like her children and treats them as such.

I jog over to her. "When were you going to tell me Bottled Wonders made an offer on Bishop Brews?"

"Sage, watch your tone. I am not one of your little friends." I refrain from rolling my eyes. "I didn't mention it because it's grown folks' business. I'm not selling, so you have nothing to worry about."

Nana reaches for the basil. I wiggle my fingers and gently remove it from the soil for her. With a wave of my hand, it lands in the basket at her feet. "Did you know he's been trying to bully his way into Blackclaw? He was at the Garden Genie," I say.

Nana sighs. "Your aunt mentioned a prospective buyer. I doubt she's serious about selling."

"We can't let him get away with this."

"If the man wants to expand into Blackclaw, there's not much I can do to stop him. We should focus on fixing the magic. Without it, a greedy businessman will be the least of our worries."

"So you've noticed that the magic's been weird too!" Ximena can't control when she shifts, Mercer's been having trouble doing readings, and I can't get my tonics to glow. It's the magic, and Nana knows it. "What's happening?" I ask.

"I'm not sure." She points at a cluster of oregano. I collect it the same way I did the basil and drop it into her basket. "Magic is not limitless. It's a resource, and like any resource, it can be depleted if too much is used. It's odd, because we've never used more than we can handle."

"Maybe someone else is," I murmur, recalling the dark patch of dead trees in the Hemwood Ximena showed me.

Nana gently rakes her hands through her garden's soil like she does with my hair when I'm sick. That's when I notice that a lot of the herbs are scraggly, their color closer to yellow than green. In fact, the stalks of lavender I sowed a month ago should reach halfway up my thighs, but they barely hit my knees. The purple petals are so pale they look gray. The poppies along the side of the house are usually bursting with color, but today even they appear muted, their leaves dangling helplessly.

"I'll check the grimoire," Nana says, saving me the effort. "In the meantime, only use the herbs we've already harvested for tonics." She nods at the basket. "I'll test these."

"But there isn't enough to last us more than a week, and we only have two days left to cure Leigh."

"Then I'd better work fast," Nana replies dryly.

)·)·)◐●◑·(·(

I've decided that riding shotgun in Ximena's truck while driving through Blackclaw is my new favorite activity.

She keeps one hand on the steering wheel and the other in mine as we head back to Bottled Wonders. Fletcher bumps through the speakers as we head east toward the early morning sun. We pass all the best places that make this town home: Bewitched Blossoms, Mystic Muffins, the basketball courts, and the Marigold Inn. I won't let John Winters run Blackclaw's family-owned stores out of business.

Leaving Blackclaw doesn't feel nearly as heart attack–inducing as before. In fact, I don't feel any anxiety when we cross the town line. Hope flowers in my chest. Occasionally exploring other places might be nice, particularly if Ximena is by my side.

During the drive, I do some research on John Winters, typing his name into Google. His smug face and silly mustache pop up, along with a LinkedIn profile. He claims to be an entrepreneur and businessman. He should add killing small businesses as a skill set.

The Bottled Wonders website and its social media also populate. Looks like the store has multiple locations, including out of state. Shit. This man is not playing around.

The Crimson Grove town sign springs up on our left, this time framed by a dead patch of trees. The forest is getting worse by the day. "Ximena, can you pull over? I want to check something." Time to see if I can feel any weirdness in the soil.

She parks her truck on the side of the road and follows me toward the edge of the Hemwood. I kneel on the ground and sweep my hands along the gritty earth and through the thorny underbrush. When I close my eyes and concentrate, I feel . . . nothing. No magic thrums under my palms or across the tips of my fingers. There's only a deadly stillness that matches the trees around us.

"There's no magic here," I whisper.

This must be because of Bottled Wonders. Their overflowing shelves, stream of new tonics, and horde of customers require *a lot* of magic. No wonder the employees look so depleted. Bottled Wonders is officially on my shit list. Greed turns people into monsters, and anyone willing to overuse a natural resource to turn a profit is as greedy as they come.

I'm fueled by a renewed sense of determination as we return to the car and head to our destination. Outside Bottled Wonders, Ximena links her hand with mine and we enter through double glass doors for the second time, and hopefully, the last. Already, I see new products on the shelves.

The employee we spoke to previously is beaming as she shows off a tonic to her coworkers. Someone got a bonus.

Of another worker, I ask, "Do you sell any specialized tonics? I'm looking for something personalized."

"I'm sorry, none of our tonics are made-to-order. The café across the street used to sell custom teas with magic added to lengthen the effects, but that was before we bought the store earlier this year," he replies.

"Bottled Wonders owns the café across the street?"

The employee nods. "And a few other magic shops in town." He stifles a yawn. "Can I help you with anything else?"

"Is the owner in?" I ask.

He gestures toward the back of the shop and then leaves. Before I can come up with a game plan, a door swings open. I instantly clock the man's slicked-back hair, crisp shirt, and handlebar mustache. John Winters.

"Who's supposed to be restocking the all-in-one creams?" he asks the worker who just helped us. "And you"—he points at the pimply faced teen who was assisting Morris during our last visit—"customers need help." John swears under his breath and then adjusts the phone against his ear. "Sorry about that. What were you saying?"

I open a voice note and hit record. It's unlikely I'll catch him talking about the break-in, but maybe I can get leverage against him. I just need to get closer so I can better hear what he's saying. Only, John has seen my face.

Ximena grunts when I pull her in front of me to stay hidden. Her body is warm and soft against mine. Her breath tickles my cheeks, and her eyes shine with mischief as she bites her bottom lip.

*Focus, Sage. You can kiss her later.*

"It's fine. There's plenty of magic in that forest to go around and we hired the best witches in Crimson Grove. . . . As for Bishop Brews? It's not going to be in business much longer anyway, not if you hold up your end of the deal. Get Hazel Bishop to sell, and I'll make your daughter's cure."

I shift my weight and my bag hits the counter, rattling the tonics I keep with me in case of emergencies—a Fever-few mixture for migraines and a Butterbur brew for allergies. John turns toward the noise, and Ximena kisses me.

My heart jumps as she runs her hands along my sides and smiles against my lips. I can't hear John or anyone else in the store. All I can hear is my pulse in my ears and the hitch of my breath.

"I didn't want him to see us," Ximena explains once she's moved back a millimeter.

"I hope he keeps looking. Wait. No. That sounded creepy."

She laughs and takes my hand. "Come on. Spending any more time here with John barking orders will only end up with us being made. Let's debrief and head back to Blackclaw." Her lips brush the shell of my ear when she whispers, "I might even kiss you again."

I waste no time tugging her outside and across the street.

"Hold up." Based on its total lack of charm, I'd guess this is the café owned by Bottled Wonders. All the more reason to scope it out and see exactly what deranged changes John has in store for Blackclaw. Instead of colorful stucco and hanging ivy, the storefront is off-white without a single plant in sight.

"John knows Bottled Wonders is using too much

magic, and he doesn't care," I say as we approach the shop door.

Ximena holds it open for me. "What are we gonna do?"

"Tell the coven? Or the council? There must be a law protecting the Hemwood, right?"

Ximena grabs her phone. "There's something called zoning ordinances, which dictate the use of natural resources between towns. I bet Bottled Wonders is in violation of one."

An older man stands in line, fumbling for his wallet. A fern leaf wriggles around his wrist curiously, a little dose of magic keeping it alive. He's a witch.

The woman at the register sighs audibly. "Sir, please. There's a line."

I scowl. "It's fine."

The man pulls out a five-dollar bill, hands it to the cashier, and turns to me and Ximena. "Sorry about that. This is a black hole," he says with a wave of his overstuffed wallet.

The man takes a seat at a nearby table. I skip out on ordering to talk to him. "You're a witch," I say, nodding at the charming little fern now inching toward me.

He pushes up his glasses. "I am. I used to own an apothecary too." He jabs a thumb toward Bottled Wonders. "Until that monstrosity forced me out of business. At my age, finding another job has been tough." He shakes his head. "I'm sure you don't want to hear an old man ramble. But the only thing the owner of Bottled Wonders cares about is money and making more of it at any cost."

"How do we stop him?" I ask.

"Wish I knew, kid. Tell you what, if you find a way and need a hand, give me a call." He slides his business card across the table.

ALBERT BAUMGARDNER: APOTHECARIST

I pocket the card with a smile. "Bet."

I watch him for a second longer while a server brings his coffee. I'm struck by how much he reminds me of Nana, with his vibrant shirt, steel-colored hair, and kind eyes. This could easily be her if Bottled Wonders has its way. I'm not letting Bishop Brews go out of business. People come to Blackclaw to escape burnout, get rejuvenated, and bring joy to their lives. You can't bottle and mass-produce that kind of small-town healing.

But how am I supposed to stop John? And with only one day left before Leigh's memory loss becomes permanent, is there even time?

# 24

After leaving Crimson Grove, Ximena and I head straight to Bishop Brews. Although we don't usually work on Saturdays, we picked up an extra shift to give Nana and Tiva time to prepare for the coven meeting tonight. We're going to discuss Bottled Wonders and tomorrow's deadline to produce a culprit for who poisoned Leigh. And while those very serious issues have been at the forefront of my mind, Ximena has this maddening trait of being nearly irresistible. Now that I've stopped trying to fight the raging crush I have on her, I can't seem to stop myself from pulling her to me any chance I get. I think Ximena feels the same. As soon as we get inside the apothecary, she presses me against the shelves and we kiss like it's the only thing we were made to do.

Lately there are only two things that can blot out my

doubts: magic and Ximena. Being with her is a kind of magic in and of itself—grounding and sure. I shouldn't get in too deep for all the reasons already stated, but I also can't seem to stay away.

Ximena pulls back first but doesn't go far. She rests her nose against my cheek. I feel the tug of her mouth against my skin when she smiles. I do the same, and it doesn't capture half of the giddiness filling up my head and my heart.

"Not that I don't want to make out with you all day, but shouldn't we be trying to figure out who's behind all of this so we can save our new kissing spot?" Ximena asks jokingly, hooking her fingers through the belt loops of my jeans.

I can't think with her this close. "Yes. Um, we still need to clear Poppy and Morris."

Ximena chuckles. "Okay, let's go to Poppy first. No sneaking around."

"There's a coven meeting tonight. I'll present everything we have. I hope Poppy still has that sweatshirt so Mercer can read its history and determine exactly where it's been. If it's gone or Poppy refuses to cooperate, maybe Mercer can read something else of Poppy's to see if she was involved or not."

"That's a solid plan," Ximena says. She's close enough for me to feel the words on my skin.

I need to kiss her again. Just as our lips touch, the shop bell rings out, signaling the arrival of a customer. Ximena pulls away with a sigh. Duty calls.

I swivel toward the door and say cheerily, "Welcome to Bishops Brews, where all our tonics are brewed with love!"

While Ximena assists the customer, showing him around the store and mentioning the sale we have for the Spring Harvest Festival tomorrow, I prep his bag. The stack of tissue paper next to me buzzes. I sweep it aside to find Ximena's phone lighting up with a new message. I don't mean to be nosy, but I can't help it. Everything slows to a halt as I read the words on the screen.

**Unknown:**

Just take whatever tonics Sage has been working on, and anything else worthwhile.

My mouth opens and closes as I try to gulp down air, which has somehow vanished from the shop. Even the plants wilt, the devil's ivy melting toward the floor and the tulips in the vase by the door closing their petals. I glance over at Ximena, shaken.

She runs her hand along the outside of my arm as she moves past me to ring up the customer. I flinch and her lips pinch together but she doesn't comment.

As soon as the man leaves with his bag full of crushed lotus flowers, I whirl on her. "How could you?"

Ximena shakes her head. "I don't know what you're—"

"How could you do this to me and my grandma after everything? I believed you when you said you weren't involved, but the truth was staring at me the whole time.

You were here during the break-in, and you could have easily unlocked the door for someone else."

Ximena's wide eyes are as moist as mine. "Sage, what are you talking about?"

I shove her phone at her. As soon as she starts to read, her face falls.

"Sage, I—I can explain." She frantically flicks through the messages. "I know this seems bad, but I promise, I'd never give this person your tonics. I don't even know who this is! They started texting me, and I figured I could at least try to lure them out." Her words are rushed, her body trembling with nerves. "Can I show you the text chain, please?"

I shake my head, hoping time just magically reverses itself to before I saw that text. I storm into the back room. I don't trust myself to speak without yelling or crying. I can't even look at her.

Ximena is quick to follow. "Sage, let me explain!"

I shove aside the jars of herbs cluttering the counter to keep moving. If I stop, I'll break. "I don't see what there is to explain. That text was clear. You're still not being honest with me. Even after everything."

"And you still don't *trust* me. I don't know how else to prove to you that you can." She tugs on her hair, a frustrated groan breaking past her lips. "Please, read the rest of the texts."

I swallow down the hurt and silence the voice in my head telling me not to believe a single thing she says and grab her phone.

**Unknown:**
Stop digging.

who is this??

**Unknown:**
Stop investigating the break-in or else.

tell me who this is or I'm giving this number straight to the sheriff.

**Unknown:**
As if I'd use my real number.

ha. you think they don't have technology to trace this?

**Unknown:**
Fine. How about we help each other out, then?

and why would I help you?

BYE. good luck staying out of jail.

**Unknown:**
You need money for college, right? Isn't that why you've been working at Bishop Brews? I could give you a bonus. All I'd need is a tonic or two.

how do you know that?

**Unknown:**
It's a small town. It's easy to overhear things.

**Unknown:**

Someone offering you the rest of the money you need for UCLA.

**Unknown:**

Just take whatever tonics Sage has been working on, and anything else worthwhile.

When I get to the end of the thread, Ximena says, "See? I told you! I don't know who this is, but I think they're our thief. If I can get them to meet with me—"

"When were you going to tell me about this?" I ask, gesturing toward the phone. "That first message is *four days old.*"

She nods. "Because I know how this seems. I was going to tell you, I swear, but I wasn't sure how much this person knew, if anything. I was trying to help."

I resume my anxious cleaning, taking the wet rag hanging on the faucet and wiping down the counter. "Were you going to take their offer?"

"Only to lure them out. I'd never steal from you, Sage."

I should believe her. So why do I feel queasy?

"I *promise* I was going to tell you." She reaches for my hand to still my movements, but I pull away. "Don't you believe me?"

And that's it, isn't it? I want to, but I also know she wants to be free of this town as soon as possible. If an opportunity to do that presented itself, of course she'd take it. She wouldn't stick around. I should have known that taking a chance on us was too risky, and I was foolish to let us get this far. I shouldn't have let Ximena kiss me, shouldn't have listened when she said she liked me.

When I still haven't answered, Ximena steps back and a chasm opens between us. I try to hold back the pricking of tears. The words stick in the back of my throat. I swallow twice to dislodge them. "I want to believe you."

She clenches her jaw so hard her teeth click. "Don't do this."

I swipe at my eyes with the back of my hand before the tears can fall. "Do what?"

"Don't use this stupid text as an excuse to push me away!"

"You mean like you pushed me away four years ago?"

"I apologized for that. I *am* sorry, Sage, but I was a kid! I didn't know how to handle being a wolf and I'd hurt my mom. I wasn't going to hurt you too." Ximena's hands are shaking at her sides. "I'm not running now, though. *You* are."

She's right. I feel like an asshole for bringing up our past. We were thirteen. What else was she supposed to do? And yet, I don't trust that I still know her. Not when we have very opposing beliefs. I don't want to push her away, but I can't deny that she'll leave regardless.

Ximena waits for a response. When none comes, she

storms out of the store. The door slamming in her wake feels final.

I throw the rag into the sink and collapse against the counter. A single thought circles my brain as the silence folds around me.

*What have I done?*

# 25

I sit in the shop for a long time, listening to the hum of the ceiling fan above me, the cranky old pipes, and the building's settling foundation. The plants are still wilted and sad. Not even the impending deadline can move me from my spot.

Except maybe the shop doorknob jingling.

I rush to the front of the store. I'd give my left lung for Ximena to come storming back in here the same way she went out, scowling and calling me out for being a coward.

But it's not her. Sheriff Dunn stands before me in uniform, his hands strung through his belt loops and his dusty boots clicking against the hardwood floor.

He nods in greeting and then asks, "Is your grandmother here? It's important."

That, plus his frown as he surveys the store, kicks my pulse up a notch. "I'm the only one in. Is everything okay?"

"Can you call her?" The sheriff walks in a slow circle. He inspects the tinctures on our shelves and inhales a batch of our hand-poured candles. He hums approvingly.

I call Nana but it goes to voicemail, so I text her, telling her the sheriff is at Bishop Brews. "What's this about?"

"The case." He continues to peruse. It's almost like he's stalling, which means he doesn't want to tell me why he's here, but I've got a right to know what's going on.

"My grandmother will tell me anyway," I say. "I'm here nearly as much as her, and one day this place will be mine. Tell me the truth."

He raises his eyebrows and rubs his chin, considering. After a beat, he lengthens his spine then recenters his belt buckle. "Fine. I don't want to do this, Sage, but I'm getting heat from the council. Your coven hasn't been as helpful as we'd hoped. Hell, your grandmother proposed my own kid as a suspect. It's a liability to keep the store open until we find out who's behind the break-in and can ensure no one else is at risk of consuming more misbrewed tonics. We're shutting you down."

"WHAT? Y-you can't *do* that!"

"The council voted, Sage."

"You mean the *founding families* on the council voted, because Nana and Mrs. Carver would never."

Sheriff Dunn tilts his head back as if trying to find patience woven into the air. "I want to see you succeed. Your grandmother's strep throat recipe is better than penicillin, plus nothing helped get rid of my wife's chronic sinus infections better than that special tea Tiva brews."

I grind my molars. "Then convince them not to do this."

"I've tried," he says lightly, as if this is simply another day for him and not the worst day for me. "The Lawsons pushed for this the hardest. Your grandmother still hasn't found a cure for Leigh, which tells the council Hazel *is* losing her touch, especially since the Lawsons found a witch at Bottled Wonders who claims he can help Leigh."

I'd bet my last tonic Mrs. Lawson made good on her threat to complain to the council about the failed cures. The Lawsons have no idea John Winters can't actually help them because he doesn't know which ingredients I used for my heartache tonic.

Sheriff Dunn grabs a fistful of the rose quartz sitting in a bowl on the nearest shelf. His energy is in full contrast with the crystal's healing properties. I'll have to cleanse them to get rid of his ineptness.

"Bottled Wonders is using more than its fair share of resources and draining the Hemwood magic. If this goes on much longer, we won't have a drop left."

Now it's the sheriff's turn to be surprised. He tosses the crystals aside, the stones clinking against each other, and steps forward. "How do you know that?"

"The owner said so himself. He's been growing his business so fast that he's overusing the magic. Now he wants to expand into Blackclaw. He's convinced the Lawsons that he can help with Leigh's memory loss, but he can't because his magic is probably messed up too."

"I'll need proof of that," the sheriff says.

"I have a voice note. Just promise to keep the store open."

"That's not how this works. I'm not negotiating with you. I wasn't even going to say anything without Hazel here." He rubs his beard. "Listen, have her call me down at the station as soon as possible. Send that voice note. If what you're saying is true, then we could have a serious breach of the county's ordinance on land usage."

So Ximena was right. Bottled Wonders is breaking the law. "What are you going to do to stop them?"

"Whatever needs to be done." He meanders to the door and taps his knuckles against the wooden frame. "Is there really an issue with the magic?"

I nod once.

His chin drops. "Have your grandmother call me," he says again. Before he leaves, he posts an official notice on the door: CLOSED BY ORDER OF THE COUNCIL.

My chest constricts painfully. I call Nana again. She picks up this time, starting to explain that her phone was accidentally on vibrate, until she realizes that I'm nearly hyperventilating on the other end. I can practically hear the steam coming out of her ears as I relay the sheriff's message. She tells me to lock up and come home. Before I do anything, I text Ximena.

> The sheriff was here. He closed the store.

> I'm sorry about earlier, okay? I panicked.

> Please answer.

She leaves me on read.

That feels like the final nail in the coffin. My throat tightens, and all I want to do is cry. I messed up big-time. There's only one place I go when things are tough like this. Without a second thought, I click the lights off, flip the Open sign to Closed, and lock the store. Then I jump on my bike and make a beeline for the woods.

)·)·)·)●(·(·(·(

Willow Creek winds along the southern half of town before it fizzles into a narrow stream a mile into the Hemwood. The sapphire-colored creek is bordered by wildflower fields and tall, skinny redwoods, a sight beautiful enough to rival the arboretum. The clear water shines like diamonds as sunlight kisses the surface.

I should be home for the coven meeting and yet I'm running from my problems like I accused Ximena of doing. I sit in silence by the water for a time, listening to the trickling creek, chatting crickets, and cawing birds.

The last time I was here, it was with Ximena. I'd give anything to go back to yesterday. I felt so light I could float. Now this twisting remorse in my gut makes me heavier than limestone. For the last week, I've felt like I was dangling on the edge of something huge. I kept waiting for Ximena to push me away again when *I* was the one holding her at arm's length. Now she's gone, which is exactly what I feared would happen.

The drum of footsteps starts low, then crescendos as

someone approaches from my right. They're loud enough to be deliberate. I turn to find Tiva in her signature linen shift dress and clogs.

She sits on the log next to me. "I thought I'd find you here."

"Come to bring me back?" The coven meeting should be starting soon. I'm sure Nana has tasks for me. Not even a broken heart can get me out of chores.

"Yes, but I also wanted to see if you're okay." Her voice is soft with sympathy when she turns toward me and says, "I heard about the store. I know how much it means to you."

I carve a narrow path in the dirt with my boot. "It was Mrs. Lawson. She's pissed we haven't been able to help Leigh. Once we do, the council will have to let us reopen the store, right?"

"I hope so." Tiva's quiet for a moment, seemingly enjoying the view, like me. "You know, of all the rivers and lakes I've seen, this one is my favorite."

Tiva spent her early twenties backpacking across the country before finally returning to Blackclaw. Her travels are inspiring, but Blackclaw is the place for me.

"Why see all those other lakes and rivers, then?" I ask.

"For the experience." Tiva nudges my shoulder and grins. "If I didn't see them, how would I know for certain that *this* is my favorite? So far, at least." Tiva admires the frothing water, foam sluicing over algae-covered rocks.

"You sound like Ximena. She can't wait to get out of

this town. How am I supposed to be with someone who wants the opposite of me?"

Tiva smooths down my curls, not even remotely fazed to learn that Ximena and I are together. Figures. My feelings are basically tattooed on my forehead.

"There's nothing wrong with leaving, nor is there anything wrong with staying," she says. "If you want a relationship with Ximena, you'll have to give up some control. Truly being with someone means letting go, compromising, merging your two dreams. It's knowing that they could hurt you but wanting and trusting them enough to take that risk. I think you should find a way to make it work. Even if the path isn't a straight one. Don't let the uncertainty keep you from going after what you want." She pats my knees affectionately. "Now come on. I told your gran I'd bring you back in time to help set up."

Tiva doesn't wait for me before she starts back home, giving me a little more time alone before I have to face the music.

I didn't realize until now how comforting Ximena's become this past week. Without her, everything feels raw and way harder than it should. I need to fix things.

The sun sits low on the horizon as I head home, painting the world in hues of orange and purple. Folding chairs are set up on the back porch. We're hosting the coven meeting again, even though it isn't our turn. Nana needs help determining our next steps now that the store is temporarily closed, and I need to update them on Bottled Wonders.

Poppy and her mom, followed by Mercer and her dad, arrive a few minutes after we're done prepping. I do a double take when Poppy sits across from me. Her box braids, usually styled in a fancy updo, hang limply around her face. She's wearing her glasses instead of contacts and is sans makeup. I'd never tell her, but I think she looks good like this too, even though it means something's probably wrong.

Mercer immediately clocks the change in Poppy. She sits next to her, and they whisper to each other briefly before Poppy shakes her head and clamps her mouth shut, seemingly done with talking.

Once everyone is here, we acknowledge the Hemwood for all it does for us and pass around the lemon myrtle and peach tea Tiva made for uplifting spirits. When I drink it, there's a spark of magic mixed in with the zesty notes and my belly warms with it, my muscles loosen, and my mind clears. It isn't much, just enough to shake off some of the weight pressing down on me.

Then it's time to confront Poppy and play the voice note I recorded at Bottled Wonders. I stand, and eight pairs of eyes bore into me. None I feel more than Poppy's. I can see myself reflected in her glasses and her expression. She doesn't seem worried about being caught. She seems stressed. Next to her, Mercer subtly shakes her head. You don't hit someone when they're already down, right?

"I have a recording to play for you," I say, instead of

forcing Poppy's hand. I still can, just in a more private setting.

I hit play on my phone. John's voice rings out. Murmurs spread through the group once the recording ends.

It's Poppy who speaks up first. Her grip is so tight on her seat that her skin pales. "Is it possible to use up the Hemwood's magic?"

"It's possible," Shaye replies. "The Hemwood is vast but not endless, same for its magic. Like life, it requires harmony and respect. Abuse it, and it'll respond in turn." Hums of assent flutter around the room.

"We're all affected by this Bottled Wonders nonsense," Nana says tightly. "The town council voted to temporarily close Bishop Brews at the urging of the Lawsons. We need to prove to them that witches aren't losing their touch but are being affected by that mega-apothecary in Crimson Grove."

The adults delve into discussion on additional concerns to bring up with the founding families. I can't bring myself to focus on their back and forth, so I sip more of Tiva's tea, the magic properties untangling the knots in my mind. The magic is still working enough for Tiva's tea to loosen my thoughts and Nana's counter brews to glow, so why aren't they restoring Leigh's memories? We're missing something.

Mercer, ever the empath, senses my mood. She texts me and Poppy, a group chat we rarely use, suggesting we ditch the rest of the meeting for ice cream. Poppy's lips twist like she's actually considering it before she shakes her head.

**Poppy Carver:**

> Rain check. I don't feel like being interrogated tonight.

> I've only been asking questions bc I'm trying to save Bishop Brews.

**Poppy Carver:**

> For the hundredth time, Sage, I wasn't involved!

**Mercer:**

> Both of you chill! Can we just go to 1000 Scoops like we used to?

> They're having a sale ahead of the festival like Mystic Muffins.

**Poppy Carver:**

> Y'all go ahead.

**Mercer:**

> Aw, c'mon, Fun Goblin!

Poppy waits for us to turn her way, and then rolls her eyes and tucks her phone away. I know I've been suspicious of her, but there's more to her mood than my questions. She's usually annoyingly put-together and always ready for the coven meetings to end so she can get back to Morris or cheerleading or whatever she's obsessing over at the moment.

Mercer stealthily loops her arm in mine and leads us outside. 1,000 Scoops is a five-minute walk down the road. It's always been our favorite ice cream parlor of the three in town for late-night snacks. We buy a banana split to share, and then we head for the playground two blocks south.

Mercer grabs a swing then jumps back. "Ew. Don't sit here. Some kid peed on it earlier today."

We find two clean swings and tear into the banana split while the moon watches. Even with everything, I manage to find a spoonful of happiness with strawberry ice cream on my tongue and my fingers tightly wrapped around a swing. It's a different kind of happiness from what burns through me when I'm with Ximena. Less consuming. It's easy and soft, like mist hovering over the valley on a lazy Sunday morning. With Ximena, happiness is hot, bright, and dangerous. A summer wildfire.

"Are you going to tell me what happened, or are you going to keep brooding?" Mercer raises a single eyebrow as she swings past me, wind rushing through her dark locks.

"Who's brooding? Not me. I'm enjoying my ice cream."

"You're in your head. Spill."

I put our banana split on the ground, kick my feet, and rock back. The world blurs as I hang halfway upside down, blood rushing to my head and the wind whistling in my ears. "I messed up," I confess.

A gust of citrus perfume blows over me as Mercer sways. "Then make it right."

"It's not that simple."

"It's as simple as saying 'I'm sorry.' My mom always says that life's hard, but love's harder. Whatever you did, apologize. Ximena will understand."

I tighten my grip on the metal chains and stare at my feet. "Who said it's about Ximena?"

"Oh, *please*."

I grumble my displeasure with her being able to read me so easily. I kick again, then dip low. "Fine. It's about Ximena."

Mercer leans back on the swing, gaining more height. "You really like her, huh?"

"I do. She's funny and thoughtful and she listens to me. She pushes me to face my fears. She tells me I'm capable of anything. I'm not sure I believe her, but I want to. I think she knows that too."

Ximena's patiently waited for me to sort out my heartbreak tonic even though she's the reason I came up with it. She's encouraged me every step of the way—even tells me I can find a way to have everything. Ximena, both knowingly and not, has helped me see just how much I'm missing out on by staying in my comfort zone. She doesn't let being a wolf get in the way of going after what she wants. Her ability to keep striving for more inspires me to do the same.

"And I understand her better than she realizes," I add. Ximena's had to hide the coolest part of herself for years. Staying hidden doesn't mean she's any less courageous than those of us who aren't.

Mercer's uncharacteristically quiet next to me.

"Why are you making that face? You look like a startled deer."

"That's because I am. I completely underestimated this." Mercer shakes her head. "How long have you been in love with her?"

My breath catches in the back of my throat, and I nearly lose my grip on the swing. Like her? Yes. But *love*?

What even is love? Is it what leaves my heart a quivering mess every time I see Ximena? Is it the maddening thoughts of her that won't leave me alone? Or is it the feeling of weightlessness when she gazes at me, the same feeling I get as I reach for my magic?

"You should tell her how you feel," Mercer says. "That'd be a good start toward fixing things between the two of you."

"She's not answering my texts. I pushed her away."

"Did you apologize?" Mercer asks.

I nod. "Didn't work."

"Hmm. She might need a grand gesture." Mercer hits an impressive height, throws her feet out, then hurtles herself through the air. A leap of faith. She lands with a thump and a snort of laughter.

Butterflies dance in my stomach as I tip my head to the midnight-blue sky sliding back and forth. I keep my gravity centered so I don't fall. Although, if the burgeoning feeling low in my chest at the thought of Ximena is anything to go by, I think I already have.

# 26

Ximena hasn't returned any of my calls or texts since storming out of Bishop Brews. Ghosting me is one thing, but what if she *can't* reply? Could she have completely lost the ability to keep her wolf at bay? If it got bad enough, would her parents make her leave for LA before finals? Would she even tell me or just dip like before?

All night my thoughts have been as tangled as the pair of headphones at the bottom of my bag. Now it's nearly midnight, and I'm still bugging. Nana and Tiva are already in bed, but I can't sleep with everything going on. The Spring Harvest Festival deadline to cure Leigh is tomorrow, and we still don't have a counter brew.

The one thing besides Ximena I can usually count on to unravel the mess in my head is magic. Nothing can reach me when I'm practicing my craft. It's like I slip into a daydream where there's only the power of holding an impossibility in the palms of my hands. That I can only use it near the Hemwood makes Blackclaw special.

And yet, where Ximena has mostly had to remain hidden because of her magic, I've been gifted relative freedom. All she wants is to have that same liberty, but to get it she has to leave.

What if she didn't? What if there were protections in place for her here—a community of like-minded people like I have with my coven? Leaving is her choice, but she should *have* a choice like I do. For that, Blackclaw would need to change. The adults in my coven are meeting with the town council tomorrow. Could I ask them about protections for everyone with magic, like the Reyeses or even my great-aunt who no longer practices? Ximena deserves at least peace of mind that she'll be safe here if anyone finds out about her being a wolf.

This idea energizes me, though my thoughts are still cluttered. A little magic will help. I decide to give my tonic one last shot. Except, when I try to work on it, not a drop of inspiration comes. Something else, then. An enticing, long-lasting perfume, maybe? It's fun and easy and isn't technically a brew. The new rug in the kitchen should thank me.

It's clear when I reach for the slowly browning petals in the vase on the windowsill that my gift has weakened. There's less to draw on when I attempt to liven the flowers. It takes more effort than I'm willing to exude, so I end up using the premade essential oils Nana keeps in a drawer by the stove.

I grab the almond oil, which I'll use as a base to dilute my essential oils (lavender and jasmine), and pour two ounces of each into a jar. Then, for an extra hint of sweetness, I pop the buds off the roses in the vase, crush the petals with the mortar and pestle, then dribble the sticky juice into the blend. It smells divine. I hold my hand above my mixing bowl, and gradually, so as not to use too much, let my magic flow. It starts glowing immediately, and I sigh in relief as I dab a bit onto my wrist and inhale. The scent is perfect. Like trees and wildflowers and sunlight.

It hits me like a punch when I realize the perfume smells exactly like Ximena. *Damn. I've got it bad. Send help.* Okay, I officially need to fix what I did and soon. I can't lose her. Not again. I'm done playing it safe. So how do I show her I'm sorry and that I care about her as much as I do Bishop Brews and my own magic?

I drum my nails against the counter. Hang on. Ximena. *She's* the reason I can't focus on my heartbreak tonic because I'm not heartbroken anymore. Though my heart aches for her, it's still intact. Intentions are *everything* when it comes to brewing tonics and mine have been muddled from the start. And with the magic acting spotty, the intention behind every brew must be precise. When I made misbrew number twenty-two, it was my first day working with Ximena at Bishop Brews, and I'd just realized how royally screwed I was because she was still as enigmatic and intriguing as ever. I don't think my intentions were solely focused on forgetting my heartbreak. A small part of me still liked her. And since Ximena has taken up real estate in my head and my heart, why not make a tonic that makes the drinker feel like I do? In love. Who wouldn't want the impression that they can do anything? *Be* anything. Like they're enough all on their own. That's what's going to ensure Bishop Brews outlasts the competition.

First things first, though. Operation: Bring Down Bottled Wonders.

)·)·)·)●●●●·(·(·(·(

"I'm glad you've finally decided to listen to me and make up with Poppy," Mercer says, her voice ringing through my earphones as I pedal to the end of my driveway.

It's early Sunday morning. The Spring Harvest Festival starts in a couple of hours, and today is the last day before Leigh's memory loss becomes permanent.

"I wouldn't exactly call this making up, but I'm giving her some slack and seeing where that gets me," I tell Mercer.

I've been approaching Poppy all wrong. Instead of trying to strong-arm her into confessing, I could get on her good side, maybe even try to understand her before I blame her for something she insists she hasn't done. Today's about trying a new approach. I still need Jason's sweatshirt so Mercer can read where it's been. Her readings are about as fickle as my brewing, but it's worth the shot of proving to the rest of the council that witches are still up to snuff and that closing Bishop Brews only hurts our community. Getting Poppy on my side again can be the start of witches coming together to heal the Hemwood. Restoring Leigh's memories won't happen if we can't fix our magic.

By the time I arrive at the Carvers' house, I'm out of breath. I don't make it up the drive before Poppy comes storming outside carrying a box and beelining for the garbage cans lined up outside her garage. She groans when she sees me.

"What do you want, Sage? Come to convince me to turn myself in? Or maybe you're here to snoop around my room some more? You won't find anything." She shakes her head tightly.

I let my bike fall into the grass and close the distance between us. Her eyes are red beneath her glasses, like she's been crying. The box she's holding is overflowing with random items. Video games, a beanie, a silver chain, a notebook, but the thing that catches my eye is Jason's Blackclaw Valley High sweatshirt. "What happened?"

Poppy scoffs. "Why do you care?"

I sigh. "I'm sorry, okay? You're my covenmate. We're supposed to be family. I should have listened when you said you didn't have anything to do with the break-in. And I shouldn't have snuck into your room."

She shakes her head. "I appreciate the sentiment, but it doesn't help me now."

"Are you going to tell me what's wrong, or do I have to pry it out of you? You were off last night too. I'm high-key offended you didn't want to get ice cream with us. Mercer was secretly hoping you would change your mind—don't tell her I told you that."

"She was?" Poppy fidgets with the box, and I swear a hint of a blush creeps across her face.

"I know we aren't as close as we used to be, and that's okay. I still want to help. I've learned that it's better to talk about the hard stuff, even if it's scary, than to let it fester," I tell her.

Poppy groans again, but I can tell I'm getting to her by the subtle slump of her shoulders. She drops the box. "It's Morris, all right? I found an anonymous texting app on his phone. He's been using it to text someone and then deleting the messages. I—I think he's cheating on me."

"Seriously? I'm so sorry, Poppy."

"He's been acting weird for the last couple of weeks—always on his phone or canceling plans. That day you saw us, I practically had to beg him to come to Mystic Muffins with me, and even then, he left the bakery early and showed up late to the fundraising rally. I thought he was worried about finals or his mom's MS." She shrugs limply. "Turns out he was texting other girls and doing who knows what else."

His mom has MS? I had no idea. Maybe that's why his dad asked about a custom tonic for pain when he stopped by Bishop Brews earlier this week, and why Morris picked up a pain management tonic at Bottled Wonders.

I glance at the box at Poppy's feet. "Is this Morris's stuff? Mercer could read this—"

"I don't want to involve her in my relationship drama.

She's too good for that. Besides, I trusted him to tell me the truth. Most of this is Morris's but I think the hoodie is Jason's. Either way, Morris is always wearing it."

My sleuthing senses start to tingle. I gesture at the sweatshirt. "Mind if I take a look?"

Poppy crosses her arms and stares me down. After a beat, she sighs. "Fine. Whatever. If it gets you to finally believe me, be my guest. I'm tired of defending myself."

I wince. "For what it's worth, I was never fully convinced you were involved. I just . . . *need* to know. My brain won't rest until I'm certain, and not just about the investigation. About everything."

Poppy seems to deflate. "I guess you've always been persistent. If I'm honest, it's one of the things I admire about you," she mumbles.

"Poppy Carver, did you just compliment me?"

"Don't make me regret it."

My lips tug into a smile. I need to know what's going on, what to expect, and ideally what to wear. I like plans and lists and playing things safe. I'm a Virgo. Sue me. But I'm also learning that being so rigid can mean missing out on the fun.

I reach into the box and pull out the hoodie. There, just where I remembered, is a stain. Something white and rectangular falls out of the pocket before I can examine the smudge more closely.

Poppy snatches it off the ground. Her forehead creases. She hands it over. "It's a business card for Bottled Wonders."

"Why would Jason have that?" I ask.

"I don't know," Poppy replies.

I flip the business card over. The name John is written next to a phone number.

"Poppy, do you remember the number Morris was texting?" I ask.

She shakes her head. "I never saw him texting long enough to memorize or write down the numbers, and he always deleted the messages. I do remember the area codes. One was a five-three-zero, and the other was seven-zero-seven. I thought the second number was a little odd because most people in Blackclaw have five-three-zero."

Ximena does, so I'm willing to bet hers is one of the numbers Morris was texting. Bottled Wonders's area code, according to the business card, is 707. It could be a coincidence.

I rub the stain on the sleeve of the sweatshirt and then inhale. Beneath the slightly dusty scent of closet, sweat, and fading fabric softener is something sharp and pungent, the same smell emanating from all my failed tonics.

It's not Ximena or Poppy or Jason or Olivia. It's Morris. He's an athlete, went to Mystic Muffins, and arrived at the rally late. But what does he have to gain from stealing from me or hurting Leigh? Then again, perhaps that's where Bottled Wonders comes in. What if it's not Bottled Wonders *or* Morris, but Bottled Wonders *and* Morris?

"When did the texting start?" My voice is pitchy and fast, causing Poppy to glance up from nervously picking her nails.

"Um, a week or two ago? Why? What are you thinking?" she asks.

"I'm thinking that your boyfriend is working with Bottled Wonders, and he stole from Bishop Brews." How'd Morris get involved with John Winters?

Poppy shakes loose a single tear. "That doesn't make sense. Why would Morris do this? He knew this could hurt me by damaging the coven's reputation."

"I don't know, but we need to find out before we confront him. His dad's the mayor and a council member. He'll be anything but pleased if we point to his son as the culprit without definitive proof."

"You got any ideas?" Poppy asks.

"One." And it involves Ximena. Just thinking about her makes me jittery. "I might need your help."

"Anything." Her mouth furls into a tentative smile. A week ago, I'd have said she didn't have it in her. Now look at us.

I return the smile. I didn't realize how much I missed things being good between us. "Can you get Mercer and meet me at the festival?"

"Sounds easy enough. Where are you going to be?" she asks.

"Right behind you. I have to do one thing first."

# 27

Can I execute my plan without Ximena? Maybe. Do I want to? Hell no. Ximena has been with me on this investigation from the start. And she's helped me in more ways than one. Not only is she a good detective, but she's also a good teacher. Without even meaning to, she's changed how I think about myself and my town. She's pushed me in the best way. Change doesn't mean leaving behind my magic, or my family, or my experiences. I carry everything from Blackclaw with me. Always.

When I arrive at Ximena's house, her car's not in the driveway. Of course, life can't be that easy. When I call her phone, it goes straight to voicemail. Neither of us has school or work today. I could ride around searching for her, but I don't know if we have that kind of time with the festival starting in an hour.

If I was rejected by my first crush, I'd go somewhere to clear my head. Could she be hiking?

I park my bike in her driveway, take the steps two at a time, and ring her doorbell.

Mrs. Reyes answers. She has a soft, knowing expression on her face. "She's at school," she says before I can even ask. "Go get your girl."

Grinning like a fool, I throw my leg over my bike and race toward Blackclaw Valley High. Ten minutes later, I spot Ximena's truck parked in the school lot. The doors are unlocked on the weekends for tutoring and extracurriculars.

What's Ximena doing here? And then it hits me. At the bonfire, Olivia mentioned Ximena was always in the music room. I've only been there a handful of times to meet Mercer. It's a small room between the art studio and the auditorium. The halls are empty. My Converse squeak against the linoleum as I jog toward the sound of a piano. Even notes filter through the dusty vents.

The door is open.

Ximena's seated at the piano. Her fingers gracefully float across the keys, each chord perfectly formed to make a dreamy melody. Her expression, while mostly unreadable, bares a hint of surprise when I step into her line of view. She keeps playing and starts to sing, a slow love song about drifting apart and coming back together.

I hardly breathe. Once it ends, she glances at me expectantly.

"That was beautiful. What's it from?" I ask, cringing internally at how squeaky my voice sounds.

"It's an original. Been feeling inspired lately." Ximena

pulls her feet onto the bench and hugs her knees. "What are you doing here?"

"Can we talk?"

"Come to your senses?" The lightness of her tone doesn't exactly match her closed-off body language, but I'll take it.

"Something like that. I want to apologize," I say.

She pats the bench—an olive branch I grasp like a life vest. I leave an awkward foot of space between us.

"I'm sorry I hurt you. I should have trusted you. I *wanted* to, believe me. Even after all these years, between my parents and you disappearing, it's hard when the people I care about leave."

"I'm not going anywhere," she says with a sigh. "Leaving town has nothing to do with how I feel about you."

I nod. "I know, but it made me worry that once you see how amazing and wonderful the world is, you'll realize I don't measure up." Ximena opens her mouth, likely to protest, but I press on. "I *want* you to have adventures. Just come back every now and then and tell me about them?"

I could never imagine leaving the place where I made all my memories—good ones, like learning magic, and the not-so-good ones, like losing my parents. My roots and my legacy are here. I still want Ximena to have a fresh start, so long as she doesn't forget about me.

Ximena releases a harsh sound. It's barely a laugh. She has a fire in her eyes, and I let it burn me. "All week, I've been trying to show you I'm not going anywhere, even if I leave Blackclaw."

"I'm a little slow on the uptake." She watches me,

unrelenting. Her shoulders are still stiff with tension. It's hard to keep my voice steady when I ask, "Can you forgive me?"

Waiting for her response is practically torture with the bombshell of information I'm sitting on, but I have to know she forgives me before I tell her what I've found.

"Of course I forgive you," she says, her lips pinching to the side. I release a breath, feeling weightless, and match her timid smile. "But not the sheriff. I can't believe he closed Bishop Brews! Pushover. How are you holding up? I was going to come find you at the festival. I shouldn't have ghosted you. I'm sorry."

I take her hand. "It's okay. I'm better now."

Ximena's gaze softens. "For what it's worth, you definitely measure up, Sage. You're the most amazing person I've ever met. I hope you know that."

"I am pretty great." If she keeps this up, I'm not going to be able to stop myself from kissing her.

Ximena chuckles. She positions my hands on the keys. Her skin is warm and soft atop mine. We play a few chords that sound pretty nice considering I've never played an instrument before.

She gestures for me to continue playing the chords while she moves farther up the keyboard. "Is the apology what was so important you had to stalk me to tell me?"

I flush. "Your mom told me where to find you. Gave her blessing and everything. So I didn't *stalk* you."

Okay, I sort of stalked her, but that's beside the point. What matters is that she forgives me. I can't stomach us being on the outs again. Funny—a week ago I would've given anything to never talk to her again. Now all I ever want to do is hear her voice.

When she catches me staring, she nudges my shoulder. I'd say our fight is mostly behind us. Which brings me to the second reason why I'm here. Time to rip the Band-Aid off. "But no," I continue, still playing the chords she taught me. "There's something else. I know who's been texting you."

Her hands freeze. "Who?"

"Morris," I reply.

"Seriously? How do you know?"

I relay everything that happened at Poppy's house as quickly as I can.

"But why would Bottled Wonders want to steal from Bishop Brews? They're kind of killing it on their own. No offense," Ximena asks.

"A little taken. John was in our store when he heard me talking about creating a tonic unlike any other. If he gets his hands on my heartache tonic before it comes out, it gives Bottled Wonders an advantage over Bishop Brews in the market, and he's likely betting we won't have the resources to compete, which makes us more likely to sell. Nana won't be able to turn him down again."

Ximena shakes her head. "Damn. So, what do you want to do?"

"I want to lure Morris out. If you text him back, pretending you want to meet at the Spring Harvest Festival to exchange my tonic, maybe John will be there and we can catch them together."

"Are you sure he'll want to meet in such a public place?" Ximena asks.

"I think it'd be perfect. Everyone will be too focused on the festival to notice you and Morris."

She rests her knee against mine, and I lean into the contact. Ximena grins and the last bit of weight holding me down evaporates. There's so much more I need to say to her. I want to tell her how much I care about her, how I might even *love* her. I have the words parsed out in my head. As soon as this investigation is over, I'll tell her. For now, at least, I can finish this.

"Should I text Morris?" Ximena asks.

I nod. "Tell him to meet you somewhere out of the way, like behind the stage."

"Okay. What if he doesn't show?"

"He'll show. Morris messed up. Somehow Leigh got ahold of my tonic instead of John. Besides, we know John is greedy. I'm sure he wants more than the basic tonics Morris grabbed the first time. He's after something bigger. And I have just the thing." I pause for the effect. "The heartbreak tonic. Tell Morris I cracked it."

Ximena lights up like a firefly at night. "Did you?"

I shake my head. "He doesn't need to know that, though."

Ximena gives me a devilish little smirk to let me know she's game. I stand up and pull Ximena with me. We need to make a pit stop at the apothecary, and then the only thing left to do is set the plan in motion and let the pieces fall where they may.

# 28

The festival is a collage of colors. A local band plays on a raised platform near the town hall. Harsh notes from a decent guitarist and the rhythmic pounding of drums fill the two blocks with more noise than I'm accustomed to listening to. The song mingles with the roar of haggling residents. The sun blazes off the white tents and catches on the green banner strung from opposite lampposts welcoming residents to the seventieth annual Spring Harvest Festival. The festival is a day where small businesses set up booths to advertise and sell their products to residents and tourists. There's also a parade, featuring floats from all the major businesses in town (most of them belonging to the Lawsons), and even different clubs at my high school participate.

Ximena and I slip between vendors stationed along the sidewalks. Every time I glance in her direction, she's staring. She flushes when I catch her. It's a game of cat and mouse that entertains me more than it should.

I brush past a swarm of people, slightly claustrophobic as I make my way toward the stage. I dodge a man handing out flyers for roofing services and a brightly dressed woman with a shapely bob offering 20 percent off kids' haircuts. There's no sign of Morris or John, but Morris did reply to Ximena, confirming he'd be here.

Behind the stage, cute cobblestone buildings frame the famous statue of witches and wolves working together. I used to think the statue symbolized a folktale, but here we are, a witch and a wolf facing off together against a threat to the town's well-being.

"Are you sure this is going to work?" Ximena asks as we approach the meeting point.

"Nope, but we've got to try."

I hand Ximena the tonic I quickly brewed before coming here to fool Morris into thinking it's the real deal. All Ximena has to do is make the exchange, and I'll secretly be recording the entire interaction.

The stage sits on wooden slats about four feet high. A white curtain trails around the structure. I take my place underneath it while Ximena stands nervously a few yards in front of me. She holds the tonic close to her chest and stiffly rocks from foot to foot. She checks her phone regularly. It's half past noon and most people are eating lunch, taking pictures, or browsing. No one's paying us much attention.

A few minutes later, Morris winds through the crowd, heading right for Ximena. It was one thing to guess he was involved, and another thing entirely to see him shadily approach her with a baseball cap sitting low on his head and his hands tucked inside the front pockets of his jeans.

Ximena's eyes widen as Morris approaches her. "I can't believe it's you," she says. "Did you seriously rob Bishop Brews?"

Morris's gaze darts around. "Where's the tonic?"

Ximena sighs, her frustration audible. "Answer my questions first. Why are you doing this, Morris? There's got to be a reason."

He rolls his eyes. "Don't worry about the reason. Do you want the money or not?"

"You have it?" Ximena asks.

Morris nods. "Show me the tonic first, and I'll Cash App you."

Ximena uncrosses her arms, revealing the tonic that was tucked into the crook of her elbow. Morris glances over his shoulder once more.

Morris reaches for the tonic, but Ximena steps back before he can take it. I smile. We may not have John, but we do have Morris. I've got the whole thing on video. This should be enough to prove he was partly involved.

"Where's your partner?" Ximena asks.

"What partner? Just hand over the tonic."

I could keep recording and wait, but Morris isn't the

big catch here. We need John Winters, and the only way to lure him out is by using Morris.

I make a quick decision to keep recording and rise to my feet. "Give it up, Morris. We know you stole from us, and that you're working with Bottled Wonders! Why'd you do it? What could they possibly offer you that you don't already have?"

Morris glances wildly between me and my phone. He seems to waver between running, lying, or telling the truth. But there is nowhere for him to go with Ximena behind him and me in front.

He whips around, likely assessing his options, and chooses wrong. He lunges toward Ximena. Her reflexes are inhuman fast, and with a growl, she snatches his shirt and drags him back toward me.

"Ow! Okay! Okay!" He shrivels like an underwatered plant. "Geez, you're strong."

His weight remains tipped onto the balls of his feet, like he's ready to run again. Ximena's eyes flare amber, and she bares her teeth. Her sparkly blue nails lengthen into sparkly blue claws that she conceals behind her back. Seeing her wolf side shouldn't be as hot as it is. Then again, I'm hopelessly gay and likely madly in love with her.

Morris has sense enough to at least appear guilty, though he doesn't deflate as much as I'd anticipate for someone who's been caught. "I'm not telling you anything."

"We already know about your deal with Bottled Wonders," Ximena says.

"Tell us how you're involved and help us catch the owner, or we'll turn you in to the sheriff," I say.

His eyes widen, and his jaw slackens. He doesn't resemble a big bad thief now. Probably because he isn't. He's just a pawn.

"Oh, wonderful! Can the three of you help me set up this booth?" Henry, the owner of the Enchanted Emporium, flags us down at the most inopportune time. He's a round man with short, graying hair. In his arms is Licorice. The black cat hisses at Ximena, and I bite back a laugh.

Henry gestures toward the folding table and a box of decorations helplessly. "I have to get a few items from the store. You kids don't mind helping, do you? My back isn't what it used to be."

*Oh my god.* "We don't really have—" I start.

"Sure thing," Ximena says with a gentle wink.

Morris clearly wants to bolt, but one low, threatening snarl from Ximena and he settles down.

"Grab this." I point to the glittery silver cloth meant to cover the plastic table. "Now tell us the truth."

He's too preoccupied with the cloth and Ximena to notice I'm still recording what he says. We need a confession.

"Fine. All right. I—I took your tonics," he stammers.

"Start from the beginning," Ximena urges, setting up the folding sign that says "The Enchanted Emporium" in bright silver letters.

"She hasn't told many people, or come out publicly

about it, but my mom has MS. Nothing the doctors have prescribed reduces the burning pain. Some days are better than others, but I'm tired of seeing her suffer. I can't leave for college without knowing I did everything I could to help her. Two Sundays ago, I met John at the farmers market. I guess he was scoping out the magical stores that have stalls at the market? Anyway, he saw my mom struggling, and while she was busy talking with her PTA friends, he told me he had a tonic that could eliminate her pain. I just had to do something for him first."

"Steal," I say, letting the dots connect.

Morris rubs a shaky hand down his face. "You don't know what it's like watching someone you love suffer."

"My grandmother couldn't get out of bed for weeks after my parents died. I know what it's like to feel helpless," I reply. "I'm sorry she's sick. But if you had come to me like your dad did, I would've done everything possible to help."

Morris rubs the back of his neck. "He just sounded *so* confident that he could help her, you know?"

"I bet." With a roll of my wrist, four purple buds from the jacaranda tree next to us land in the palm of my hand. I snap my fingers and the petals separate so I can scatter them across the table. "How'd John know about my tonic if he visited Bishop Brews for the first time the morning of the break-in? If he wanted our regular tonics, he could've just bought them."

"He knew you were working on a tonic that was going to take Bishop Brews to the next level. You told your coven, right? Poppy told me you were working on an original tonic. She seemed really impressed. So when John asked me if your apothecary sold anything innovative, I mentioned it."

I grind my teeth. I should've kept that heartache cure a secret until it was ready to hit the shelves. "So he only wanted my tonic to boost his sales?" I ask.

"No. Taking it was a way to ensure Bishop Brews fails, so it's easier for him to either buy you out or crush you once he finds a location in town to open another apothecary." Morris takes a few items out of the box Henry left at his feet—an antique clock and a shiny pendant. He tosses them haphazardly onto my delicate flower petals.

"John won't stop," he continues. "He wants to open a dozen more businesses across the country, all selling magic products. Crimson Grove isn't the only place he's invaded—just Google apothecaries outside New York, Chicago, and Atlanta. They've all shut down, only to be replaced by Bottled Wonders. He's been scoping out other magic sources besides the Hemwood so he doesn't have to ship perishable products. Our deal was to steal the brew that was going to put Bishop Brews on the map in exchange for me getting a tonic for my mom. I saw your notes for the heartbreak tonic, but I wasn't sure if it was the mixture in the cauldron or one of the unlabeled tonics next to it, so I took everything."

"Were you wearing Jason's sweatshirt?" I ask, fixing the presentation of the antique items with a little too much force.

"I didn't want to spill anything on my jersey before the game. It was the first thing I saw at Poppy's house that would fit me," he confirms.

"What about Leigh? How was she involved?" Ximena asks.

Morris shakes his head. "She wasn't. That was a total accident. All of the tonics were already bottled except the one in that cauldron. I had to improvise, so I used my water bottle to collect it. Poppy was blowing up my phone the whole time since we'd just fought, and she can't let anything go." He drags a hand across his face. "I didn't have time to go home first. And then I saw Leigh rushing toward school. I gave her a ride, and she drank the tonic. I guess she thought my water bottle was full of the electrolyte mix I usually bring to games. I tried to label it, but I don't think she noticed." He shakes his head. "No one was supposed to get hurt."

"Well, people did!" I yell, suddenly furious. "And not just Leigh, but my family's business and my coven. You betrayed our community."

Morris crosses his arms and avoids making eye contact with me and Ximena. As he starts to close off, I force myself to deflate. There's no use putting him so far on the defensive that he won't help us. "You can still make it right," I tell him.

He peeks at me. "How?"

"Text John. Tell him you have my tonic and that you want to meet in the town square within the next twenty minutes, or you'll give it to another interested party," I reply.

Morris frowns. "But no one else is interested."

"He doesn't need to know that. You'll be bluffing. Keep up. Get John to talk about the plan. We'll be nearby recording the entire thing. Do this, or we'll tell Sheriff Dunn and the rest of the council that you're solely responsible for the break-in and Leigh's memory loss," I tell him.

John isn't going to confess to anything shady. He's got too much to lose. But maybe we can force his hand.

"You're not really leaving me with much of a choice here," Morris complains.

"That's kind of the point," Ximena replies, finishing the last of the decorations just as Henry returns with another box, the cat in tow.

"Wow! This is great!" Henry's smile is warm. Licorice is clearly plotting Ximena's demise.

"I'm glad you like it, but we've got to go," I tell him.

"Oh yes. Go on. I'm sure you have your own booth to set up. Mercer should be here soon, anyway. Thanks again," Henry replies.

Ximena subtly steers Morris across the street.

"I'll text John," he says. "He's cautious. He's not going to meet in the open like this." To make his point, Morris nods at Henry, who waves.

Meeting somewhere public is safer, but I have Ximena and my magic and a drive to see this through to the end no matter what. "The town hall, then," I say, noticing the stone building across from us. "It should be empty with everyone at the festival. As soon as you give John the tonic, get out of there."

"Why?" Morris asks.

"You said he's cautious, right? If he doesn't like what he's getting, he'll blame you."

Morris is quiet for a moment. "This *is* the heartbreak tonic, right?"

"Of course, but it hasn't been tested," I lie, hoping we're all long gone before John notices anything off about it. "Now let's go."

)·)·)·)●(·(·(·(

The town hall is filled with offices belonging to lawmakers and council members, an archive room, the great hall where senior prom is held in the spring, and the auditorium for town meetings.

Ximena and I are squished together behind the welcome desk, arms and legs pressed together, faces a hair's width apart. I try to regulate my breathing so it doesn't seem like I'm struggling being this close to her.

"Don't be nervous," Ximena whispers, misreading the situation. "He'll show, and we have a good angle."

"I'm not nervous about that."

"Then what?"

I shake my head. Hiding behind a desk while we wait to lure out a thief is not where I want to confess my feelings. "Tell you later. Promise."

Across from us is the long glass case home to town artifacts like a brick from the batch used to construct the town hall. Also displayed are dozens of black-and-white photographs of the original settlers, the founders included, in dark trousers and waistcoats standing next to the town sign. And there are sketches of the Indigenous peoples who inhabited this area long before California became a state and greed marched in to claim the land. The Locklears had them commissioned to honor their ancestors. And Nana had one made of our own ancestor, Ruby Bishop, who worked as a florist, saving every penny until she had enough to buy an acre. And then another, and another, and three more. Recalling our history now, I hope I can do right by them in protecting our town.

My phone buzzes in my pocket again. It's been doing it nonstop since I left Poppy's house.

**Mercer:**
Girl, where ARE you?

**Mercer:**
We're at the festival. What's the plan to catch Morris?

**Poppy:**
don't go MIA on us now

Before I can reply, a familiar figure enters. He's tall and lean, and has a blond mustache that curls at the ends. Seeing him in person again boils my blood.

I hold my phone out and try to stop my hand from shaking. Mercer's and Poppy's texts give me an idea, and I switch to the Bishop Brews Instagram account Ximena and I created and start livestreaming. Mercer was our first follower. With any luck, she'll see this. Along with our other loyal customers.

John spots Morris immediately. "Do you have it?" he asks brusquely.

Morris keeps the vial tucked in close, his hands shaking with nerves. He's going to give us away if he keeps it up.

"You're still going to give me the tonic, right? I did everything you asked me to do."

John sighs. "I said I would."

Morris shuffles his feet. "It's just that—uh—I need reassurances that this won't come back on me and that you won't ask for anything else."

A vein in John's forehead pulses. "I won't. First, you give me a bunch of basic tonics, all of which we already sell, and then you misplace the actual tonic I wanted."

"How was I supposed to know which tonics are basic or not?! I didn't think Leigh would drink it." Morris scrubs the patchy stubble speckling his chin. "I actually feel really bad about that."

"Then you should've kept a closer eye on it! Suffice to say, I don't trust you as far as I can throw you. Our little partnership is over. Hand over the tonic before I lose my patience."

My hand's trembling and my lungs burn from holding

my breath. It's worth it, though. I got it on video. This should be enough to prove my coven's innocence.

And then Morris makes the mistake of giving him the tonic and sticking around long enough for John to inspect it. It's a serious miscalculation on my part to think John wouldn't notice the liquid's matte coloring and that Morris would listen to directions and flee the second he handed it over. As it is, we're screwed.

John takes one glance at the tonic and instantly knows. Of course he does. The tonic I made before we came here is not my heartache cure. It's not a working tonic at all.

"It's misbrewed," John murmurs.

"What? Uhh . . . No, it's not," Morris stammers.

"Yes, it is. It isn't even glowing!"

"Um . . . well, that's because . . ." Morris is visibly sweating now, so when he looks directly at where Ximena and I are crouched beneath the desk it really shouldn't be a surprise. What I'm not anticipating is him blurting out, "I'm sorry," and then racing toward the doors.

*Shit.*

There's no time to run. John extends his hand. The Boston ivy clinging to the exterior of the building untethers from the wall and wraps itself around the door handles. Morris throws himself against it but it's no use. The doors don't budge.

A sharp knot forms in my throat. John isn't just the owner of Bottled Wonders. He's also a witch. One that can manipulate plants, like I can.

Heat radiates off Ximena and even if I wasn't next to

her, I'd know her wolf is clawing just beneath the surface, begging to be let out. Gray fur sprouts on the tips of her ears and her knuckles.

"I know someone else is here! Show yourselves!" John yells.

Ximena's eyes spark a warm amber. Does she have her wolf under control? I touch her arm, trying to convey that it's okay if she needs to stay hidden. She doesn't have to risk someone finding out she's a wolf. But Ximena only smiles.

Together, we stand.

"Well, well. What is this supposed to be, some sort of trap?" John asks.

"It's over," I tell him calmly, though my pulse is anything but.

John stalks forward. Ximena juts her arm out protectively and makes a low threatening sound. This is not the time to flush hotly, and yet . . .

"Give me the real tonic," John demands.

I manage a smirk. "I don't have it. I never did."

"No. There's a tonic that's going to put Bishop Brews on the map. You said so yourself when I visited your apothecary. I *need* that tonic. Bottled Wonders is doing well on its own, but imagine if we had something truly special. We'd be unstoppable. Give me the tonic," he demands.

I shake my head slowly. "Sorry to disappoint you, but there really isn't a tonic. You're a thief—one that's been caught. And you've been stealing extra magic from the Hemwood. The forest itself is proof enough."

John raises a single blond eyebrow. He's trying to seem unbothered, but his flimsy mustache is twitching, and his face is turning an impressive shade of red. "So I'll pay a small fine for violating the ordinance."

I wave my phone at him. "We have you admitting to coercing Morris into stealing for you on video too."

In his anger, John smashes the tonic against the floor, just like I hoped he would. I didn't use just any misbrew. I used attempt number twenty-one. My accidental battle tonic that destroyed Nana's kitchen rug.

As soon as the vial breaks, wild green bubbles escape and charge at John's feet. They lap at his fancy shoes and corrode the hardwood beneath them.

I shouldn't laugh to see him kicking at the little monsters, but I do. The sound dies in my throat the moment John flings his arm out. The cactus sitting on the welcome desk flies toward me and hits my wrist. Thorns dig into my skin and the momentum knocks my phone out of my hand and into the angry foam rushing for my feet.

I don't have time to mourn it. John's on the move, heading straight for the door. He's fast but not wolf-fast. Ximena throws herself between him and the exit. Her fingernails stretch into claws, and the fur on her knuckles scatters down her arm.

Morris shrieks, John stumbles back, and an office door down the hall bangs open. Swift, uneven footsteps head in our direction.

"Good lord, can't I practice my speech for the festival in peace? What is going *on* out here?" Mrs. Brown, the mayor's wife and Morris's mom, stops next to the display case wearing a navy power suit and sporting a sleek cane for better mobility and balance. The cane must be new, because I haven't seen her using it before. Her brown hair is slicked back into a tight bun. She regards us with sharp, winged eyes and a slight grimace.

John takes this brief interruption to attempt to flee. The vines securing the front door fall away at his command. He takes a beat to steady himself against the doorframe, no doubt the magic slowing him down. Before he can open the door, a set of familiar faces speckled with concern do so for him. My grandmother is here, along with Poppy and Mercer.

Nana blocks John's path. "You can try to run but we know where to find you. It's better to cooperate," she says.

For a second, I fear he'll knock her over to escape. Then she shifts her weight. Sheriff Dunn is behind her, already reaching for his handcuffs. John must see him too, because he shrinks.

"I didn't do anything," John says, the lie as smooth as syrup.

"He's a criminal," Ximena snarls next to me.

"Don't listen to her." John jabs a finger at Ximena. "She's some kind of . . . *monster*."

By now, Ximena has tucked her wolf back inside like a loose bedsheet. Her responding head tilt is seemingly innocent, but I can see the twitch of her jaw and the sparkle beneath her walnut-brown eyes.

The sheriff nods at the vines still loosely looped around the metal door handles. "Preventing someone from leaving an enclosed space is false imprisonment. It's a crime. We also have a video confession of you orchestrating the break-in at Bishop Brews. Suffice to say, you're under arrest." The sheriff steps aside as his deputies handcuff John and drag him out.

"What's going on?" Mrs. Brown asks once the sheriff and John are gone. "Who was that man, why aren't you kids at the festival, and what is this stuff *eating the floor*?" She slinks back from a scorching bubble as it threatens to devour her shiny kitten heels.

"I'll tell you outside, Mom," Morris replies, pale from either the excitement or all his bad choices coming to a head. He takes her arm and helps her toward the door.

Morris and Poppy have a tense moment as they pass each other. Morris opens his mouth like he wants to say something but snaps it shut. Either Poppy's closed-off expression or Mercer's scoff of disgust have him thinking twice. It's bad enough to anger one witch, but an entire coven? I feel sorry for him. Morris is going to have to do some serious groveling.

Which reminds me. I kneel and attempt to fish my phone out of the burning mess. A bubble snaps at my finger, and I hiss.

Poppy makes her way over. Her arms are folded across her chest, and her nails drum against her skin in a lazy rhythm. Dare I say, she appears mildly glad to see me?

Without a word, Poppy steps around me and grabs my

phone from the pile of fizz. The tips of her fingers turn an angry red, the skin growing tight and burnt. But she shakes off the pain, and a second later, new skin weaves together over the old like tree roots.

"Show-off."

Poppy's eye roll is practically the equivalent of a smile. She puts my phone on the desk. "It's dead."

"Perfect," I reply sarcastically.

"I wouldn't worry too much." Mercer shows us her phone and the livestream video I started on Instagram. "I already showed it to the sheriff. I can't believe we had to rescue you."

"How did you find us?" I ask.

Mercer grins. "Find My Friends. I told you it'd come in handy. And you thought it was creepy."

I pull Mercer into a hug. "It *is*. But I am so glad to see you."

"Yes, I am a beacon of light." She lowers her voice and leans in conspiratorially. "Also, when were you going to mention that your girlfriend is a werewolf?"

I choke on nothing. *Girlfriend? Werewolf?* I glance at Ximena. Everything appears normal, and then I notice the single sparkling orange claw on her pinky finger.

Amusement brightens Mercer's face like she didn't just pull the rug out from under me. I long to tell her that the wolf legend is real, and that Ximena is nothing to fear, but it's not my place. "She's not—"

"It's cool. *Really* cool. Wolves are clearly misunderstood

and should be free to be themselves. I'm so glad y'all made up." Mercer gives me another squeeze.

"Who made up?" Nana comes to stand beside me. She pulls me into the crook of her arm for one of her rare hugs and then pats my hair.

"Me and Ximena," I tell her. "Your plan for us to team up was a success," I tease.

"Nanas always know best. Now let's get to work. Save the cheerleader, save the apothecary."

# 29

Nana's able to set up an emergency council meeting for later tonight to break down the investigation and discuss how we'll protect the Hemwood against future threats like those posed by Bottled Wonders. In the meantime, we have to do something about the waning magic. Leigh only has a few hours left before her memory loss becomes permanent.

The counter brews are failing because Bottled Wonders is overusing the magic and, by default, messing up ours. My coven can still use magic, but it's sparse and spotty, like bad Wi-Fi. The counter brew, my tonic, Ximena's bracelet, and everything else magical won't work properly until we heal the Hemwood.

At home, I flip through our grimoire in a last-ditch effort to find a solution. I stop at tips for assisting plants to grow and flowers to bloom, an idea forming. What if witches can cultivate new growth on a larger scale, say the Hemwood itself? The forest gave inhabitants magic to protect it from harm, and John Winters exploited that gift for his own gain. Could we replenish what's been lost? Healing the Hemwood, even a little bit, could boost the counter brew's potency.

I fish out the business card of Albert Baumgardner, the older man we met at the café in Crimson Grove, and dial the phone number. He's a witch and must know others who were affected by Bottled Wonders. I'll need all the witches I can get to even have a shot at this working.

"Hi, Mr. Baumgardner, it's Sage Bishop, the girl you met at the café the other day? You said to call if I had a way to take down Bottled Wonders. I have something better—a way to restore the magic John Winters took from us. Can you, and as many witches as you know, go to the Hemwood and try to give it a boost with your magic? Instead of drawing power from the forest, maybe we can give some back by healing the dead parts. I don't know if it's possible, but we've got to try." I don't breathe as I wait for his response.

"Give me thirty minutes," he replies.

*Yes!* When I get off the phone, I'm literally shaking. We're cutting it so close to the deadline. If this doesn't work, Bishop Brews will be permanently closed, and the founders will never trust my coven again.

I relay my plan to Nana, who group calls the rest of our coven, including my great-aunt Genie. Tiva, Poppy, and Mercer are already here and eager to assist. Once everyone arrives, they run to where the Hemwood butts against our property.

Twenty minutes later, when Mr. Baumgardner calls to say he's in position, Nana and I link hands around the brewing pot we keep at home. I conjure up that same feeling I had a week ago, right before everything went wrong. I think of Ximena, how she caught me off guard singing in Bishop Brews and how perfect she looked in our uniform.

Meanwhile, Nana adds in the opposites of the original ingredients. Instead of carnations and lemon balm to calm the nervous system, she uses ginseng, known to boost energy and memory. She's careful to put them in the same way I did and in the right quantity. Once all the herbs are in the pot, we focus our intentions. I wanted a tonic that would make me forget my heartache. Now I only want to remember all the ways I'm loved.

Ximena watches from across the room. Her dark hair is loosely pulled back, with a few wispy strands framing her face. She smiles when she notices me staring. A familiar warmth courses through me at the sight.

Finally, the counter brew glows.

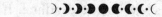

Council meetings normally take place in a small conference room in the town hall, but today the members agreed to open the floor for public comments, so it's been moved to the great hall.

My coven and I get there early to meet the Lawsons. To say I'm anxious would be putting it mildly. If this counter brew doesn't work, Bishop Brews will remain out of business, and the Lawsons will never forgive us. They still might not, but having a daughter who remembers you must count for something.

Nana hands Leigh the counter brew, and she only hesitates a moment before downing it in one gulp. The herbs, bound together and enhanced with magic, must taste awful because her lips pucker. Once it's down, the magic takes hold. Leigh's face flushes pink, and her body sways from the rapid onset of the tonic. Her parents steady her, and when she opens her eyes this time, they are wide and knowing.

She glowers when she sees me, and I grin. It's over. Maybe now that I saved her, she can forgive me for the tenth birthday fiasco and stop trying to one-up me in these last few weeks of school. Not gonna lie, I'll miss our competition.

"I—I remember everything," Leigh says, rubbing her temples.

"You know who poisoned you?" Mr. Lawson demands. "Was it Morris Brown?"

Her mother grips her shoulder. "It's okay. You can tell us."

"That's just it. No one did." Leigh gazes directly at me. I can't decipher her expression.

"I don't understand," Mrs. Lawson says.

Leigh shakes her head, seemingly trying to get the right

words to form. "I've been feeling lost lately. Cheerleading doesn't feel the same. Everyone seems to have it all figured out but me. The icing on the cake was when Jason told me he didn't want to commit to long distance. I should've known he wasn't down to make it work. I didn't even want to go to the fundraising rally, but the team would kill me if I missed another performance." She runs a hand through her hair and stares at her sandals. "On the ride to school, I saw the tonics in Morris's bag. I drank one. I didn't even care what it did. I just wanted to feel better, and that's usually what your brews accomplish. Except this time—"

"The tonic made you forget everything," I finish for her.

Mrs. Lawson scowls at Leigh. "You did this to yourself? Over a *boy*? We're talking about this when we get home."

Leigh groans, but her annoyance morphs into surprise when she notices Ximena. "Hey, didn't I see you in the woods? You were . . ." She trails off, likely remembering the giant wolf she told the cheer squad she saw. My head throbs as I hold my breath, hoping she doesn't expose Ximena. Leigh shakes her head. "Never mind."

I release a harsh breath. The Lawsons appear more confused than ever. Nana seems entertained.

The auditorium doors open, and my great-aunt and Mrs. Hart from Bewitched Blossoms enter. Residents are allowed to observe certain council meetings, and since this one was called to discuss protecting independent businesses in Blackclaw, I'm not surprised to see familiar faces.

"How are we punishing Morris?" Mrs. Lawson asks Nana. "Will you be pressing charges?"

"I haven't decided yet, but I'm open to your thoughts. First, I'd like to know more about your involvement with John Winters." Nana says that last bit to Mr. Lawson.

He blanches. "I was only doing what I thought was best for my daughter. In hindsight, I never should've trusted him."

"You lost faith in me. We need to trust each other if we're going to survive outside influence on this town." Nana levels Mr. Lawson with one of her no-nonsense glares. He shrinks like a popped balloon.

As more people file in, the sheriff corrals us to the front of the hall. "This conversation isn't over," Nana warns the Lawsons before pulling me aside. "Sage, before we start, I wanted to tell you how proud I am of you. Your parents would be too."

My throat tightens at her words. "Thanks, Nana."

She pats my head. "Are you ready for this? You can make your proposal, and then the council will open the discussion on how best to protect the Hemwood and the businesses in Blackwood."

"I'm ready." It's time to make a change.

Nana, Mrs. Carver, the founders, and two other elected officials take their seats at the long wooden table. Nana pulls the mic closer. "Good evening. We're here to discuss the possibility of enacting new ordinances for Blackclaw. You'll hear from my granddaughter, Sage, before we open the floor for public comments and concerns. If there are none, the council will draft a proposed ordinance to be heard at the next public hearing."

Nana gestures for me to take the mic. As soon as I do, my mind goes totally blank. Seriously, no thoughts, just nerves. What am I doing up here? Why do my legs feel like they're made of pudding?

In the back of the room, someone clears their throat. I follow the sound and see Ximena. Her smile snuffs out all the anxious thoughts burning through my mind. I can do this. For me, for my town, and especially for her.

I inhale and steady myself against the mic. "Some of you may know John Winters, an entrepreneur and witch from Crimson Grove who wanted to expand his business into Blackclaw. He made offers on our stores and pressured us to sell. He was using more than his fair share of Hemwood magic, threatening Blackclaw's economy. We can't let this happen again. There must be protections in place for independent businesses, like limits on how magic is used and financial assistance for small businesses in trouble." I find Ximena in the crowd again. She nods encouragingly. "And it's not just our stores that need protecting. People with magic do too." Whispers spread through the audience. I'm not going to change a hundred years' worth of bias with one speech, but speaking up is better than staying silent. "Everyone needs to feel safe here."

The room is too quiet. A sinking worry weighs me down until Mrs. Hart gives me two thumbs up. Across the aisle from her, Henry nods approvingly. Agnes, from Mystic Muffins, beams. Everywhere I turn I spot someone I know signaling their support.

"Any comments or objections to the council creating protections for Hemwood magic, businesses using magic, and residents with magic?" Nana asks.

There is total silence. It feels like submerging my head underwater, only when I break the surface, the room erupts in cheers. The council members nod to themselves, even the stuffy Lawsons.

"As I hear no objections"—Nana brings the gavel down hard with a smile—"so moved."

# 30

TWO DAYS LATER

The sun is perched high, its warm rays lancing through the windows of Bishop Brews like golden swords. Ximena is radiant in her work T-shirt tied at the waist and a pleated blue skirt that shows off her tan legs. The store is officially reopened, and Nana has us clearing space on the front shelves for new merch. I finally have a tonic ready to debut. The vial glows brightly when I show it to Ximena.

"Is this your heartbreak tonic?" she asks, pausing her dusting to grab the bottle.

I shake my head. "Something better. This makes the drinker feel how I feel right now."

Ximena tilts her head. "And how do you feel?"

"Loved." My cheeks are hot at the confession. "I used the counter brew for Leigh as a base for my love tonic.

Mrs. Carver gave it the okay yesterday. She or Poppy test all our glowing tonics for any negative side effects since they can heal themselves."

Ximena spins the bottle between her fingers. "This is definitely going to put Bishop Brews on the map."

"It also helps that Bottled Wonders has been fined for overusing the Hemwood, and John has been arrested."

"Semantics. This is gold," Ximena tells me with a cheesy grin.

We restock in comfortable silence for a while. I throw out the wolfsbane charms and replace them with trinkets containing nettle and burdock root, nutritive herbs best known for their adaptive benefits.

And then Ximena grabs my hand. "I really am sorry I ran after you saw those text messages from Morris. I told you I wasn't going anywhere, and that means even if things get rocky."

I rub the space between her index finger and thumb just like she used to do for comfort. Ximena trails her free hand along my arm, her fingers leaving tingles in their wake. "It's okay. I'll hear you out next time. I trust you. There is something I need to tell you, though. I—I think Mercer might know you're a wolf. She saw a claw at the town hall." Ximena freezes, her muscles locking into place. "But she won't tell anyone! You can trust her, same as me."

I've ruined this. I should have waited. I should have—

"It's okay." Ximena resumes her soothing caress up and down my arm. It's like she can sense when the anxiety is working its magic and knows just the thing to calm its plight. "Between that, John calling me a monster, and the close call with Leigh, I'd say I'm pushing my luck. I've been talking to my parents. They always wanted to lobby for change, but they were worried residents would suspect them, which is too much of a risk with the boys being so young. But after learning about your speech at the council meeting and hearing how well it was received, they want to talk to the council members to make sure those protections you proposed become official."

"The council should be supportive, especially given how much you helped."

Ximena nods. "I'm mostly excited to come home for breaks once I start at UCLA. I won't feel so stressed if someone learns I'm a loba."

I grin, glad Ximena has found some peace in Blackclaw. "In the meantime, the magic should go back to normal soon. Nana's been doing research in the town archives. She found that the Hemwood is like a well. Even if it's drained, eventually it will refill. I want to help the forest rejuvenate by planting redwood seeds in that dead patch you showed me. Are you still changing against your will?"

"Yep. It's a pain in the ass, but I've started to anticipate when it's going to happen. And when it does, I use the time to explore more of the Hemwood. It's really helped connect me more to my wolf. I've even found a few new dens and overlooks."

"Oh? Will you show me some of these new favorite hideaways?" I ask, nudging her shoulder.

Ximena's expression softens. "Duh. I was thinking of you when I found them."

A customer enters, and Ximena quickly helps them while I continue clearing and restocking the shelves. The box at my feet is stuffed with love tonics ready to sell. I never thought this day would come. Now that it has, I couldn't be happier.

"Any news on Morris?" Ximena asks once the customer is gone.

"We aren't pressing charges, but he is getting a lot of community service. Nana seems to think that's punishment enough, especially since his parents have been making him do extra work here." I point at the freshly washed windows and repainted walls. "All Morris's doing. Can't say I feel too bad." As I add Bishop Brews labels to my love tonic and proudly place the bottles on the shelf, it hits me. "I think, with a little customization on Nana's part, we can use the counter brew to heal not only the mind and heart but the body as well. It could help with Mrs. Brown's MS. Such a versatile tonic would rocket Bishop Brews into new heights, no doubt."

"Genius." Ximena grins. "I take it you're happy?"

"I'll be happy once the magic is back to normal. My gift is getting stronger every day since Bottled Wonders has been fined and closed for evaluation. Even Poppy and Mercer, who haven't been able to stop making heart-eyes at each other, have seen an improvement in their gifts."

Ximena chuckles. "I meant in general."

"Oh." That misguided feeling I had at the start of all

this is gone, and I'm excited for what's to come. "I am. Are you?"

Ximena nods. She grabs a handful of labeled love tonics from me and helps put them on the shelf. "More than I've been in a long time. A friend invited me to a game night after school next week. I'm gonna go."

"You? Spend time with friends?" I press the back of my hand to her forehead. "Are you sick?"

"It's your fault." Ximena's smile is big and bright. "You've gotten me to let you in, and now I can't seem to stop. Don't get me wrong, I still want to keep my wolf hidden for now, but I'm not as afraid as I was about people finding out. I don't want to run from who I am. You make me want to embrace every part of myself."

I take her hand. "You said you liked musicals because you can pretend to be someone else for a while. Is that still true?"

"I'll always love falling into a story and imagining myself there, but I still want to have my own adventures. The more things I see, the more material I'll have when I write my own stories one day."

From my pocket, I grab the sheet of paper I've been carrying around with me all day. It's a little wrinkled when I hand it to her. "Good, because I got you something."

"What's this?" Ximena skims the paper and I see the moment she realizes what she's holding. Her eyes double in size and the corners of her mouth slowly lift. "Two tickets to *Chicago*, the musical . . . in Los Angeles? I don't understand."

"Your offer still stands, right?" I force a lighthearted laugh and hope it does. I used a whole paycheck to get these.

Ximena's face lights up like a freshly brewed tonic. "You're coming?"

"For a week at the end of the summer, if that's okay with you and your aunt? Nana already said I could go. By then, we should have the funds to hire Mr. Baumgardner. So I'll have some free time."

Ximena lunges for me. She wraps me in her arms and nuzzles her nose against my hair. I miss her warmth when she pulls away. "But won't you miss Blackclaw and your magic?"

"Yes, but I'm not leaving forever. And I want to share new experiences with you, although the past week has felt like an adventure all on its own."

Ximena kisses my cheek. "That's very sappy of you. I'm honored." She rubs the back of her neck. "I—I, uh, wanted to ask you something. I've been thinking, and I know it's almost the end of senior year, but I really like you and I want to give us a go. If you do."

I face her fully. "Are you . . . asking me to be your girlfriend?"

"Yeah. Yes. Will you?"

My heart feels like it might burst. Her enamored expression mirrors my own. Neither of us has garnered the courage to name the feeling yet, but seeing it on her face is a gift, and having her here with me is everything I never knew I needed. I finally give in to the sensation of needing *more* bursting out of my chest. It's scary and unfamiliar and that's okay because I can handle it. With Ximena by my side, I can do anything.

"I love you," I whisper.

Her eyes spark amber, her lips glisten, and when she grins, I catch a glimpse of her wolf canines. She's been staring at me all day, but right now, it's like I'm the last thing she'll ever see. "I love you too."

I don't even hesitate. On her lips, I taste redwoods, blue summer skies, and a rainbow of wildflowers. When we kiss, there's love, steeped in magic, and a freedom so sweet it could rot my teeth.

# Leigh's Counter Brew & Sage's Love Tonic

## INGREDIENTS

2 cups Hemwood spring water
4 roses
honey, so much honey
1 tsp. ground cinnamon
2 oz. ginseng

1 ginkgo biloba leaf
1 rosemary leaf
1 apricot pit
2 tsp. bee pollen

## DIRECTIONS

1. In a brewing pot, bring spring water to a boil. Soak the roses until they lose most of their color.

2. Pour in more honey than reasonable, then add ground cinnamon and ginseng. Stir.

3. Toss in the ginkgo biloba leaf and rosemary leaf. Let simmer on medium heat for 5 minutes while you pretend you're a contestant on *The Great British Bake Off*.

4. Lower heat. Throw in the apricot pit and add bee pollen. Stir. Stir. Stir.

5. Let the mixture steep for 2 minutes.

6. Close your eyes and think of healing memories: joy and affection and all the best stuff in between.

7. When ready, tie the properties together with magic.

**Reminder:** *The best tonics are brewed with love.*

# Acknowledgments

Getting to publish a book like *Brewed with Love* is a dream come true. I've been writing since I was a little girl. My mom knew I'd be a writer before I did, so I'd be foolish not to thank her first. Mom, thank you for fostering a love of reading in me. Thanks for buying me books and encouraging me to write down my thoughts. Thanks for always being my first reader and biggest supporter. And huge thanks for telling me I should pursue traditional publishing. Solid advice!

To my grandma, who's like a second mom to me and let me read and write curled up in the back seat of her Buick while we ran errands. I adore you, Nana.

To my readers: Stories about queer love are my absolute favorite. We deserve happy endings. I hope this one left you feeling as warm and fuzzy inside as it did me.

To my fabulous agent, Rebecca Podos, who has been on this journey with me from the very beginning. Thanks for reading all my stories with enthusiasm and selling my debut! It's been a long road, and I'm glad you were with me for it.

To my editor, Bria Ragin, who took a chance on my witchy little book. You've made editing this story a breeze. All your notes made *Brewed* so much better. I'm floored with how far this has come with your guidance. Thank you for giving it, and me, a chance.

And the same goes to Nicola and David Yoon, wonderful creators of Joy Revolution. I'm amazed that you thought my story would be a perfect addition to your list. Thank you for reading my manuscript multiple times and helping me shape it into a real book. It's been such an honor to work with you both.

I want to give a huge shout-out to everyone on the Random House team who helped make *Brewed* shine: Wendy Loggia (I'm glad you like apothecaries as much as me), Beverly Horowitz, and Barbara Marcus. Thanks to Casey Moses, who designed my incredible cover and jacket along with Betsy Cola, who created the fantastic cover art. Thanks, Michelle Canoni, for the interior design work; Colleen Fellingham, production editor; and Tracy Heydweiller, production manager; as well as Alison Kolani, Melissa Kavonic, and Tamar Schwartz for their amazing copyediting and proofreading skills.

To my sounding board and bestie, Alaya: You always know how to get me out of a jam. In case I've never said it, you're brilliant. Thanks for always being patient and listening to me ramble off ideas. Ready for Book 2?

To Mr. Toby Page, my seventeen-year-old bichon frise, who may have a cameo in this book: I wish I could give you a Pooch Potion, bud. Thanks for being a great little assistant while I wrote this. You're my best boy, you know that?

Aida Shonibar, you are such a great listener. Thank you for always supporting me and having last-minute video chats to calm my nerves.

My Do The Words crew, who have been so great throughout this journey: I cherish you all and our talks.

*Brewed with Love* once went by a different name and had two different plots before this one. So, thanks to the many writing friends who have helped me hone the many versions of this book: Alex Brown, Justine Pucella Winans, SJ Whitby, Ash Van Otterloo, Leira Lewis, Amber McBride, Rebecca Danzenbaker, Sonora Reyes, Vanessa Montalban, Jen St. Jude, Destiny Rae, and Paula Gleeson. Y'all are so great. I'm probably missing people, so if you're one of them, my bad. You're the best!

I always forget to celebrate my accomplishments, so to everyone who has hyped this book, and me, over the years, especially on social media, I am so grateful to you. You've kept me excited.

And last, but definitely not least, to all the authors who have inspired me over the years, I wouldn't have turned my passion into a career without reading your words first.

# About the Author

SMALL CAPS Shelly Page is a young adult contemporary fantasy romance and horror writer. By day, she's a practicing attorney representing unhoused LGBTQ+ youth. By night, she's writing stories about love, magic, and mystery—all with the hope of providing genuine representation for queer readers of color. Shelly lives in Los Angeles with her dog, Toby, and a collection of half-dead plants. *Brewed with Love* is her first solo novel.

shellypage.com